I0619338

SONS OF THE SYNDICATE

ALEX J FISCHER

For my Family and Friends

PROLOGUE

A multi-story building had a sign out front. It read 'Wester Adoption Ministry'. A lone light above the front door was lit, pointing down on the front porch area. There were homes nearby, but none of their lights were on. An unmarked van stopped in front of the prominent building behind the sign.

The van's side door slid open without pause. A large group filed out. They wore formal suits, helmets, and vests strapped over their clothes. All of them had assault rifles. Straps looping around their necks held the rifles in place as they walked. They filed out of the vehicle in lock step. They approached the front door and got into position around it. One of them worked on the lock without pause. He worked fast, and the door was opened quickly. All of them marched inside, apart from two who were stuck outside on guard duty.

The ones inside went up the nearby stairs. The air was dusty, and it was dark in the hallway. Their boots scurrying across the floor were the only sound, aside from the occasional creaking from the floorboards of the dark interior.

They turned, opening the first doorway marked 'resting area' nearby. Once all filed inside, they closed the door and flicked the light switch.

Rows of cribs were housed in the expansive room. The light coming on started a cascading domino of crying to erupt from the infants.

"Find him," a female voice said. "Double check the birth date, to be sure. Bernard's here somewhere."

The group spread through the rows, searching efficiently and without wasted time. They moved with speed and purpose, leaving nothing to chance. They checked every crib and every label, being quick and efficient. Failure was not an option. Their orders had demanded perfection, and that was precisely what they aimed to deliver.

"I found him," a male voice said. The man reached into a crib near the room's corner and lifted a cooing baby swaddled in a blue blanket.

The female member hurried over and took the child from him. "We've secured the package, sir."

"We're leaving. Get outside," the male said.

The lights outside the door turned on and the sound of rapid footsteps approached, along with panicked voices. "What in heaven's name?" one female voice asked. "Someone's in here."

"There's a car outside. Call the police!" a male voice said.

The leader of the armed group reached up and tapped his ear. "I don't want any calls leaving this location."

"I'm already on it," a male voice said in his ear. "It's being redirected to me. Hold one moment."

"Good, looks like we'll have to deal with these fools. Do not fire unless I order it so," the male said. "You two, follow me," he said to the two nearest. "J, leave while we deal with the nosey witnesses." He approached the door and kicked it open.

A nun in a black and white habit tumbled backwards and fell to the floor across the hall. The male priest rushed over to her and tried to help her up, but he paused when he heard a round chambering behind him.

"Whoa." He turned around with his hands held high above his head. "Please don't do this."

The leader kept the business end of his rifle aimed at the priest and stared down at him. "Get him out of here." He didn't look behind when the baby holding member slipped by and headed for the steps leading downstairs. This left the leader with two of his crew standing nearby, staring down their noses at the two helpless innocents.

"Who are you?" the nun asked. "Why are you doing this?"

"That's not your business," the leader said. His finger was resting near the trigger, not on top of it as he spoke.

"Just return the child," the nun said. "God will forgive all of this. Just don't take the child. He's finally found parents. They are on their way to complete the adoption tomorrow."

"That will not happen," he said. "Now, how shall we deal with you two? Should we send you to meet your God? Can you keep a secret, though? Something tells me no."

The man grasped the cross hanging from around his neck. "We do not fear death, you poor lost soul. We wish no harm to any of you."

"It's good to hear you're not afraid," he said. "Are there any others here?"

Neither of the two answered, fearing what their answer would bring about.

"On second thought," the man said, "someone needs to care for those kids until the authorities show. Eh, fuck it," he said. "They'll be here in the morning. Fire." He aimed at the priest while the two at his side mercilessly executed the nun.

Both raised their hands up in front of them to block the lead projectiles from piercing their flesh. They were unsuccessful, as evidenced by their dying screams of pain. The life quickly left their bodies, and they went limp on the floor with a rapidly expanding blood pool underneath.

"Let's get out of here," he said, jogging down the nearby stairs with his men and out the building's front door. "We're leaving, boys and girls. Saddle up."

Everyone filed inside the van, and the sliding door slammed shut. The van roared to life, and they left the crime scene they'd just created. The leader took his helmet off in the safety of the van's interior to reveal Chris. He looked over at the nearby soldier holding the kid. "How's he doing, Jackie?"

"He's fussing a bit." She cradled his neck as she held him close. "It looks like he's unhurt and perfectly healthy."

"Lee, tell me you got everything scrubbed that needed it."

The nearby pudgy man didn't look up from his laptop. "Camera footage is no longer available from inside the Ministry, thanks to quick manipulation and deletion. No emergency phone calls went out. So long as you didn't leave evidence inside, we're in the clear."

"Good. The boss lady should like that."

"I still wonder why she sent us after her aunt's baby," Jackie said. "They don't get along on the best of days, and she does this massive favor?"

"I don't pretend to know the boss's intentions and motives," Chris said. "I just make sure she gets what she wants. You'd be wise to follow my example. Questioning orders is not a wise career move."

"Noted," Jackie said. She felt a tap on her shoulder and saw one of their troops passing her a bottle filled with formula. "Thank you." She looked down at the infant with a smile and spoke in baby talk. "Are you hungry?" She received a cooing as an answer. "Here you go. Drink up. You've had a big day, little guy." She gently placed the nipple end into the baby's mouth and slightly tilted the bottle up so he could drink.

"Now, to return home and deliver the kid," Chris said. He leaned his weary head against the side of the van and stared at the cabin's roof. "They'll be happy the last of their precious bloodline is under the same roof, finally."

"Yeah," Jackie said. "They'll be one regular old-fashioned happy family."

"I sense the sarcasm, but that family is anything but old-fashioned." Chris, Jackie, and the others shared in a hearty laugh. Once it died down, he spoke up again. "Everyone did a good job in there. I'll inform the right people. It was clean, efficient, quiet, and professional. You did well, but don't rest on your laurels."

"Yes, sir!" the group inside the cabin said.

The sudden loud noise caused the child to burst out into tears.

"Now stay quiet. I don't want to hear that incessant crying the whole drive back." Chris covered his ears with a wince.

A much quieter "Yes, sir" was his only answer, besides the swaying cabin.

"Lee, call the police anonymously," Chris said.

"Why?"

"We killed the caretakers," he said. "There's no one left

inside to take care of the babies. I won't allow them all to die because of us. You get me? Make it happen."

"Right away. It's not a problem."

"Did we really have to kill them?" Jackie asked.

"We were just being cautious. We didn't need either of them getting brave about their own piousness and trying something stupid. Even if nearby neighbors heard the gunshots, there's no guarantee they'll call the cops to investigate. Besides, I don't like witnesses talking to police. I don't play with children's lives. That's the line."

"Maybe this will calm the older Ms. Morris down," Jackie said. "She's always kind of snippy. I can't even imagine what it'd be like knowing your baby is somewhere else, and you can't go get him."

"That is a consequence of the life she chose - we all chose. We knew a life of crime wouldn't be sunshine and rainbows. We didn't choose it for that. It was for money, and the foolhardy among us chose it for adventure and action."

"I notified them," Lee said. "I sent an anonymous email from one of my burner accounts. They'll be there in the morning, no doubt."

"Good, that's one less thing to worry about."

"Did your ass ever figure out how to drive, dude?" Jackie asked.

"Laugh it up," Lee said, clearly not amused. "Where did you hear about that?"

"It's all the gossip. Rumor is you nearly fucked the boss over when she was rescuing Elizabeth Morris."

"The old boss sent me to driving classes. Yes, I can drive now. Thanks for bringing that up."

"Relax, kid," Chris said. "She's just ribbing you. You'd best get used to it. It is a hilarious story that's immortalized in this family's gossip."

"That doesn't make me happy."

"You're well known. Some men kill for notoriety inside a respected criminal organization."

"They usually want some fear and respect, but true," Jackie snickered. "I guess you take what you can get."

"Fuck you two…"

1

EIGHTEEN YEARS LATER...

R oger and Bernard had grown up over the last nearly two decades. Roger himself had brown hair, brown eyes, and was slightly shorter than Bernard's six-foot frame. His short hair was freshly cut compared to Bernard's slightly unruly black mane. He was clean shaven and kept himself orderly. His casual t-shirt and jeans were in stark contrast to the man beside him.

Bernard had black hair, harkening back to his mother and uncle. There was a prominent scar adorning his face. He had a constant smirk as the pair walked around the family's property outside. He had his family's dress suit and jacket on. As they walked, he puffed out his chest.

"You should come along with me on my next assignment," Bernard said, walking side by side with Roger. "You wouldn't have to live with the pocket change that mommy dearest gives you in allowance." He rubbed his fingers together to indicate the money. "I'm talking about making some real spending money, like me."

"Fuck you." Roger pushed Daniel away with a laugh. "What does she have you doing?"

"It's nothing big," Bernard said with a shrug. "I go with the buy groups. We collect the guns, and we pay at a separate location. I build street rep, get cash, and gain some respect from the family members. I'm telling you, you need to put in honest hard work alongside us. You'll gain more respect from folks. They won't be able to murmur any mama's boy bull anymore."

"It would be freeing to leave." Roger looked up at the chilly night sky filled with twinkling stars. They were being serenaded by insects echoing in the night sky. The moon was full, staring down at the pair on the cool evening. "I'm going stir crazy in this place. I wonder why mom doesn't want me working for the family."

"Who knows? You're her kid. By all rights, you should learn how this outfit works for when you're in charge. It's even more reason you should come with me on my next job. You'll learn the business better than I could explain. It'd show your mother you're not some little babe in the woods. She'd entrust you with more jobs afterward."

"Or she'd scream at me for putting myself in danger. That's her famous saying. Remember the time I snuck out with you and headed for the shooting range when we got our pieces?"

"Who knows what her problem is?" Bernard asked. "You're eighteen now. You're a man. We can do what we want regardless of what our mothers want. It's the joy of youth, man. We can't be cramped up in this place our whole lives," Bernard said. He turned and walked backwards and extended his arms out to his sides. "We can get any woman we want. We can do what we want. Don't you want to experience all life offers? Or would you rather stay under mommy dearest's thumb your whole life?"

"Alright already," Roger said. "You've convinced me. When is your next job, anyway?"

"Tomorrow morning." Bernard had a shit-eating grin on his face. He stopped and turned with Roger as they walked toward the back of the Morris property. They passed a patrol of two men and waited until they were out of earshot before they continued their conversation. "Meet me out front at eight-thirty a.m. Do not be late. We'll leave before most wake. The team knows I usually drive there alone. You'll be accompanying me. The deal's not until nine. We have time to find trouble afterward."

"Eight in the morning? I thought I'd get to sleep in after Lauren's homeschooling."

"Don't bitch, little prince of crime," Bernard said. "Your mother's too scared to turn you into a man, so it'll be your best friend's job."

"Like you know more than I do," Roger said, rolling his eyes.

Bernard brought them to the fence surrounding the compound and leaned on it with Roger, staring out into the dark tree line. "That's where you're wrong," he said. "Mother has been teaching me what it means to be a working man inside the family. She wants me to rise through the ranks. You're lucky you're my friend, because I'll share the secrets with you. Just don't blab about it."

"Like I'd ever rat on you, you idiot," Roger said. "I never did, even when you used to slip firecrackers into Ms. Taylor's desk."

The pair broke into laughter at the memory he'd brought up. Lauren had jumped up from behind her desk and started screaming uncontrollably, yelling for help before she ran for the door. Their prank had resulted in nearly a dozen men with fire extinguishers running into the room within two minutes. The children were infinitely more amused than the panicking adults.

"She flipped her shit that day," Bernard said. "It was totally worth the ten laps around the place for that."

"Ten? She gave the both of us thirty."

"I guess I'm in better shape than you. It felt like ten."

"Always the braggart, aren't you?" Roger asked.

"If you got it, flaunt it, as my mother says. Why hide your gifts? That's what guides you in life. The same goes for your hard work. The more people that witness you working, the more they will respect you. No one likes a spoiled, worthless nobody."

"I know you're not trying to reference me," Roger said. "I pull my weight around here."

"Doing what?" Bernard looked to his left at Roger. "Don't say fielding complaints from the grunts. That shit doesn't count. They only tell you because they don't view you as a threat. The fact you won't tell Rachel who's bitching is the other reason. That's trustworthy enough, I suppose, but it's not putting in hard work for the family. Let's not kid ourselves."

"I said I'm going tomorrow already," Roger said. "Anything I should know?"

"Bring your six shooter."

"You hate I use that thing, don't you?" Roger backed away from the fence. "What's your beef with it?"

"It's inefficient," Bernard said, following his friend a few feet back. He placed his hand over his hip and pretended to draw a weapon, aiming into the darkness. His index finger squeezed as he enunciated the sound effect. "Bang. It's so much faster than trying to play cowboy with a six-shooter trying to fan the damn thing."

"Because double action revolvers aren't a thing, right?"

"You only get six shots before you have to reload at a snail's pace."

"There are speed loaders too, you know. You just don't like it because Mom told you about the man they named me after," Roger said, the smile fading from his face. "He used a couple of six shooters you know."

"I have no clue why your mother named you after that traitor." Bernard spat on the soil beneath before placing his foot over the spit. "My mother named me after the original patriarch of the family."

"I asked her once." Roger looked up at the clear night sky above. He could see his breath float up into the heavens with every breath. "You want to know what Mom said?"

"Yeah."

"She told me she named me after the greatest man she'd ever known."

"What about her pops?" Bernard asked.

"Grandpa Daniel? I don't know. I was too young to remember, but I heard stories from folks during the past decade. Most of them revolved around his combat prowess and occasionally how he was a genuine man of the common soldier."

"That's what I mean, dude," Bernard said. He reached a hand out and laid it on Roger's shoulder. "The family respected my uncle. Tales are still told of him. What's so bad about that? Why would she choose to name you after that reviled traitor everyone knows about? He ratted on the entire Morris crime family to live with a girl who wanted to leave. Talk about selfish, brother."

"I'm not here to argue about family ancient history," Roger said. "I'm relaying what she said. If I had my wish, she'd have named me Daniel, to be honest, but that's not for me to decide."

"It's moot anyway, I suppose," Bernard said. "It's not my place to question her, as mom always tells me."

"You rag on me about my mom, but what about you? You do her every command."

"She's training me how to be a leader, so I can rise through the organization's ranks and not simply be Elizabeth Morris's kid anymore - to be my own man. Don't you want that? If someone with her amount of experience is teaching me, I'd be stupid to turn my nose up."

"Whatever you say," Roger said. "Let's head inside. I'm getting cold."

"Make sure you set your alarm nice and early. Oh, and dress the part, you bum. You'll be representing us. No shirt and jeans shit. Wear a nice suit like this." He grabbed the expensive jacket. "Remember what I said."

"I got it." Roger turned and headed for the nearby back door and disappeared inside, leaving Bernard out in the cold alone.

"He'd better show up tomorrow." Bernard reached inside his jacket and pulled out a pack of cigarettes before plucking one out and sticking the end in his mouth.

The back door opened, along with heavy footsteps. "Hey, buddy," a male voice said.

Bernard looked and saw an authority figure he'd come to recognize from a young age. Everyone knew who he was and respected him for his dedication to the group, to his friend's mother specifically. "Hey, Ben," he said. "Did you see Roger?"

"We passed by each other. He said he was going to bed already. It's a little early for him, isn't it?"

"Maybe he wants to catch up on his sleep. Who knows what he's thinking half the time?" Bernard asked. He jammed his hand in his jacket pocket and pulled out a lighter. He flicked the wheel, trying to spark a flame.

"Those things will kill you, you know," Ben said.

"You were the one who said once I was eighteen I could smoke."

"You are an adult, sure," Ben said. He turned, waving at a nearby patrol coming into view from around the building. "Hey," he said.

The pair greeted him with a hearty. "Hello, sir."

"Carry on," Ben said, looking at Bernard. Ben's face was no longer the baby-faced, timid wreck Rachel had met all those years ago. It was covered in stubble, and his timid demeanor from almost two decades back was replaced with a mask of indifference, often bordering on calculating. Still, often a spark of warm concern tinted his voice, particularly toward those he knew and liked.

"What are you doing outside this late?" Bernard asked. "Are you checking if there's any slackers?"

"Aside from you, I have found none."

"What are you talking about?" Bernard said. "I got my job tomorrow morning. I'm not a slacker anymore. You don't get to say that."

"I guess you're right," Ben said. He had his hands in his dress pants pocket.

"How's Crystal doing?"

"Why do you want to know about Crystal?" Ben narrowed his eyes at Bernard. "Are you two scheming something again? You'd better tell me if you are, and maybe I can fix it preemptively."

"No, it's nothing like that," Bernard said.

"It better not be." Ben's voice was stern. "If I catch word one that you're planning on involving her with your little job, being bored will be the least of your worries."

"I'd never dream of it," Bernard said.

"What were you and Roger talking about out here that you needed privacy for?"

"Is this why you're out here? It was nothing."

"Is that right? I don't know that I believe that with you two young bucks. Well, get inside. You shouldn't be out here this late unless you're on patrol. I can rearrange you to patrol tonight if you'd like to stay out here." He reached forward and grabbed the cigarette from between Bernard's lips. He threw it onto the grass below and stepped on it. "Get inside."

"Yes, sir." Bernard bit his tongue and left the conversation while he still could. When he reached the top of the stairs, he was halted by Ben.

"Be careful out there tomorrow, kid," Ben said. "The simple jobs can go bad in a second. Always be prepared. Treat no job like it's going to be a cakewalk, and you'll be one step ahead. Always be watching for a threat."

"Thanks," Bernard got out before opening the door and slamming it behind him. He rushed with ease through the rooms he'd memorized over a decade ago, speaking only when spoken to, and never stopping his movement toward the stairs. He climbed the steps and another familiar face stopped him in his tracks.

She had heavy black mascara on, along with black lipstick and more than a few piercings, ranging from her ears, nose, and eyebrows. She had an impish grin on her face as she approached him at the top of the stairs.

"I bet you're nervous about tomorrow," the young woman with platinum blonde hair said. She was only one year his junior in age. "Let's hope if worse comes to worst, you don't piss your pants and run."

"Preposterous," Bernard said as he continued walking. "It's not my first time working. I'm used to it now."

"Uh huh," Crystal said, following along. "Is that why you dragged my brother out there with you to talk?"

"You were watching us," Bernard said.

"You idiots were below my window. Do you think I don't occasionally look outside?"

"A guy can't hang out with his best friend? We were talking is all."

"Whatever," she said. "If you don't want to tell me, you won't. Where are you going? You're not going to bed already."

"I need all the rest I can get before tomorrow morning. I'm responsible - something you know nothing about," Bernard said. He heard the stomping behind him get quicker. He could see her at his side.

"You're an ass."

He reached his destination and grabbed the doorknob. He reached into his pocket for the key and inserted it before twisting. "If you'll excuse me, I'm going to bed. I suggest you do the same. You have finals soon, don't you?" He shut the bedroom door and locked it behind in time to feel a large amount of force pushing against his door. It knocked him a few inches forward. He heard a loud stomping before it was finally quiet again in his room.

He wandered over to his closet and flung it open. Over a dozen suits hung there, along with some flashy casual wear. He got his next day's outfit together and folded them. He placed them on the windowsill near his bed. "Finally, I can get some rest..."

2

Roger had on one of his few formal suits that his mother had gotten him for formal occasions. It matched the work wear of the members that surrounded him daily, so he was sure it'd work. He made sure he wore his revolver holster around his waist after he got dressed. It was rare he wore it, but this was warranted. *Mom is going to kill me when she finds out about today, but fuck it,* he thought.

He exited his room and entered the wide hallway. As he descended the stairs, he heard a whistle.

"Is today a special occasion, kid?" Chris asked. He sat in a recliner in front of an enormous television in the large living room. "You're usually in something more casual."

"Leave the kid alone, old man," Jackie said from a nearby seat. "He probably wants to impress some lady today on a date."

"Is that right? You have a date today, kid?" Chris asked with a grin. "I can give you some tips if you'd like. With my advice, you'll bed her on the first date."

"I keep telling you not to call me kid," Roger said.

"I'm sorry. It's just hard when I've watched you grow up," Chris said. "You're like a little brother I never had."

"At your age?" Jacqueline laughed. "Try a son or nephew you never had."

"Ouch." Chris feigned hurt by clutching a hand to his chest. "You're always vicious, Jackie. You'll never find a husband acting like that."

Jackie's long, toned, dark leg reached out and kicked in the older man's direction, along with a lone finger. "Stay in your own dating lane, and mind your own business. Didn't your mother ever teach you that?"

"So, I'm right?"

Roger read the room and made his escape while the two continued their petty bickering inside the living room. He quickly exited via the front door. The other person who saw him leaving the house he met outside.

Crystal was sitting on the bottom step of the house. She had a cell phone in her grasp, and it looked like she was texting.

"Damn it," Roger said under his breath. It caught her attention, however.

She stood up and turned around. "Dear Brother, what are you doing up and at them so early? Surely this has nothing to do with that secret meeting you and your troublemaker friend had yesterday. My, what fancy clothes you're wearing. Aren't those the same as Mom, Dad, and everyone else wears? I thought you hated those because they made you feel stuffy?"

"Maybe I wanted to appear nice for a shopping trip? Did you ever think of that? Why are you here this early?"

"Duh," she said, as if the upcoming answer was the most obvious concept. "I wanted to investigate what you two were planning in secret. I knew you were up to something from your partner in crime's dodging my every question. Almost like he had something to hide. What about you? Why are your eyes so shifty? Why don't you have a bodyguard if you're heading out? Neither of us is allowed off site without accompanying security. That tells me you're sneaking out."

"You've just been sitting out here all morning because you're bored? Shouldn't you be prepping for your upcoming tests and not coming up with conspiracies to charge me with?" Roger asked.

"I'm ready for them already."

The front door opened, and Bernard exited. "Ah hell," he said. "Why are you out here too?"

"How rude," Crystal said. "I'm just minding my own business out here. We should move before the patrol comes around the house if you want to escape unnoticed."

"Escape? What are you talking about?"

"She's not buying it. I've been trying," Roger said.

"Damn it all. Head inside and don't tell anyone," Bernard said.

"I'm going with you if you're going anywhere, or I'm spoiling the whole thing. What's it going to be?"

"Fuck it," Bernard said, grabbing her arm. He dragged her toward the nearby car. "Get in the back then."

"I knew you'd see it my way." She threw open the back door and climbed inside.

"Dad's going to kill us," Roger said, climbing into the front passenger seat.

Bernard got in and started the engine. "You're not getting out when we get there, and that's final. This is official family business you know. We can't have our image sullied by a seventeen-year-old girl showing up in her little skirt."

"I'm just happy to get out of that damned mansion."

Crystal had a wide smile adorning her face as they passed through the infernal gates she saw every day.

"You got your piece on you I trust?" Bernard asked.

"What?" Crystal leaned forward between the seats. "Why do I need a gun?"

Roger placed a palm on her face and pushed her back into the backseat. "He meant me," he said. "Yeah, I got it on me. Hopefully we won't need it. I cleaned it before bed to be safe and have a few speed loaders on me."

"Good of you to remember," Bernard said. "We'll make a soldier out of you yet."

"Like Mom or Dad would allow that," Crystal said. "I don't envy you two when we get back home."

"I am an adult now," Roger said. "They'll deal with it, or they won't."

"Big words from you now," Crystal said. "We'll see if you feel the same when we get back. I'm betting you won't. You're acting big for your buddy here is all."

"Be quiet for once," Roger said. "Who are we meeting with here?"

"I'm supposed to be there in about ten minutes. We're meeting with Oleg. Have you met him yet? He's been one of our suppliers for close to two decades now. They don't seem to talk much, or maybe that's just since I'm new."

"If they knew who you were, I bet they would have," Roger said.

"It doesn't matter. No one said shit last time. I expect it will prove similar today."

"How much do you usually earn on these jobs?" Roger asked.

"Last time I pulled down over ten thousand by myself," Bernard said. "I wouldn't expect a payday for you, though. You're a guest here."

"What does that make her then?" Roger asked, jabbing a thumb toward Crystal in the back.

"A stowaway, I guess."

The two young men shared a laugh at their passenger's expense. She just folded her arms and huffed. She looked out the window as the passing trees gave way to open fields. A large metropolitan city loomed on the horizon. "I don't guess we could go shopping while we're in the city?"

"After the job, possibly," Bernard said.

"We're already in the fire. We should enjoy today afterward," Roger said. "You shop online every day. You still have things you want, though?"

"I don't get to shop in person. It's a totally different experience," Crystal said. Her eyes were glued to the enormous buildings in the distance. "Just getting to walk around in public is a foreign exercise. We're missing out on our youth being stranded out in that mansion with Mom, Dad, and the family."

"She just wants to keep us safe," Roger said. "It's nice to get out and about, admittedly."

"Aren't you glad you tagged along?" Bernard asked. "Now get your game face on. We'll be there within a few minutes. We're meeting along the riverside, like last time. Few people stick their noses where they don't belong down there. They know better than indulging their curiosity after last time, according to Warren."

"That guy creeps me out," Crystal shuddered. "He hangs around like some damned ghost, just watching. I've heard stories he used to be the guy throwing bodies into the nearby Great Lake. That's sick, handling dead bodies like that."

"He's security," Roger said. "It makes sense, even if it is unnerving. What are we doing when we arrive?"

"Just stay by me," Bernard said. "We're only there as a formality. The dealer has already been appointed, and they'll hand over the goods. We're there to ensure it goes off without a hitch. Don't talk once the Russian's get here, and don't look like you're about to piss yourself. Also, keep your hands where they can see them. Don't make any sudden moves."

"Oh, is that all?" Roger asked.

"Yeah, really simple," Crystal sarcastically said.

Bernard slowed the car down as they entered the city proper. "Just a quick turn coming up, and we're almost there," he said.

A horn blared behind the car thanks to Bernard's reckless crossing into the right-hand lane.

"I had assured clear distance. Screw you." Bernard flipped their follower off.

Crystal turned and noticed the driver behind was not happy, judging by his face. "You need to practice your driving," she said. "I'd also be mad if I were in his shoes."

"Bah," Bernard said. "Let him deal with it. We've got places to attend and people to meet."

"Uh, he's following us," Crystal said, peeking over the back seat.

"Is he now?" Bernard asked, peering into the mirror on his left. "Oh, that's why. I see now."

"You know them?" Roger asked.

"They're our team. Boy, this'll be funny when I explain after we exit," Bernard said with a nervous chuckle.

"Oh, this will be fun," Roger said.

Bernard slowed the car down as they approached the waterfront. "We're meeting just up here in front of the docks, as usual." He pulled over and stopped.

The car from earlier passed them and parked in front of them.

"Best work your magic then, boss," Roger said.

Bernard withdrew the key from the ignition. "I got this. You two worry too much," he said.

The pair of young men exited the car while Crystal stayed inside the back.

The car in front had multiple armed individuals file outside, with the driver approaching. "Learn to drive, you idiot. You nearly killed us all." Once he had finished his complaint, he became silent. "You..." he paused. "You're Elizabeth Morris's kid, aren't you?" He glanced over at Roger. "Oh shit. You're the boss's kid too? Why the fuck are you present without protection?"

"He's with me," Bernard said. "Now get your head in the game. They'll be here soon."

"You two stay to the side. We'll handle this and then take you back home."

"Sure, whatever you say," Bernard said. "We'll be over here waiting then. Don't have a stroke over this."

The man reached into his jacket pocket and pulled out a pair of sunglasses. He put them on and returned to his group near the car. They leaned against it, aside from one who sat on the hood of the car, and kicked their legs out every so often.

Roger adjusted the tie around his neck and cleared his throat. "I wonder if it'll be running laps or if it'll be cleaning duty for this one?"

"You need to remember my life advice and live your preferred way, dude. You're enjoying being out of that place, yeah? Live in the moment. You'll be happier that way."

"For the moment anyway," Roger said.

"Pipe down, they're here."

A larger SUV arrived further down the road and stopped.

The annoyed family member had his phone buzz in his pocket. He extracted his phone and checked the newly arrived message. He texted a response and shoved the phone into his pocket again.

A group of obviously armed men emerged from the SUV. They had machine pistols strapped to their hips in plain sight for the world to see.

"Mr. Artyom, how nice to see you again." The man who complained at Bernard stepped forward with a wide smile. He reached a hand out toward the aging Russian man as he approached.

Artyom's bald head shined in the sunlight coming from above. He'd kept in shape. Even through the formal uniform he wore, you could almost see the muscle hidden beneath. He had glasses and a special red pin attached to his suit that his other crew did not. Adjusting his suit and tie, he moved forward toward the formerly angry driver. He shook his hand and looked over at Bernard and Roger. "Is that who I think it is?" His voice had lost a bit of its old accent.

"Him? Yeah, he's the boss's kid. He wanted to see how our business is run in case he takes over. Learning on the job thing."

Artyom immediately left the Morris employee in the dust without another word and walked to Roger and Bernard.

"Hello, Mr. Morris," he said.

Roger kept his voice calm and controlled. "It is nice to finally meet you, Mr. Artyom." Roger stepped forward and met Artyom halfway. He heard Bernard keeping pace behind him, a fair distance away.

"I never thought we'd get to meet you. It's truly a pleasure. Your boss keeps you nice and locked away at that makeshift base of hers."

"She is a mother," Roger said. "Mothers try to keep their kids safe, but boys will be boys."

"You snuck out?"

"Perhaps," Roger said. "Are you going to report me?"

Artyom burst out in laughter.

Artyom's men and the family's men alike all looked very surprised at Artyom's sudden boisterous outburst. Their eyes were wide, and one even had his mouth hanging open.

"I like you," Artyom said. "You remind me of myself twenty years ago when I joined my boss. No, kid, I'm not going to report you. If I know your mother, she already knows you're gone. She always was a smart one. If she asks, I will tell her I didn't know you'd be here. This was all your idea."

"Yeah, fair enough," Roger said.

Artyom looked over Roger's shoulder. "Who is that? Your bodyguard? He looks familiar."

Roger glanced over at Bernard before turning back to face Artyom. "That's Bernard. He's been to these meetings before. You can think of him as my bodyguard if you like, but he's my friend."

"Any friend of Rachel's son is a friend of mine. Come over here." Artyom gestured the young man over. He reached his hand out. "Nice to meet you."

Bernard extended a hand and felt his hand wrapped in the iron tight grip of Artyom. "It's an honor," he said.

"I like you two, so I'm going to tell you a secret." Artyom's voice grew low. He peeked over his shoulder and turned back to Roger and Bernard. "You should leave. Right now!"

"Excuse me?" Roger asked.

"You picked the worst shipment ever to tag along on,"

the enormous man said. "Get back in your car, and tell your boss that Mr. Oleg isn't happy."

"I don't suppose there's anything we could do to change that?" Roger asked.

"How bold to take command at your age and on your first outing to boot." Artyom never let the uncharacteristic smile fade. "It's an issue that's been boiling for years. Nothing any well-meaning young upstart could do would make any difference. No offense intended."

"None taken. I'm new on the scene. You have any advice for a young whippersnapper?"

"Yeah," Artyom said instantly. "Go to college and get a regular job. You won't make as much money, but you'll be happier. However, if you're dead set on following in your grandfather's footsteps, then on your head be it. I've said my piece. May I sit in your car and have a bit of a private discussion?"

Roger watched Artyom's men and his own family members before looking back at the noticeably large man. "Sure. What kind of envoy for my mother would I be if I refused a request from one of our most valuable suppliers?"

"That's the spirit," he said. He reached out and poked Bernard's chest. "You come too."

They heard assorted mumbling from their group as they complied with Artyom's request.

Roger opened the back door and held it open for his guest. "Right this way. Scoot over."

Crystal followed her brother's command and looked at Artyom. "Hi there."

"You get in first." Artyom got in after Roger, staying near the door. "A pleasure to meet you, Ms. Morris. I assume you are Rachel's other child, yes?" He looked back at Roger. "Your bodyguard can sit up front."

Roger sat beside his sister. She was on his right, with Artyom flanking him on the left. Bernard was up front in the driver's seat.

"You will not enjoy what happens next, all of you. I wish the girl wasn't forced to witness this, if I'm honest. Close your eyes, girl."

"I beg your pardon?" Roger asked.

"It's not your pardon I require, it's your compliance," Artyom said. "When I press this button, all hell is going to break loose outside. Now I brought you two in here because I recognize you, and we don't want to cause a blood feud. I may like you two, but not enough to disobey orders." Without delay, he pressed the button on his phone.

Roger was in a daze as he looked at Artyom's men. They all pulled out their phones before jamming them into their pocket.

"Back us up," Artyom said. "Do it now."

Bernard looked at Roger, who was nodding his head in agreement. He backed the car up a few dozen yards until Artyom spoke up again.

"This is quite far enough," he said in his deep masculine voice. "Tell me, friends, have you been in a life-or-death situation before, or has mother dearest sheltered you your whole life?"

"Are you threatening us?" Bernard asked. He had his hand over his weapon in the front seat, out of sight of Artyom.

"I'm trying to keep you two alive. If you pull your weapon, you will not survive. I guarantee that. That goes for you too, Mr. Morris. Don't make your sweet little sister see your friend get his brains blown out because you want to be a hero. You might kill me in a rush, but not before I turn his head into a bloody canoe. You wanted my advice earlier?

Know when to fold; otherwise, you'll die early. This is one of those on-the-job training sessions I've heard about. Aren't I kind, doing this for free?" He pressed another button on his phone while his other gloved hand was inside his jacket. As soon as he pressed the button, he pulled his hand out, revealing he was grasping a handgun the whole time. He pointed it toward Bernard. "I see that hand move, I fire, no hesitation."

"Dammit," Bernard said. A bead of sweat trickled down his temple.

Neither of the young Morris boys had time to analyze their situation, as many gunshots went off in front of their car. Roger felt two arms wrap around his right arm. He could feel Crystal shaking against him. He wrapped his arms around her, trying to use his body to shield her from any potentially stray bullets.

"Christ," Roger said.

Artyom raised his voice to be heard over the gunshots outside. "Your mother should have known better than to stiff us. Inflation is a bitch. We told her to increase our pay, but she gave us pittances. We are tired of it; therefore, we are terminating this business relationship. You," he grabbed Roger's collar, "you will be our envoy and tell them precisely that. Are we clear?"

Roger watched men and women he knew get gunned down in front of him in cold blood. Some he'd known his entire life, others only for a few years. One thing was obvious - they were not prepared for the sneak attack, as they barely got a shot off in self-defense. He watched as the bullets ripped through their skulls at close range, and their bodies fell to the ground below in heaps. The horrific screams coming from outside of the car as some ran amplified the gore he was witnessing. Others stood and tried to fight. Something inside of him went numb at this sight. He barely heard Artyom as the horrifying scene embedded itself into his mind for all time.

"I asked, are we clear?" Artyom asked again with more force.

"Yeah." Roger shook himself out of his daze. "I get it."

"Good." Artyom's voice returned to its normally calm demeanor. "Now get out of here quickly. The cops will arrive inside ten minutes. You don't want to get caught in that mess, trust me. You have enough to explain to mother about today. What a day you picked to sneak out!" Artyom laughed. He slid away from Roger and opened the back door, keeping his weapon trained on Bernard's skull all the while. He slammed the car door shut and backed further away from the vehicle as the last gunshots died in the morning air.

"They're dead," Roger said.

"No, no, no," Crystal cried into Roger's shirt. "This cannot be happening. Tell me this isn't real."

"That bastard," Bernard said through clenched teeth. "We don't have a choice. We need to leave." He turned the car around with the squealing of their tires screeching above the ringing in their ears. "We're fucked," he said.

"I can't believe they're dead back there." Roger looked over his shoulder to see Artyom's SUV was following them. He absentmindedly rubbed Crystal's back as the chanting had escalated into full on wailing into his chest.

"Keep your head down," Bernard said. "There's no telling if he was lying earlier." He slammed the gas down and pulled out into traffic.

"They turned the other way," Roger said. "Besides, he wouldn't have gotten us out of harm's way, only to shoot us when he already had the chance."

"You're far too trusting of that psychopath," Bernard said. "What the hell are we going to tell your mom and dad?"

"The truth is the best option I imagine," Roger said. "It doesn't matter if I get in trouble or not anymore. People are dead, and it looks like more may become deceased in short order."

Crystal finally calmed herself a bit. She wiped her nose with her finger and spoke up. Her voice was hoarse. "We're not going shopping, are we?"

"No," Bernard said. "No, we are not..."

3

Rachel sat behind her desk with the large window behind her. Ben stood on her right with both his hands tucked neatly behind him. Neither of the pair looked especially happy. Elizabeth stood nearby on her left.

"Let me see if I understand you correctly," Rachel said. Her once youthful face was now middle-aged, still beautiful, but being in her mid-thirties was a far cry from her late teens. "Two groups of ours get killed while you two survived."

Elizabeth's hair was now nearly fully white. Wrinkles had taken refuge in her face. Her twilight years were upon her, at nearly age seventy. She still possessed the appearance of a predator hidden in her eyes, and they showed her disdain. "It's smart of them to take the money and keep the product if this is the end of our business relationship. Almost like a severance package."

To round off the leadership of the syndicate, Warren was directly behind Rachel's seat, towering over it. He had his arms crossed and didn't look too pleased. "Severance paid in both blood and money, maybe."

"Why did you three attend this deal?" Rachel asked. "You know what? It doesn't matter why you were there. You two will be punished. For now, we deal with this treachery."

"I told you it would happen eventually," Elizabeth said. "We were lucky they dealt with us as long as they did. It was inevitable."

"A simple phone call would have sufficed. My employees didn't have to die brutally." Rachel's hands balled up into fists.

"He's old school," Ben said. "Maybe he figured you wouldn't get the message."

"I received it loud and clear," Rachel said. "Honey, get Rog and Crystal outside. Leave Bernard here."

Ben nodded and moved over to grasp Crystal's wrist and Roger's.

Roger shook free of the grip. "I'm not going anywhere."

"Boy," Ben growled.

"If you want me gone, you'll have to knock me out. I am not leaving of my own volition," Roger said, a scowl on his face. He backed away from his father figure.

Elizabeth watched this whole thing with great interest and a small smirk.

Not one to be outdone by Roger's youthful perseverance, Ben got Roger into a headlock. "You're coming with me. Don't make this worse on yourself."

Roger was serious earlier, however, and stomped on his father's foot as hard as he could manage with the heel of his shoe. He used the opportunity of Ben's surprise and escaped the hold. He held his fists up. "I said I'm not fucking going anywhere, old man. You hear me? I'm tired of being treated like a child by the pair of you."

"You wanted this? You got it, you little shit." Ben regained his composure and charged with a barbaric yell.

He tackled Roger and lifted him off the ground. The pair crashed through the door leading into the open hallway.

"Damn it." Warren maneuvered around the desk and chased after the pair.

He wasn't the only one, as Bernard broke rank and dashed out the door, following everyone.

"Why tonight?" Rachel sighed. "He can be such a pain in the ass." Rachel shook her head. She looked up at the tall ceiling before asking. "Why me, Lord?"

"Damn it!" Ben's voice came through the open door. "You'd better get this out of your system. Hit me. Will that make you feel better?"

"For fuck's sake." Rachel slammed her fists on the desk and got up. "I'll break this shit up. Apparently my son has lost his mind today. If you will excuse me," she said.

"By all means," Elizabeth said.

Rachel saw Roger and Bernard standing side by side. Bernard, for once, was the timid member of the pair as they stood opposite from Ben and Warren. The two older men approached the teenagers and the two pairs started fighting. Roger squared off with his father, but was clearly no match for the combat veteran. Ben did not retaliate or strike his son, but tried to immobilize him; however, the youthful energy kept Roger moving just out of reach.

Bernard, however, looked like he was only defending himself from Warren's attempted strikes, but he dodged or blocked all of them.

"Enough!" Rachel elevated her voice. Everyone around her froze in place. She marched over to the pair of eighteen-year-olds. She grabbed Roger by the ear and yanked it hard. "That's enough of this bullshit. You have the audacity to sneak out, and then, to add insult to injury, you assault your father?"

"I'm fine," Ben said. "He only got a cheap shot in. I've had far worse."

"I know you are dear," Rachel said.

"It looked like it hurt, though," Warren said. "There's some potential there. You've gotten better, kid," he said to Bernard. He cracked his knuckles. "You remind me of your uncle. The stories I heard of him in combat were the stuff of legends. You've got the same spark in you, I can tell."

"Be quiet," Rachel said.

"Yes, boss," Warren said with a clearing of his throat.

Roger looked to the side and saw Bernard watching over his shoulder. He also noted that Elizabeth was as well.

Rachel gripped his face and turned it back to her. "You will calm down, Son. Right now. Don't look away from me. Now apologize to your father."

"No. I don't think I will."

"You are just like your grandfather. I swear to God," Rachel said. "Did you get this disobedience out of your system? If I let you free, are you going to act like a civilized human?"

"So long as you realize I'm staying in there, sure."

"You want to hear business talk? Fine. Just realize you're not in the family business." Rachel let go of his ear. She turned to her husband. "Calm down, dear," she said.

"You try anything again and you'll receive worse than a tackle, Son," Ben said.

"Now get back in there," Rachel said.

The trio walked into Rachel's office. Roger took his spot next to Bernard, and Ben stayed near Roger's side, keeping a close watch on his son.

"Have fun?" Elizabeth asked the returning mother.

"Boys will be boys. You know how it is. Remember when Bernard and Warren got into it during training?"

"He was just angry," Elizabeth said. "It was his first time getting struck."

"Well, same for my son here. Now let's move on and talk business." She looked at her son. "Yes? I can infer you wish to speak. What is it?"

"Artyom had a message for me to deliver to you."

"You couldn't lead with that?" Ben asked. "Is that why you were so adamant? Why didn't you just say so?"

"You all didn't give me the chance to."

Elizabeth couldn't hide the small laugh that escaped her mouth.

"You be quiet, old woman," Rachel said.

"Sorry."

"Which of you troublemakers wants to spill what that hunk of concrete desired to send?" Rachel placed both palms on the imposing mass of a desk with a loud slap.

Bernard spoke up, cutting off Roger. "He said he'd told you before that they wanted a higher price and you ignored them. Therefore, this was the price exacted. Then he sent the order on his phone to kill the team there."

"He shielded us," Crystal spoke up. "Don't forget that part."

"Excuse me?" Ben asked. "What did you say?"

"I said he moved us to safety before he ordered the team killed. He said he didn't want a blood feud and that he liked these two for whatever reason, so he didn't want them killed."

"Explain how this happened," Elizabeth said.

"He wanted a private conversation, or so I thought," Roger said. "He wanted to sit in our car and discuss something, so we obliged him."

"The son of a bitch pulled a gun and pointed it at my

skull," Bernard said. "Right before ordering me to back the car away from our team."

"Quite the Samaritan, isn't he?" Ben asked. "What were you jokers doing while this happened?"

"Trying to not piss him off so he wouldn't blow Bernard's head clean off." Roger nodded toward Bernard. "Besides, my gun arm was indisposed."

"What?" Rachel asked. Her eyes wandered toward her daughter directly next to her son. She saw her clinging on to him. "Right. I see."

"Who cares about the minutiae?" Elizabeth asked. "He killed ours. We need to decide on our next course of action."

"If he wanted to piss us off, he'd have killed them too," Ben said.

"In his mind, we're even now," Rachel said. "If we retaliate, we spark a brand-new war."

"If we don't, we look weak and invite similar action from any new business partners we have," Elizabeth said. "It's the conundrum that's plagued man since the inception of organized crime."

"Thanks for the philosophy lesson."

"Oleg might not want a blood feud, but he knows killing our personnel is a declaration of war," Rachel said. She clasped her hands together on the desk. Her eyes gazed at the mahogany desk sitting in front of her, flittering back and forth, as if searching desperately for the answer she desired.

"We do not need their supply anymore," Warren said. "We've built up enough of a supply chain that the guns themselves are immaterial. It'd be for either political or vengeful reasons if we strike back."

"Father would have struck back. I know before you repeat it," Rachel said, looking over her shoulder temporarily at Elizabeth before turning to face the boys and Crystal again.

"The man had his faults," Elizabeth said. "Both of your leadership styles have pros and cons. Yours works if your partners respect you. You both make money, and no one dies. Yours fails when they test you."

"His failed when the cartels tested him too, as you'll recall. We were this close." Rachel held her thumb and index finger closely together. "They almost killed the syndicate before it was properly started."

"Might I make a suggestion?" Ben asked.

"Give me something," Rachel said.

Ben reached up and stroked the stubble on his chin. "Why not simply place a bounty on Oleg's head anonymously? It'd get our point across and keep us out of it."

"No sane hitman will take that job," Elizabeth said. "They'd have the whole of the Russian mafia after their asses, and no one is that greedy. We'd have to send our own personnel, and that's the opening shot of the war. We're better off getting this over and done. A war is brewing. We have the manpower, and we have the pull on the streets. Why are we tiptoeing around that pissant Oleg anyway?"

"He's no longer a pissant, as you so colorfully describe him," Rachel said in an annoyed tone. "He's the head boss in the US for his organization. You know what? I'll call and feel this out. Sitting and jerking off about our options won't solve anything. If he wants a war, we will not cower. Now be quiet."

She picked up the nearby landline phone and dialed the number she'd memorized over the last eighteen years.

"Funny you should call," Oleg's voice greeted her. "What do you want?"

"This is how you escalate wanting higher payment?" Rachel asked.

"Artyom let your little boys and girl live, didn't he?" Oleg asked. "I cannot see how you'd be all that angry. Think of it like a severance package. You fucked me for nearly twenty years, so I took your men out. It's business. Don't take it so personally, like your old man would've."

"Do you want a war?"

"Even if I did, you always were the peacemaker, weren't you? Some on the streets question your resolve to do what needs to be done. I guess they'll see soon. Besides, I doubt your outfit needs our supply anymore. What's the big deal?"

"A pile of dead bodies. I doubt you'd be so cool if I killed a group of your men. Never mind if it was a supposed business partner. You'd be foaming at the mouth."

"Good thing you're so tolerant and understanding then." His mocking tone tinted his voice.

"You planning on another strike?"

"Where'd the fun be if I told you beforehand? I always enjoyed a good surprise. I guess you'll find out in due time. Why would I inform you? So you can dox me and my men before threatening to kill them and their families? You think word doesn't travel after what you pulled on the cartel leadership?"

"I could do that anyway, depending if you piss me off," Rachel said. "Don't think I won't if it comes to it."

"I'll take my chances. Your little group is so hard focused on your income, you're not known for your viciousness anymore. Your father had his faults, but he knew how to stay respected on the streets. Even if he was a bloodthirsty fool who picked fights he couldn't win."

"You want to be evasive and not answer questions, fine. I'll consider you hostile in that case."

"You do what you want. We're through with the Morris Syndicate. You're coasting on name recognition alone at this point. The organization is an embarrassment to Daniel and Bernard Morris of the past. That's because of you, if I hadn't spelled it out quite clear enough, little girl."

"You want to act like that? I've heard enough. Hope your family dies in a fire then." She slammed the phone down and grumbled to herself. She looked up at her kids and then over at her advisors. "What? He deserved it."

"I'm sure he did," Elizabeth said. "So, we're at war then?"

"He was shifty and never answered. He didn't deny or confirm it. Put everyone on notice. I don't want anyone going out alone."

"You got it," Ben said. "I'll put the word out to watch for the Russians - that they're no longer our partners."

"That is not a green light. Defend themselves only. Got it?"

"Of course," Ben said. "I hope this isn't a war, but I don't hold my breath with that guy. I never trusted him."

"They know where this mansion is." Rachel wore a sour look on her face. "We can't stay here if this escalates into a war. Hell, we should move now. They may try an assassination and take us all out at once."

"We're implementing plan C then?" Ben asked.

"Make it so. As for you kids, I want a word with each of you privately." She pushed the rolling chair out from behind the desk and moved around it until she stood in front of the three troublesome youths. "Everyone else, get out."

Elizabeth and Warren quickly followed orders and left. Ben trailed behind and whispered something in his wife's ear. Afterward, he leveled a pointed glare at Roger before leaving and following behind the pair.

"That leaves us with you three. What will I do with you

dolts?" She reached forward and poked Roger's chest. "Especially you."

"I want to fight if we're in a war with those Russian assholes," Roger said.

"Out of the question."

"It's not a question."

"What was that?"

"I said," Roger said, locking eyes with his mother, "it's not a question. If you lock me up, I'll get out and go anyway. You know I will."

"Why can't you just make your mother's life easier?"

"He killed men and women I've known for years. All that death and misery for a stupid reason like insufficient payment pisses me off. Jeff and the others didn't deserve that. They had no bearing on the weapon prices."

"You're saying it was my fault then?"

"I'm saying I want Russian blood."

"You're certainly hot headed like your grandfather," Rachel said. She reached up and rubbed her forehead. She looked and saw the revolver her son had equipped. "What if I told you I still won't allow it?"

"Then I'd head out alone."

"Not totally alone," Bernard piped in. "I'd be with him."

"Yeah, that doesn't help. No offense, Bernard, but you're a rookie for all intents and purposes. Your entire unit was killed, so you need another one. Lord, help me. I see a solution that would make you both happy, but I can't make my peace with it."

"I want to stay with him," Crystal said.

"You are not heading into the field. Even if this idiot of a son of mine wants it. He's at least been practicing with that piece. What skill do you have that'd be useful?"

"Lee has taught me lots when he wasn't on a job."

"You too, Crystal?" Rachel asked. "Why can't you two be like me when I was your age? I wanted to steer clear of this dangerous life, but I was dragged into it; and now one of you can't wait to throw his life away. I vowed when I became a mother I wouldn't allow it, that I'd be a better mother than my father was a father. You are putting me in quite the position. If I say no, you go out alone just asking to die. If I say yes, you're out on the front line and may die. I hate lose-lose situations. You know that?"

"Life isn't fair," Roger said.

"Says the spoiled brat who's gotten everything handed to him in life," Rachel said. "You're dumb enough to follow through on that threat. Today is proof enough of that. God dammit," she said. "Now, even assuming I did this, you realize you wouldn't be the vanguard. You'd be the rear watch, so to speak. Defending our turf, not attacking."

"So long as I get to show Artyom what happens when he kills my friends," Roger said, "I don't care."

"Son, have you ever heard the saying, 'When preparing for revenge, dig two graves'?"

"I do like the idea of double the body count."

"I know you're not as dense as that. It means prepare your own grave. Don't be willingly ignorant. It's not a good look. No one likes a smartass, and don't even use the dumb ass retort. I've used it too much to make a point. Now stay quiet and let me think." She paced in front of the three teenagers. "This mansion is a target. I can't have you all stay here. Loathe as I am to admit it, assigning you all to a unit and putting you in our territory at an undisclosed location would keep you safer."

Bernard saw Rachel was deep in thought and elbowed Roger in the ribs, wearing a smirk.

On Roger's other side, he felt Crystal holding onto his arm.

"Alright, fine," Rachel said. "You want to be a gangster? You want revenge? Trust me when I tell you, it won't make you feel better. Your mother knows how you feel better than anyone here, Son. However, given the circumstances, I don't have a choice. Go to your father and tell him to test your shooting abilities. I will have you ready to defend yourself before I send you out and about. That brawl earlier told me you need improvement."

"Should be easy enough," Roger said.

"Temper the arrogance," Rachel said. "You may be our son, but the standards do not differ from another family member. You will be held to the rank and file's standards." She stepped to her left in front of Bernard. "As for you, you'll be transferred to another unit effective immediately. Report to Ben for your assignment."

"May I ask a question?" Bernard asked.

"If I was a teenager, I'd tell you that you could ask another. Go ahead."

"Could I be in your son's unit? He's always needed me to watch his back."

Rachel looked at her son, who was silently comforting his sister, and back to the slicked black hair of Bernard. "We will see if Roger passes his tests. Make your request to Ben, and tell him I approve. My son will need a bodyguard, and you just volunteered. You two have always been thick as proverbial and literal thieves."

Crystal raised her free hand.

"Yes?" Rachel asked.

"What about me?"

"You're to report to Lee and have him ensure you're

43

ready for what you volunteered for. They will need an information gatherer and overwatch. It is a ton of responsibility. I used to do it. You're skilled with computers, but this is another league. You will always wear a vest anytime you are not in your safe house. Also, you will never leave the vehicle mid-operation. If you agree to those terms, I will allow it." She reached out and removed her daughter's grasp from Roger's arm. "Stand on your own." She shooed them away with her hand. "Now get out of here. That's an order."

Downstairs a bit later...

Roger, Bernard, and Crystal sat around a table placed in a far corner of the living room, secluded from others.

"Can you believe it?" Bernard couldn't hide the glee in his voice. "You're going to be working soon."

"Provided he passes Dad's test," Crystal said. "Speaking of which, have you talked to him yet?"

"He said to show up tomorrow morning at the shooting range," Roger said.

"It's easy enough," Bernard said. "You practice every other day. I assume you've practiced against the targets when they're moving, right?"

"Of course."

"Then you'll be fine. You're always jogging on the trail behind the property, so your endurance will pass too."

"It's the only way I can escape this prison temporarily."

"Then you'll pass the mile jog like it's nothing."

"You realize she put us with Chris and Jackie," Roger said. "She doesn't trust us in the least. Why stick us with long time veterans?"

"She wants to keep us safe," Crystal said. "That's all. She

knows they're skilled and will do everything they can. That's why. She can't assign Warren or Father just to us. They're her guard. We get the best of the best soldiers."

"What about you, princess?" Bernard asked. "Have you talked to the shut-in Lee yet?"

"I did," Crystal said. "He quizzed me a bit, had me go through some basic hacks and tasks - like ringing a phone, messing with the camera system, and even infiltrating our network. That last one was very difficult though, since it was his own system and he's damned good."

"You're already cleared?"

"He said he'd report to mother," she said. "I'm already good to go."

"That leaves me then," Roger said. "Fuck it. I'm going to find Father and attempt the test. We have lights down there. It's not a matter of visibility, and we all know it. He's dragging his feet."

"He's probably pissed at you, dude," Bernard said. "I would be if my son took a cheap shot and embarrassed me in front of the syndicate leadership."

"He was treating me like a child," Roger said. "Look what it accomplished. I'll be joining you both on jobs soon enough because of that outburst. Besides," he said, "you advised me to seize control and fight. I was just taking your advice for once."

"That's your first mistake," Crystal said. "He always gets you in trouble. How you've never learned yet is a mystery."

The group heard a smattering of greetings. They looked over and witnessed a group of members saying hello to Ben, who'd just entered the room. He returned the gesture before heading toward the teenagers. His smile morphed into a scowl.

"Get ready," Bernard whispered. "He doesn't look happy."

"That's because I'm not," Ben said. He moved behind Roger's seat and reached down. He placed both hands on his son's shoulders. "I just heard from a birdie that you desire a test to measure if you're as competent as you believe. While I know your fist fighting skills are lacking from earlier, what about shooting?"

"I'll pass whatever test you give me, old man."

"Old man?" Ben asked. "You've got some guts after that outburst earlier."

"The kid can manage it, boss," Chris said, walking over to the group.

"Why can't you mind your own business?" Jackie followed closely behind Chris. "Sorry about him, sir," she said.

"I'm used to him," Ben said. "He gets a pass because of his proven skills, but this naïve idiot has yet to prove himself. What makes you so confident in him?"

"He's down at the target range three times a week. I also taught him tricks here and there over the years," Chris said.

"I remember telling you specifically not to." Ben glared at Chris.

"Hey," Chris raised both palms up in front of him, "I was down there sharpening my skills, and I saw the kid struggling. What was I supposed to do when he asked his uncle figure for tips? Just ignore him?"

"The good Samaritan act only works if you're actually a good Samaritan," Ben said.

"Which you are definitively not," Jackie said.

"Come on, kid," Chris said. "Back me up here."

"He's right," Roger said. "He taught me a lot about how to shoot."

"Well, now you're going to learn from me," Ben said. "Right now."

"Remember what I told you about nighttime shooting, kid." Chris clicked his tongue. "You'll amaze your dad and be one of us."

"Get up, lazybones," Ben slapped Roger's shoulder. "I meant right now."

Roger hopped out of his seat and followed his father out of the room.

"Remember what I said about squeezing the trigger, not pulling it. Oh," Chris said, cupping his hand around his mouth to amplify his voice toward the retreating pair, "remember about exhaling for longer shots if you want it to be accurate."

The teenager and his father figure exited the back door and started the trek toward the nearby shooting range. Ben flicked a switch outside the door and enormous lights turned on in front of them, illuminating the shooting range they'd built all those years ago.

"Even if you pass this so-called test, I know you can't fight hand to hand worth a damn," Ben said. "I don't think you're ready myself. However, I know you're as stubborn as a mule, and you'll sneak out even if we forbid it. You are an adult now, and I suppose I must treat you like one. Don't expect leniency, for you will receive none from me or your mother."

"I don't need leniency. I need respect and revenge for all those lives lost. It's weird, knowing that I'll never see them again."

"That's the life you're so desperate to join. This is a dirty life, Son. You sure you wish to rush headlong into this life-style like I did years ago? I guarantee if you do, you're going to see people you love die. Is this little revenge fantasy worth it?"

"I won't let them get away with it. End of story."

"Oh, you're a big man I see," Ben said, still leading his son across the backyard. He opened the gate and shut it behind his son. "I was your age myself once, you know. I'm trying to spare you the heartache and pain that your mother and I went through at your age. Of course you're young and dumb, so you won't listen - just like me. I'm doing this because I love you, Son."

"Gee thanks, Dad. I'm uh..." Roger scratched the back of his head, trying to force the words he knew he should say. "I'm sorry about earlier."

"Hm," Ben said. "At least we didn't raise a total shit bag."

"Fuck you."

The men shared a mutual laugh as they finally arrived at the long table underneath the makeshift roof. The beams had pipes filled with wires going to wherever they needed to.

Ben flicked a nearby switch on the control board. Targets shaped like human's sprung up across the field at differing distances. Some were as close as twenty-five yards, others ranged to a hundred or further. The bright lights towering above helped a bit with visibility, but it was not as clear as daylight. Hay bales held human shaped paper targets near the rear of the range.

"Let's see your piece then," Ben said. "Hand it over." He held out his palm, face up toward his son.

Roger took the revolver out and handed it over.

"A six shooter? Interesting choice. I'd go with a semi-automatic personally. Are you married to using this?"

"It's stopping power is what I value."

Ben flicked his hand. The chambers holding bullets

came dislodged. "Thirty-eight caliber provides just that." He spun the chambers with a satisfying series of clicks before he closed them in one flick. He inspected the rest of the weapon. "It's engraved I see. What is this? Is that a skull and a rose?"

"Love and death are integral to our lives."

"It doesn't offer a tactical advantage. It's useless and for pure vanity. No demerits for it, but it is senseless." He flipped the gun and handed it back to his son. "Any others you will use?"

"Depends on the range of the target."

"Your aim is to hit the near targets, then hit the rear targets. I trust you know how to zero a rifle's scope. Or do I need to teach you?"

"Chris taught me. Now let me fetch a rifle."

Ben watched his son walk off toward the nearby building they'd erected near the range. He disappeared inside. He looked up at the mansion toward where he knew Rachel's office was. "I hope you know what you're doing." The sound of a door closing snapped him out of his reverie.

Roger returned, keeping the business end pointing down. He'd grabbed his earmuffs and donned the hearing safety equipment. He had both hands on the rifle, keeping a secure grip.

"I'm assuming he also taught you about gun safety too. You know, if you'd asked, I'd have been happy to teach you all this."

"If you'll recall, I asked repeatedly," Roger said. "You were always busy. Either escorting Mom, dealing with personnel issues, or whatever it was. I decided to just go by myself - and Bernard sometimes. We held competitions to gauge who the better marksman was."

"You're angling for a job where you rarely have time off

and work constant overtime. I'm sorry I never found time, but that's the life we live." His somber tone gave way to a more playful one Roger hadn't heard from his father in years. "Now, who usually won? Be honest," Ben said, keeping a straight face.

"It was usually a sixty-forty split," Roger said. He looked toward the targets. "Can we get on with it?"

"Who usually won?" Ben reached for the ear protection sitting on the nearby table and hung them around his neck.

"He did," Roger said. "He barely won. Alright?"

"Sure, whatever you say." He pulled out his phone and pressed the app icon that looked like an egg. A clock came up. "Now when I say go," he tapped the screen, setting the timer to thirty seconds, "you will hit every target at twenty-five meters. I had the targets replaced so we could be sure of what you hit. You should thank Chris. He jumped at the opportunity when I told him you were being tested. All I did was ask him if he knew any shit birds who needed discipline to do it, but he did it himself. You should thank him after this, if I taught you anything growing up." He put on the ear protection and hovered his thumb over the button.

"Yes, Father," Roger said. "Twenty-five yards, huh? Alright." He placed the rifle down and chose his revolver for this round. He put on the ear protection and took a deep breath. "I'm ready whenever you are."

"Go!"

Roger's arms lifted in a flash and aimed down the iron sights of his revolver. Loud firing was followed by puffs of smoke and flashes of light. Ben looked down the range, then to his son. His form was better than he cared to admit. *He's slow on changing targets. I need to check if he can hit a moving target next,* he thought.

Roger fired his sixth shot and pointed the smoking barrel upwards. "Done."

"Let's see how fast you can reload." Ben got the device's timer ready. "Go."

Roger's muscle memory took over. He flicked the cylinder open and dumped the spent rounds on the ground before transferring the gun to his left hand. His right grabbed a speed loader from his back pocket and finished loading.

"Time." Ben tapped the screen once he was done. "Seven seconds is a bit slow. Now pick up your rifle and get ready for the one-hundred-yard targets. You have three minutes to adjust it before the round starts. Take shots to zero it in." Ben once again set the timer in his hand. He watched his son look through the scope before inspecting the scope perched atop. He adjusted it and looked down the sights, then fired off a round.

"Miss," Ben said.

Roger made another adjustment and tried again.

"Hit, but not a good one."

"I see what it is now." Roger made one final adjustment to his scope before his father called out.

"Time. Hit every target. The best shot will be the only one counted, so be accurate. Go!"

Roger had the rifle configured for single shots and first fired at the far-left target, working his aim toward his right. He'd barely fired the shot on the last target when his father called out again.

"Very good," Ben said. "Now we try the moving targets. If you pass, I'll acknowledge your skill as a marksman. You have forty-five seconds." Ben pressed a different button on the control panel. A nearby machine whirred to life.

The rear of the range had multiple human-like figures

moving right and left. They were on multiple levels. Some of them were flipped and hung upside down just above the targets. One area of the shooting range had the targets climb up and down a slight incline.

"These will speed up the longer the test goes. Again, only the best shot counts per target. The more targets you hit, the better. Reload and prepare." Ben configured the machine for the correct set and hovered his finger over the button. "Go!" He pressed the button and his phone.

Ben watched his son take his first shots and saw that they had missed. *You didn't adjust. That's a farther target.*

Roger saw this and made a quick adjustment before continuing to fire.

Ben noticed the shots were landing now. He glanced down at the timer. *This will be close*, he thought. "Time!"

Roger fired off the last shot and halted. He placed the rifle on the table in front of him and turned to his father. They both took off the earmuffs.

"Let's see how you performed," Ben said. He pressed the button to stop the moving targets and then reached for another. A safety light in each booth turned on that read in bright red letters 'No firing'. No one was inside, but it was a precaution he himself had drilled into every recruit for safety's sake.

The pair checked the nearest target first.

"These look passable," Ben said. "Not perfect, but good enough."

"Those are kill shots." Roger reached out and touched the bullet-hole pierced paper. "Look," he pointed to an abdomen shot. "Center mass is perfect."

Ben kept going, ignoring his son's protests. "The rounds at the one-hundred-yard range look decent enough," he said. "Now for the moment of truth." He led his son toward the furthest back targets. "Get up here," he called out.

Roger jogged to catch up with his father and stopped beside him. "It looks good, huh?"

"Your first shot missed," Ben said. "You readjusted, but you should have done that before the round started. You know they're a different distance. That is a fault I saw."

"How many targets did I need to hit?" Roger counted the different assorted struck targets and arrived at nine targets he'd hit out of ten. "That's nine right there. Surely that passes."

"Twenty years ago the requirement was ten out of ten," Ben said. He turned to his son.

"Perfection? Seriously?"

"Lucky for you, we've since lowered it to nine."

"I passed?"

"So long as you show up tomorrow morning and jog two miles with me, you'll pass the endurance portion. If you pass that, then you're good. Make sure you are not late. We will meet outside the back door at five sharp. If you are late, I will take it as you changing your mind."

"I'll be there. Make sure you keep up, old guard," Roger said. He took his revolver and holstered it at his side. He then picked up the rifle.

"Hurry and put those away. Lock those safely out of reach, and then sleep."

The next day...

"Judging by the sweat," Bernard said, leaning away from his friend, "I'm guessing you finished your running."

"That's not sweat." Roger reached up and wiped away

some water. "I just showered after that run. I left him in the dust."

"So, you're part of the team now?"

"Officially and done," Roger said. "He said I was to report to Chris today at noon. What time is it?"

"Quarter until noon," Bernard said after a glance at his wristwatch. "Are you enjoying wearing these threads? They're stiff at first, but you get used to it."

"I'll get used to it. Now let's go hunt for our new team. I can't be late on my first day. Do you know where they are?"

"They're supposed to be back around noon. They're out securing our lodging. That's what Jackie told me when I asked. I had most of your clothes packed and sent over already while you were running with your dad."

"That's how you occupied yourself while I was testing? You just assumed I'd pass?"

"I knew you were going to pass, man," Bernard gave him a cocksure grin. "You need some spine in you. You're one of the syndicate now, brother. Act like it. We can accomplish anything we set our mind to, you and me."

Roger saw his sister walk into the room and approached her alongside Bernard. "I was wondering when you'd show up."

"I was packing," she said. She was dragging a large suitcase behind her. She handed it off to Roger. "This is the last one. Thanks."

"Sorry, I was busy with Dad's last test. It's not even noon, and I'm already tired," he said.

"I wouldn't let anyone else hear you talk like that," Bernard said, keeping his voice hushed. His voice returned to its normal loud tone. "Now let's get outside and be sure we're ready for them when they arrive." He led the group to the front door and opened it, holding it open for Crystal.

"Did you pack everything? Odds are we won't return for a while."

"Just about," she said. She walked alongside her brother and Bernard down the short flight of stairs to the soil beneath. "I'll be glad to be near civilization again. Where are they sticking us?"

"We'll see shortly." Bernard pointed down the long dirt path that served as the property's driveway. He dashed toward the gates and opened them for the approaching car. He ran back to the group. "Be on your best behavior," he said. "That goes for everybody. If we're forging a name for ourselves, let's make it a respectable reputation."

"I am always professional," Crystal said.

"Coming from you," Roger said, "that's rich."

"I'd say the same of you, buddy," Bernard said while the car passed through the gates and stopped nearby. "These are our superiors, make no mistake, and treat them with respect."

The doors opened and out came Jackie and Chris.

"I take it you passed if you're out here," Chris said. "That's good. We got our base of operations all set up. I hope none of you mind roommates because it's only a three-bedroom apartment."

"Crystal, sweetheart," Jackie said after she exited the car, "you'll be in my room, which is the master bedroom for the record before anyone argues. It's a done decision. We girls need our bathroom access."

"I suppose that means you're getting a bedroom to yourself then," Roger said. "I'm fine having a roommate."

"Good, let's head out," Jackie said. "The sooner we leave, the sooner we work. Everyone should take their own cars. We'll go in a convoy."

"Got it," Roger said. He reached into his pockets and

fished out his car key. "You want to ride with me?" he asked his nearby sister. "I'll load this luggage for you."

"Sure," she said. "Come on B. Move it."

"Don't call me B. You know I hate that," Bernard said.

"B, get a move on like the girl says," Chris called out toward the retreating girls along with a boisterous laugh.

"I guess that's your new nickname now, B," Roger said.

"Don't you start on me now too..."

4

Oleg leaned back in his chair and placed his shoes on the desk in front of him. "Is everything in place?" he asked.

Artyom nodded. "Yes," he said. "Sir, are we sure we should press this further?"

"Are you questioning my decision?"

"I am simply concerned about a prolonged war with that woman. I thought sparing the children would keep us from this unfortunate outcome." Artyom held his hands at his sides, almost like a soldier standing in formation. "It would not be wise for business. Why are we doing this?"

"You know the law of the concrete jungle. It's every man for himself. In our case, every organization for themselves. Their usefulness has run its course. Now we can use their stocks and enrich ourselves at their expense. We have to ensure we have enough money to send the higher ups their slice and still live comfortably here. That necessitates a change of the political landscape."

"What about her unique methods of targeting our loved ones?"

"Fool," Oleg snarled. "She doesn't have reach to get to them. They're back home. What's she going to do? Find an assassin dumb enough to go into our home country and kill them? We know the brotherhood protects our families. They'd be dead in a day. She knows that. She has no leverage with that trick of hers, and she knows it. That's why she won't strike first. Why not take advantage and steal inventory? It's pure profit."

"I do not debate the practical side of this, merely the consequences. Our course is set, however, and I will not question it. I have our best men on the job. If she is smart, they will be on alert."

"She has caches of the stuff scattered throughout her turf. My guess is in apartments with her personnel. They have gone back to their roots with how their original patriarch did things. Our observation has uncovered this is a reliable building for them to have supply. We have confirmation that yesterday's shipment did not originate from there, so it's a higher chance it has inventory to steal. Now, what of our previous arrangements?"

"Our men arrived yesterday, along with Mikhail."

"I love it when a plan comes together. Use him in our upcoming war with the syndicate. He'll be invaluable to us. The higher ups sent us this much personnel for a reason. We need to expand to keep up with the money demand."

"I'll put him to good use. His specialty should come in handy for my plans."

"You always have been a tactical genius, my friend," Oleg said. "Use it once more and clear this rabble from the city for me."

"That is a tall order, but I will do everything within my power. They rival us in pure body count, even with our newfound reinforcements. They've recruited heavily in recent years. Precise strikes at their income streams, I think, would be most effective. If we starve them of their money, more men may quit or desert."

Oleg tapped the side of his head. "There it goes again - always planning. After our store house raid, what else did you have in mind?"

"We know their territory. Their men stay near it for collection, decentralization, and security purposes. If we throw several surgical strikes across their controlled businesses, we can pressure them even further and gain some money for ourselves. The store owners can't pay if they already paid us. We'll tell them we're their new beneficiaries and make sure they see it our way."

"Old school but efficient," Oleg said. "I like it. Piss right on their shoes."

"Retaliation is a foregone conclusion. May as well go hard," Artyom said. "If we attack from multiple points at once, it will sow confusion; and, unless they're on their game, they may panic."

"Discord, chaos, fear - all powerful allies in battle. I'll leave the specifics to you. If you need men, weapons, or logistical support, let me know. I'll get you whatever it is."

"Our new men are already equipped, thanks to keeping the hardware we were supposed to sell to the Syndicate. It seems everything has lined up for us. We need to prepare for the inevitable retaliation. We should place scouts between us and their territory, so we'd receive an early warning in case they get the idea to retaliate in kind."

"With our new influx of men, can we defend our places of work?"

"With scouts, our buildings would possess a skeleton crew. That's counting the personnel going on raids, too. The theory is with us on the offense, it will keep them out of our front yard and in theirs playing emergency management. While our enemy is busy putting out fires, we're starting them even faster. Eventually, it will not be sustainable. Meanwhile, we'd be profiting off their misfortune."

"I might have to watch my back with that intellect," Oleg said. His jovial tone had taken a more reserved one.

"You need not worry, sir," Artyom said. "My loyalty is to you and the group. My personal aspirations are not for power, merely to live another day and live comfortably within my means."

"I'm both relieved and disappointed to hear that." Oleg brought his feet down to the floor. "You'd be a hell of a leader, but I don't want to lose you as my advisor."

"That will not happen, sir," Artyom said. "Leadership has never been my strong suit. I just execute the plans."

"Well, while you're finalizing our plans," he got up from the office chair, "I'm going to go introduce myself to our new men. Where are they holed up?"

"Mikhail is in the restaurant, at the bar specifically. I can bring him back for some privacy. The others are nearby in various apartments. I can call them and get them here if you'd like to brief them."

"Make it so. I want to address the troops and rally them for the upcoming war."

"It is as you say, sir."

5

The orange burning light of the dying day shone through the glass windows inside the main living room of the apartment. Roger, Bernard, and Chris finally got the couch where the ladies wanted it and placed it down.

"Is there anything else?" Roger asked.

"For now, no," Jackie said. "That's all the furniture."

"I know you two young men don't think that's all we're doing today," Chris said. "Work awaits tonight. We have a collection run to make before we can truly relax. It should prove an appropriate way to ease you into this life."

"It's only a few places," Jackie said. "Two groups comprising two members should be adequate. Which leaves our tech to get settled in while we're out. We won't need her expertise there. So get some rest, Crystal honey."

"That's good. I need to gauge this internet speed we've got here. Once that's done, I'll set up everyone's PC's and get them secured. You already moved hardware into each room, so I'll get those ready for when you return."

"Good," Bernard said. "I hate setting those things up. It's a proper pain in the ass."

"Yes, I too loathe going to our list of pre-approved software, going to the website, and installing them," Crystal said, sarcasm apparent. "Following directions is so difficult and a pain in the ass."

"Now to determine the pairs," Chris said. "The bosses probably want us to split up with one of us veterans with one of you two young bucks. However, I know you two would prefer going it together, wouldn't you? Two young made men, out to prove themselves on their first job."

"That would be nice," Roger said. "The collections are nearby, right?"

"I had these printed before we left," Jackie said. She leaned down and picked up the stacks of papers. She handed one to Bernard and Roger. "These are all our spots we're going to be assigned to collect from. Tonight, we're going to number four, seven, and nine. They're the ones due for payment. I think if you two are sticking together, you should try number four."

"That leaves seven and nine for us," Chris said. "Don't worry, it's only until you two get a feel for collecting. It takes a little finesse. You can't come down too hard or they shut down. You'll get the hang of it soon enough."

"What if they can't pay?" Roger asked.

"Then you get creative," Jackie said. "You're going in with a baseball bat. I'd suggest a nice swing to the kneecap. That always jogs their memory of where the money is."

"Or if you want to maintain their ability to earn for future nights," Chris leveled a sidelong glance at Jackie, "you can destroy parts of their shop. That usually gets the same message across with far less resentment. Now don't misunderstand. You still need your guns on you in case of an emergency. It's not unheard of that a stupid sucker is pissed and pulls a gun. Number four's shopkeeper has always been docile and paid on time. It's a good beginner assignment. Don't worry, you'll get tougher jobs in due time. Savor the simple jobs while you can. They don't last forever. Isn't that right?"

"From your mouth to God's ears," Jackie said. "Now let's hurry. I want to return and eat. I'm getting hungry."

"You heard the lady," Chris said with a clap. "Let's get moving, gentlemen."

Roger and Bernard followed the older pair out of the three-bedroom apartment and into the parking lot below.

"We'll take mine," Bernard said.

"Fine by me," Roger said, climbing into the passenger seat of his friend's sports car. He looked across the parking lot and watched Chris opening the passenger door of his car for Jackie.

Bernard climbed inside, drawing Roger's attention. "I can't believe we're getting the baby jobs," he muttered.

"They said it was temporary."

"They're babysitting us. Can't you see that? This is a sweet gig for them. They won't have to go out on the front lines with us. They're here to keep us pacified." He pulled out of the parking space and waved to their seniors to pull out in front of them. He wore a smile as he let them exit the parking lot first.

"You don't think the harder, more lucrative jobs will come?" Roger asked.

"You mean the arms deals? I doubt it. Collection runs pay peanuts. The real money is when you head an arms deal. With this unit, we'll be lucky to get one."

"We work our way up, starting from the bottom. We'll put our nose to the grindstone, and those opportunities will open eventually. You're not a boss first day."

"It's your first day, not mine."

"You're my partner, so call me the albatross around your neck, if that makes you feel better."

Bernard gave a momentary glance over at Roger after he pulled out into traffic and got situated. "You're a lot of things, but a burden was never one of them. We'll just prove ourselves valuable, and then they'll have to promote us."

"Hard to do that when we're doing collection runs. How does one prove themselves on jobs like this?"

"Getting it done on time, I suppose. It's my first collection run too, if I'm honest."

"You make fun of me for being the prince of crime, and you got placed into an arms dealing unit for your first post? Fuck off," Roger laughed. "You were elevated out of the gate because of your mama, just like everyone makes fun of me."

"You're not wrong. It just pisses me off that we've got something to prove, you and me." Bernard used his right hand to reach over and touch Roger's chest before returning it to the steering wheel. "We're not just spoiled little bitches. We're men who get the job done."

"Sorry to break it to you, but I'm batting zero on that front. The one job I went on, the entire team, minus us, died."

"That's different," Bernard said. "That wasn't our fault."

"I doubt that excuse flies for anyone else. Yet it did for us. Plus, let's not forget that brawl I started, and you joined in. They'd have reprimanded anyone else, at the very least - not give them another job. Face it, we're reaping rewards from our parents' favoritism."

"Point taken," Bernard said. "If we're doing that, then we should reap it for all it's worth."

"That's just like you."

"Think about it. No one else gets this opportunity. We'd be fools to waste it." He pulled the sleek car into a nearly empty parking lot. He pulled up right beside the building and put it into park. "Remember, you flip the sign from open to closed after the last civilian leaves, if any are inside, and guard the front door. You have your gloves, yeah?" He reached into his coat's pockets and donned his own black leather gloves.

Roger followed suit. "Yeah, what about our faces?"

"We'll just take the CCTV tape he uses. We just can't leave our fingerprints in there. Aren't you glad you have me to look out for your new ass?"

"Let's get this done," Roger said, gripping the door handle.

"Right you are."

Roger got out of the car alongside Bernard. They pushed open the glass door and were surprised at the scene they encountered inside. Nearby shelves were already knocked over. Bags of chips, candy bars, and assorted snacks littered the floor. Some nearby plastic containers with colored liquid had fallen, and now the floor was wet to boot. The storekeeper was behind the nearby counter. Bernard made his way over while Roger flipped the open sign to closed.

"Quite the mess you have here," Bernard said, reaching the counter. "You get a troublemaking kid or something?"

"Sir." The shop clerk was not looking at Bernard. Instead, he was staring at the newspaper in front of him. "I must ask that you excuse the mess. We had an accident earlier."

"Boy, I'll say," Bernard said. "Look at me. It's only polite when we're speaking."

The timid cashier took his time but indeed did as Bernard asked. He lowered the paper to the counter and inspected Bernard and Roger nearby. His bruised eyes went as wide as saucers. "Why are you here?"

"Someone sure did a number on you. Anyway, you know why we're here," Bernard said, leaning forward, invading the man's personal space. "It's collection day."

"What?"

"Don't act dumb. We're not fools. You know what I'm talking about. We lent you money to start this fine establishment. We only require the payments you legally owe us."

"The Russian guy said that arrangement was no longer binding."

"Russian?" Bernard lost his cool. "What are you talking about?"

"They came in less than an hour ago," the clerk said, "and already took all the money we have. They said they'd bought our debt."

Bernard reached over the counter and grabbed the cashier by his neck. "I sincerely hope you didn't give them our debt money. For your own sake, I mean."

"Look at me, man," the man pleaded. "They beat the shit out of me when I told them I wasn't giving them anything since you all hadn't told me anything. They didn't give me a choice, man. Please believe me."

Roger casually circled around the counter and moved past the scared man toward the camera system. He pressed the eject button, only to be met with a noise.

"They already took it," the clerk said.

"You're aware if you don't have money, we're forced to take collateral, right? You're not escaping giving something before we leave. Our necks are on the line too," Bernard said. "I'll be damned if my friend's opening job is going to be a failure because of this bullshit."

"It's a convenience store, man. Nothing here is going to approach the two thousand you normally take."

"This rundown shop should have an office," Roger said.

He spotted the nearby door behind the counter. "You keep him here. I'll check to see if he's hiding anything."

"That's the manager's room. He's not here right now. For the record, I'm not positive there's cash inside. It's not my business."

Roger opened the door and entered the cramped office. He moved to the desk and opened every drawer, rifling through their contents, looking for anything valuable.

"Any luck in there?" Bernard asked, never taking his eyes off the battered cashier.

"I found something alright." Roger's eyes moved from the drawers to the desk itself. It had a small safe on it. On the top of it was a note with three numbers, along with R's and L's above each number. "Your manager's an idiot, by the way." He leaned down and input the code. The miniature safe opened, and he looked inside. He saw stacks of papers and a lone diamond necklace. Snatching the jewelry, he held it up to examine more closely. "This is the only valuable, besides insurance papers and a bunch of bullshit." He closed the safe and moved back into the front room. He leaned against the counter, facing the entrance to the store.

"You have a wallet, don't you? Empty it. I don't care if this isn't your store. That necklace will not sell for two thousand dollars. We need more."

"I'll get it," Roger said. He moved behind the cashier and reached into his back pocket. He extracted the wallet and opened it to reveal nothing but his driver's license, medical insurance card, and a lot of nothing in the main compartment.

"They already took that too."

"Fuck," Bernard said.

Roger tossed the billfold on the counter and moved back to the glass doors. He sighted a black SUV just sitting in front of him. It was parked so the driver's side was pointed toward them. "We might have a problem."

"What now?" Bernard asked. He pushed the clerk with a lot of force, causing him to tumble back and fall on his butt.

Roger backed up toward his friend. "Get to cover."

"What?" Bernard looked over at his approaching friend. He saw the SUV's windows roll down.

Roger grabbed Bernard's arm and dragged him behind a nearby store shelf just in the nick of time. A hail of bullets shattered the glass of the store's windows. Both men dove, hitting the ground next to each other, and laid praying on the cold tile while lead death passed above.

"It was a trap," Roger yelled over the commotion.

"No shit," was Bernard's only response.

Both got to a knee, keeping their heads low. When the onslaught stopped, they peeked over the shelf and returned fire, Roger with his revolver, and Bernard with his semi-automatic pistol. They saw the SUV take off and pull onto the street, leaving them to their own devices.

They stood and checked on the cashier.

"Ew," Roger said, looking at the poor soul they were accosting. He was crumpled against the wall, not so lucky as them. The counter had done little to protect him from the lead being flung from its flank. He was still breathing, even as the blood pooled around him. A foul smell hung in the air. He gurgled something that was impossible to understand.

"He's gut shot and possibly lung shot," Bernard said. "That's a brutal way to die. You can smell the shit. We need to leave quick." He grabbed Roger by the wrist and dragged him out of the store.

They quickly entered their car and drove off.

"You've still got the necklace, right?"

"Indeed I do," Roger said, reaching into his coat pocket. He pulled it out. It shimmered in the dying light of the day.

"At least there's that. For the record, this wasn't our fault either. We got our second taste of this war. I don't know about you, but I'm totally ready to go on the offense."

"You and me both. That dude didn't deserve to die like that. He was just trying to make ends meet. Roughing him up is one thing, but killing him?"

"We were the targets. Don't mistake that," Bernard said.

"Hopefully Chris and Jackie are alright," Roger said. "If they hit our target, they may have gone after theirs. Should we swing by and see how they're doing?"

They were interrupted by Roger's phone ringing in his pocket. "One second," he said. He answered. "Yeah, Sis? We're busy here."

"No kidding," Crystal's voice said. "I received a call from the others. You're to come straight home. Something's happened apparently. They couldn't tell me over the phone."

"Got it. We'll be back shortly." He hung up and before he could relay the message, Bernard had guessed.

"We're heading home?"

"That was their orders. Something happened with them. I'm guessing they got out and didn't want us wandering into the Russians by ourselves."

"Regrouping is a wise idea then. You know what this means, though?"

"What's that?"

"We're going to reclaim our turf. We can't let them claim what's ours. I expect we'll receive some sort of briefing of our guidelines when we get back. Even our own turf isn't safe anymore."

The rest of the ride back was quiet as both teenagers

recalled their recent brush with death. They returned to their apartment in silence - at least until they closed the door to their shared apartment.

Crystal greeted them at the door and gave Roger a hug. "I was worried after I heard what happened."

"Why don't I receive a warm and tender embrace?" Bernard asked, holding both arms out at his side.

She pulled away from her brother. "Come inside. We have a meeting." She headed deeper inside the apartment into the main room. She grabbed her laptop and took a seat on the sofa at the end.

The boys followed, taking the remaining two seats on the sofa next to Crystal. Chris and Jackie were already present in the two recliners.

"You two are back." Chris breathed an audible sigh of relief. "I was worried."

"Something happen to you two also?" Roger asked.

"Also?" Jackie asked. "You were hit too?"

"The Russians had already shaken our guy down before we even arrived," Bernard said. "We barely grabbed some collateral before Roger dragged my ass to cover as the shooting started."

"Good man," Chris said, giving a nod to Roger. "At least you two watched each other's backs. I've seen men die in this same scenario."

"For what it's worth, Bernard here was doing the shake-down. I was just keeping watch. He was quite convincing."

"Talking up your friend is one thing, but this is serious," Jackie said. "I'd hoped this far into our own territory would be a no-go zone for Oleg and his minions, but they're serious about riding to war. Crystal, did you report these findings to your mother yet?"

"I'll do it right now," she said. Her fingers danced across

the keyboard as the conversation continued unabated amid the clacking of keys.

"We can't go collecting for the next few days now," Bernard said. "Cops are snooping around, I'd bet."

"The guy died?" Chris asked.

"Got shot multiple times. He didn't reach cover in time," Bernard said. "All we found was a necklace inside a safe nestled in the office."

"What convenience store keeps a necklace in the back office?" Chris asked. "Show me."

Roger pulled out the ill-gotten gains and held it up.

"That's worth maybe a few hundred - well below what they owed," he said. "You got rid of the camera footage?"

"It was already gone, and it wasn't recording," Roger said. "It was the third sign we found that something smelled funny."

"First two signs being the shop already busted," Bernard said. "The bruises the guy had completed the trifecta. They worked him over pretty good before taking the money."

"I'm done." Crystal finished typing. "It's encrypted and sent."

"What's our next move?" Bernard asked.

"Report to Ms. Morris and find out what she wants. She may want to use us to attack, though I doubt it," Jackie said.

"Since we're here," Roger said. "Let's not mince words here. If we were two new guys, you'd be riding to war tonight. Is that right?"

"Probably," Chris said. He jumped when Jackie reached out with her leg and kicked him in the knee. "Ow," he said, rubbing his knee. "What? We all know it's true. They're grown ass men. They deserve the truth. She will not keep from sending us out if you ask me. If they're throwing their weight around with this level of reckless abandon, she'll need every one of us doing our part."

"Nobody asked you a damned question, old man," Jackie said.

"I got a reply," Crystal said. "It's from Mother. She says we've been suffering attacks across the organization. She says we're launching counter attacks tonight."

"Are we working tonight?" Bernard asked, trying to lean over and peek at the message.

"You will find your target's name sent to your phones. Let nothing stop you. All means are permitted to strike at Oleg's men. My son wanted blood, and so he shall have it. Be careful, all of you."

Everyone's phone rumbled in their pockets. They pulled them out and read the message.

"Guess this is our newest job," Bernard said.

"It's proving to be an interesting night," Roger said.

"That excitement will fade," Chris said. "I envy that sense of wonder - back when I thought hit jobs were some big thing."

"Stop daydreaming," Jackie said. "Did you see what this place was?"

"It's a restaurant from the looks of it," Roger said. "Not a very well-reviewed one, judging from the reviews online."

"You'd think more people would put pride in their cover business, but it's a lost art," Bernard said. "I guess it's up to you two, then. What's the plan here? Personally, I'd recommend just burning the place down. It'd attract more unwanted attention to him. He wants to pressure us, let him put out his own fires."

"I'll take that under advisement," Chris said. "Jackie? You must have an idea or two. What do you think?"

"A fire would prove safer than busting inside and

shooting the place up, true," Jackie said. "We could even wait outside the exits and fire on them as they exit."

"That's screwed up," Chris said. "Effective, but not sporting. Not that they deserve a chance, mind you. Human beings when given the choice between burning to death or catching a few bullets, they'll choose the bullets. We will oblige their choice."

"I volunteer to head inside," Roger said. "Starting a fire isn't rocket science."

"How about I go?" Jackie asked. "You can be around the back. Chris and Bernard can cover the front. That means you'd kill whoever comes out the back with me."

"What about civilians?" Chris asked. "It's a restaurant. There are bound to be some."

"Not if we do this immediately after they close. If they're still inside, that's their problem," Jackie said. "After closing hours, the only folks left will be Oleg's minions. The employees would be leaving."

"We'll need our rifles for this one," Chris said, rubbing his hands together. "Pistols and six shooters won't cut it for the number of bodies that could come running outside. Now I won't lie, boys. This will be a good old-fashioned massacre we'll be committing. Neither of you two has a problem?"

"This is war," Bernard said. "They killed our men, so we're returning the favor."

"He and his thug Artyom deserve to know they're not immune from consequences," Roger said. "I witnessed first-hand a lot of good men and women killed while Artyom held us at gunpoint. They deserve it."

"Let us hope you feel that way afterward. We'll take two cars - one for the front and another for the rear, ensuring a quick getaway." Jackie said. "Alright, everyone. Get your masks, gloves, rifles, and ammunition. We'll have to assemble them on site. We can't carry fully built rifles through the apartment complex. I assume you both are proficient with them."

"You worry about yourself," Bernard said. "We've got this."

"I hope so."

6

Roger could smell the fetid decay of the nearby dumpster's contents. He was posted behind one near the rear of the targeted restaurant. He looked back the way he had come toward Jackie's car parked nearby, acting as a wall to dissuade the public from coming down the alleyway. Peeking around the garbage receptacle at the grimy door, he observed that the lone light perched above flickered every so often. "She just got inside," he said.

"Acknowledged," Chris said into the earpiece. "Hold tight. The show will start soon."

Roger waited in the dark space between buildings, occupying his time by keeping a watch around him. Paranoia told him to suspect every noise he heard. The engines were Russian's coming up to ambush him, his mind told him. Indistinct chatter from the nearby street was civilians who could rat him out if they saw him. It all caused his heart to race because of the highly illegal activity they were engaged in.

He was granted a reprieve when he heard the door shut. As he snapped to attention, he could see who exited the establishment's backdoor. He peeked around the dumpster and saw Jackie running toward another nearby trash receptacle. She got behind it and picked up the rifle leaning against the brick wall Roger had placed there earlier.

"It's done. I set two," Jackie said. "One's a grease fire. The other's an old-fashioned fire. Both are originating inside the dirty ass kitchen, which is abandoned. There was no one in there."

"They didn't even change the grease after closing hours?" Chris asked. "Must be why their reviews are shit."

"Focus, old man," Jackie said. "It'll be a minute before they realize what's happening. I didn't see any smoke alarms, so they'll have to see or smell the smoke before they stampede outside. Everybody keep a watchful gaze. You two found an acceptable perch to fire from, yeah? You're not just on the street causing a spectacle?"

"How dumb do you think I am?" Chris asked. "We're posted up in an alleyway across the street. We're hidden from the public eye, but we still have a clear shot at the front door. Our car's ready to make our getaway, like yours I assume."

"I was just making sure. Screw me for caring if you two make it."

"I might take you up on that offer, beautiful." That male voice was decidedly not Chris's.

"Don't you ever tire of being rejected?"

"Never happened to me yet. Is this a first?"

"Wait a minute," Jackie said. "Bernard?"

"Yo," he said.

"Stop the chatter." Jackie was obviously flustered - even Roger could tell. He couldn't help but smile to himself as his long-time friend got one over on the combat hardened veteran.

The restaurant's back door opened with a loud creak.

"Hold your fire," Jackie said. "They're not running out. We can't spook them too early."

The door fully opened to reveal a small child. He couldn't have been older than eight or nine years old, by Roger's estimation. He carried a large black trash bag and waddled out and down the stairs.

"A kid?" Roger asked. "What's a kid doing here? He's not supposed to be inside."

"That's his tough luck," Jackie said. "If you see a child running out, do not hit him. Is that understood?"

"Roger that," Chris said.

The child quickly dropped the sack and hurried to get back inside.

"Oh shit," Roger said. Minutes after the kid disappeared inside, black smoke billowed out from under the door. *I can't let a kid burn to death with those animals*, he thought. Without a word or warning, Roger got out from his cover and sprinted toward the building.

"What are you doing? Stand down. That is an order!" Jackie yelled toward Roger as he approached the building. "Did you hear me? Get back here right now."

"That's not an option," Roger said. "I'll be right back. I have business in there."

"Be right back? Bitch, you better return right now." Jackie's tone was one of anger. "This is how people get killed."

"You can blame me later for all I care." Roger gripped the knob and felt it was warm. He pulled it open and ducked inside. Smoke was visible, obscuring the inside. He got low to the ground and noticed a few people approaching.

"Light them up," he heard Chris say before gunshots sounded off.

In front of him was a narrow hallway with multiple doors on either side. To his side, he spotted a corner to take cover should the worst occur. Incoherent screams and orders met his ears. When he spotted a group of men, he quickly dove behind the corner and scrambled to his feet. He took a deep breath, smelling the acrid smoke, and turned. He aimed center mass on the nearest one and squeezed the trigger.

Roger felt the recoil in his shoulder. That dull ache of pain was nothing compared to the flesh he was rending with every lead projectile. The lead man fell, mortally wounded. His aim moved to the next closest, and he too fell. The remaining Russians took cover on the opposite side of the hallway, using the corner, taking a page out of his book.

"Arson?" one yelled. "That's some bitch shit right there," he called out to Roger. They returned fire. "You think you can smoke us out and shoot us like dogs? Fuck you and your matriarch. She's weak to order some cowardly bullshit like this. You're even worse. We're escaping, and that's final. You'll die in here!"

Roger ejected one magazine and placed another in with a click. "I'm just giving you all a sneak peek at where you're going. Hope you enjoy the fire," he said. He sidestepped around the corner and started firing as soon as he cleared the wall. As quickly as one target fell, he adjusted his aim with surgical precision. More hits, more screams, and more smoke came into the hallway, obscuring his vision. He coughed as the last target he saw fell.

"Dad! Where are you?" Roger could hear the small child's voice nearby in what he guessed was the bathroom. *I don't have time,* he thought.

"Our side's cleaned up. No more are coming out," Chris said. "We're heading out. How's it looking over there?"

"I'll be out in a minute," Roger said. He kept his weapon pointed down the hallway, waiting for anyone else to try their luck. It wasn't long before he realized they were dead or unconscious from the smoke.

"Out?" Chris asked. "Oh, shit the bed. Tell me you're not in there."

"He is," Jackie said. "All over a Russian kid being inside. Get back out here. Now!"

"Get out of there, kid. We're leaving. We can't stick around forever; the authorities have probably already been called."

"I'm not leaving without him," Roger heard Bernard say.

"You have your orders," Chris said. "Pull back now."

"God damn it," Bernard said. "You had better escape safe, buddy, or I'm going to be pissed."

Roger saw part of the ceiling that was engulfed in flames in the main restaurant fall with a loud crack. He saw the bathroom open. The kid ran out into the hallway. He saw the bodies piled near his feet and fell on his butt, trying to shuffle away from the bodies.

Another Russian came into view. He didn't appear concerned by the child in his way, or he didn't see him. He ran full tilt over the child, knocking him back down to the ground in his desperate plea for refuge from the flames and smoke at his heels.

Roger took aim and fired. The man fell backward, landing on top of the kid, pinning him below.

"Fuck," Roger said to himself. His coughing was becoming more frequent. He could swear the smoke was thicker than a moment ago. Slinging the rifle over his shoulder by the strap, he used his right hand to pull out his trusty six shooter. He sprinted over to the kid and dragged the body off him. He lifted the kid up over his shoulder. "I got the kid and am exiting. Don't fire." He saw another man running toward him. This one was engulfed in flames and screaming bloody murder, seemingly intent on spreading the fire by tackling Roger and the kid. He lifted his six shooter and fired three times, causing the human torch to tumble forward to the ground, still screaming all the while. Roger turned from the horrific sight and smell of human flesh burning. Running was harder with the kid, but he managed it.

He ran as fast as his lungs would allow him toward where he had entered. He heard a loud crash behind him, and the floor shook from the impact shockwave. *Sounds like where the kid was,* he thought, approaching the exit. He barreled through the door using his free shoulder. Smoke billowed out the door behind him as he stumbled down the stairs.

Jackie ran up to him. "Are you alright?" She kept a watchful gaze on the door behind him.

"Just peachy," Roger said. He gently let the kid down to the concrete below. "You're safe now, kid."

"What about my dad?" The kid looked toward the burning building.

"Look, just stay here. The police and fire department will be here soon. Alright? Your dad will be alright. Trust me," Roger said. "He's a smart guy, yeah?"

The child covered his mouth and coughed some more, trying to clear his lungs from the smoke. "Yeah."

"Good," Roger took off toward the car.

Jackie followed closely behind. "That was stupidly reckless," she said as the pair entered the car. "You could have gotten yourself or that kid killed."

"The kid would have died without me," Roger said as she started the engine. "They trampled the kid to the fucking ground, trying to get out. They didn't care if he burned to death in there."

She pulled out onto a nearby street and made some distance. "Just because they're animals doesn't mean we have to play superhero and risk ourselves."

"If you're fishing for an 'I'm sorry', it's not coming. You'd best make your peace with that," Roger said. "The plan was to kill Russian gangsters, not Russian children, and I was simply following that plan."

"You're lucky I'm driving, or I'd smack you upside your damned head for that attitude," Jackie said. "That was sentimental and stupid."

"I killed quite a few in there," Roger said. "It's mission accomplished. I'll need an extra strong shower to remove this smoke smell off me, but that's a small price to pay for a kid's life. It's bad enough I had to lie and tell the kid his dad was alright."

"You're not wrong, but I'm still pissed at you."

"Story of my life," Roger said. He looked over to see Jackie was not laughing at his attempt at humor. "You're going to get wrinkles if you keep scowling like that."

"Shut the hell up for your own sake."

"So testy tonight," Roger said. "You'd think you were the one who saved a kid and is getting dressed down for his trouble."

"Teenagers never understand when to stay quiet," Jackie said.

"I'm not wrong though, and you know it."

Back at the apartment afterward...

"We both know I'm supposed to lecture you," Chris said. He laid down on the bed and looked over at Roger leaning on his shut bedroom door. "I have questions about that."

"I expected as much."

"Why risk everything for a Russian kid who was the responsibility of his parent?"

"You want to know why?" Roger asked. "The thought of a kid barbecuing in there because of my actions makes my skin crawl. Do I seriously have to explain?"

"I imagined as much." Chris grabbed a book sitting atop an opened cardboard box full of books. He tossed the literature to the younger man. "Look at that," he said.

"A book about philosophy?"

"I think it's an admirable trait to rush into a burning building to save a child. Maybe it's a touch stupid, foolhardy, and risky. I understand the sentiment, but we cannot indulge in such luxuries. We can learn from them, know they exist, and even sometimes implement them in guilty indulgences, but they cannot be commonplace. Our lifestyle does not accommodate such greedy desires."

"I didn't know you took philosophy in high school."

"I didn't, you little shit," Chris said. He pulled his nearly sixty-year-old carcass up to a sitting position on the bed. "I've been in this game for a hot minute, as the kids say."

"I think that lingo was commonplace twenty years ago, when Mom was a teenager."

"Shut the hell up and show some respect." The older man's tone was harsh for once. "This was a one time thing. You endangered all of us with that stunt. Yay, great for you. You saved a child, but you endangered your brothers and sisters. With that delay, you and Jackie were at risk of getting out too late. It's a cold way of looking at it, but that's why we try to pick our targets. We weren't given that option this go around. Your mom gets what she wants, and it's our collective job to make it happen. You heard the message she sent us before we left. Those included kids."

"I will not say sorry. That would imply I thought what I did was wrong," Roger said.

"You going to make it a habit?"

"Disobeying orders? Hell no, I'm not," Roger said.

"Good, because your mother won't hear about tonight's complication," Chris said. He relaxed and rested against the headboard. "I already told your sister to halt mentioning your heroics. We don't need that kind of headache because of headstrong childish idiots trying to play a hero. Trust me when I tell you it's not worth the trouble."

"You know from experience, old man?" Roger asked. "They tell stories of you saving others in battle. Maybe I wanted my own heroic moment?"

"You're too damned inexperienced to be trying that. Only fools try that in a combat environment. I guess we are all fools being in this line of work - especially you, wanting to join it so bad."

"It's all I've ever known," Roger said. "My mom is the boss, my dad's her bodyguard. All my friends are members. This is my family. You don't walk away from that."

"Boy, you've drunk the punch wholesale. I guess that's to be expected," Chris said as he turned on the television they'd hooked up earlier in the day, turning it to the local news. He muted it as a helicopter view showed a brief glimpse of their handiwork before continuing to another tragedy around the city. "Make no mistake, we're not a lifestyle you should want. Surely your mother and father have told you as much."

"More than a thousand times." Roger walked around the room. He stopped at the computer system on top of the desk in the room's corner. He reached back behind the desk and connected wires as he spoke. "They want to send me off to college to get a degree. They tried to tell me from a young age they were sending me once I hit eighteen."

"It's a shame they didn't follow through."

"They tried to," Roger said. He pressed a button on the tall computer case. Its lights came on with a brief rush of fans before it settled down. The monitor sprung to life as the computer operating system started. "I told her I'd just drive back and move out if worse came to worst."

"You actually gave her that ultimatum?"

"Yes," Roger said. A small curvature of his lips rose.

"Don't be smug. She may be one of the toughest women I know, but she's still a mother I see. I suppose that's a positive. Besides, your dad's one of the smartest guys I've met. If you asked, I'm sure he'd help you sort whatever you needed out."

"Maybe," Roger said. "It looks like your computer's ready."

"I'm going to file my report before I head to bed. Something you should do like now. I bet Bernard's already in bed."

"Not possible," Roger said, moving toward the room's door leading into the hallway. "See you in the morning. I don't suppose you have a guess what we're doing tomorrow?"

"As soon as I know, everyone will know, kid. Now get out of here."

"Good night," Roger said.

Meanwhile...

"Yeah, Mom." Bernard had opened the window in his and Roger's room. He climbed outside onto the fire escape and looked over the alley below. Sounds of distant engines met his ears. "Everybody's fine. Roger had an incident, but he's safe and everything was clean."

"Define an incident, Son," Elizabeth said. "Was he hurt?"

"No. He saved a kid's all."

"Of course he saved a child," Elizabeth said. "What about you?"

"I followed every order to the T, just like you suggested." He looked right toward the street below and watched cars pass. A few citizens roamed the sidewalk, completing the city ambience.

"Good. Earn respect by prioritizing the family first, above all. Your friend's heroics, while brave, were unnecessary and reckless. I know the type of fool who thinks he's God. He has a hero complex. Take advantage of it. While he looks like a vain fool, you can be a proper soldier."

"I'm doing that. He's my friend. Besides, his disobedience was morally correct. A small child didn't deserve to die because of that operation."

"Do you value friendship, or do you prefer to become the future patriarch of the Morris Syndicate? You want power, untold fortune, and respect? There will come a situation when you need to weigh dreams and aspirations versus the brotherhood you Morris males hoot about."

"You never liked Roger, did you?"

"Preposterous," Elizabeth said. "It's not a matter of like. It's a matter of proper inheritance, as I've said before. After Rachel, the next successor will be one of three people by my wager. It's you, Roger, or Ben. I'm coming up with contingency plans. You just focus on building up an excellent reputation. Do what Chris says, and don't cause waves."

"That was the plan," Bernard said. "A war is the perfect

environment to prove my mettle and elevate up the ranks. If we play our cards right, so can Roger."

"Forget about him. He has an advantage with his mother being the boss. You focus on you."

"Some would notice I possess the same advantage as you."

"I may have been boss decades ago, but that time is long past. I don't have nearly as much pull as I used to. Now listen up, Son. From everything I've heard, this war is turning serious out there. We've been hit in multiple gun warehouses. While yes, we're attacking and retaliating, on pure resources, Oleg's men have the distinct advantage. That girl will not give you all another job. The only reason she did was to make it look like she wasn't playing favorites to the rank-and-file members stuck battling."

"You know this for a fact?" Bernard asked. "That we won't receive another job tomorrow morning?"

"I'm ninety percent sure. So, if you want my advice - if you insist on bucking the authority with your friend, make it worth it. Your uncle and his friend Roger once did it when we were at war with the Irish."

"Uncle Daniel disobeyed orders?"

"Not so much disobeyed. Those idiots wandered off without permission, searching for revenge. They ended up blowing up a building because the damned Irish ambushed me and Roger. I was nearly killed, so they took matters into their own hands. Daddy wasn't enthused about it, but he would not punish the men who killed those who attacked his daughter. If you want fame and glory, when no opportunities present themselves, make your own. Don't suddenly go AWOL like Daniel. First, offer the idea of hunting Russian storehouses."

"I suppose reclaiming guns for the family would help if

our supplies are getting hit. What if leadership doesn't want to risk playing ball?"

"You're talking about Chris?"

"That's the one."

"If he doesn't, then tell me. I have favors to cash in. If worse comes to worst, he wouldn't be able to yell at you if you brought back more guns, if you catch my drift. Nothing is out of reach if you're willing to bend the rules. Never forget that lesson. That, and loyalty is worth its weight in gold, as your uncle also learned."

"Don't recite this wild conspiracy again."

"The way Danny died doesn't fit," Elizabeth said. "Something fishy happened, and I'd bet my life on it."

"Let's not delve into that and focus on the war instead. Do you have locations I should suggest? It's not like we know where a ton of Russian storehouses are."

"We're in the process of moving our supply from the storehouses that haven't been hit as a precaution," Elizabeth said. "We captured a prisoner earlier and we're questioning him now, but we've extracted little useful information out of him. As far as locations to suggest, search. I can't give you all life's answers. Ask that girl Crystal to help find it. I doubt Oleg was stupid enough to leave digital footprints, but it's either that or go after the ones we know about. While they're an option, they're also heavily fortified if they have any sense."

"What about the warehouse where we picked up guns on my first job? It was a small mechanic's office. There weren't many men, and it was on the edge of their territory, albeit nowhere near ours, so it'd be a longer drive."

"That's an idea. Follow up on that. Wait, was that at Park Drive? The prisoner mentioned a Park Drive yesterday. Yes, do that. If it's as important as I believe, you could make a name by hitting there."

Bernard backed up a few steps and sat on the windowsill. He lifted his legs up and extended them out, resting them on the handrail he was just using. "These two have been trying to treat us with kid gloves. They always want to give us the boring jobs."

"They're scared shitless," Elizabeth said. "With good reason, mind you. They've been given the job of guarding two of the leadership's children who are headstrong, eager to prove themselves, and teenagers. They're worried if you die under their watch, then Rachel and I would take it out on them."

"Are they right?"

"They are one hundred percent correct," Elizabeth said. "This is a risky lifestyle. There are no gains without risk. Sometimes you disobey an order to make greater headway - like if Chris says no. If you pull off the job, then he looks like an idiot while you look like heroes who prioritized the syndicate more than your own asses. Conversely, if you disobey and then fail, you're in the fire. So be careful."

The nearby door behind him opened. He looked over his shoulder and saw Roger slam the door behind him. "I've got to go. Rog just got back."

"You remember what I said about him."

"Love you too, Mom." He rolled his eyes and pointed toward the phone, eliciting a silent laugh from his friend. "Good night." He hung up the phone and climbed back into the bedroom. He shut the window behind him and moved over to his bed. "Did you get an earful, Mr. Hero?"

"I received a philosophy lesson from Chris, and I got bitched out by Jackie. I barely got away from her," Roger said. "We almost came to blows. I decided to talk with Crystal. That was a mistake. For the record, if you ever piss off Jackie, prepare for the worst. She pulls no punches, so don't lose your head like I nearly did."

"I try to not piss women off."

"You're a dirty liar," Roger said, falling back onto his bed. "You love pissing them off."

"Only after they've given me a reason to. Now never mind that," he said. "I have an idea for tomorrow. You want in?"

"Chris said he probably wouldn't get orders until tomorrow."

"Maybe I got an insider tip that we'd be getting none tomorrow," Bernard said.

"Your mom said that? Well," Roger said, "I guess she'd know better than us. She is the one at the strategy meetings. What's your plan?"

Bernard lowered his voice. "I was going to bring it up to Chris tomorrow morning. She said they hit a lot of our weapon storehouses. Obviously, it's hard to be an arms dealer when someone is stealing all your arms. I know of one of Oleg's weapon storehouses."

"How would you know where one of his secret caches is?"

"My mother gave the location of the place. Apparently they've gotten a prisoner from one of the recent battles. They've been questioning him back at the mansion. She gave me the intel so we could stay busy. It'd make us look like we're keeping busy, and we'd be helping the war effort with getting back some of our guns," Bernard said.

"If he says no?"

"Then we'd have to be sneakier. We'd need to plan it out. It'd probably take a day; but if we can grab tons of weapons in wartime, that's a tremendous boost. The Syndicate members will view our operation favorably and there isn't a damned thing brass could say."

"Going over his head after I promised not to gives me an unpleasant taste," Roger said. "I just said I wouldn't make it a habit of disobeying his orders."

"You want to climb the rankings, or do you prefer to sit inside this apartment for weeks before this ends and let the chance for glory pass us by?"

"Well, when you word it like that," Roger said. "We'll see what Chris thinks. He might think it's a good idea..."

In the living room just earlier...

"My report is done and sent," Crystal said. She placed the laptop to the side and plugged it in to charge. "You know, you didn't have to be so hard on him earlier."

"Don't you start too," Jackie said, glaring at Crystal out of the side of her eye before resuming reassembling her rifle. Assorted parts of the rifle laid bare on the coffee table in the middle of the room as she sat in front of it. "He's lucky that's all he received."

"I don't see how saving a kid is worthy of being yelled at. In the civil, normal world, they would celebrate a citizen for bravery and compassion. Are we so backwards? We venerate savagery but revile saving a child? Don't you ever think about that?"

"The problem wasn't the idea of saving a child," Jackie said, keeping her flank to Crystal and looking at the flatscreen in front. "The problem is, he deviated from the plan and put us both at risk. Bernard and Chris got away on time. Roger and I escaped a few minutes late. A few minutes late can sometimes be the difference between heading home and getting a neat new jumpsuit and new friends behind bars. You see my point?"

"In my book, selflessness is still an admirable trait, and you'll never change my mind about that."

"You're too sweet then." Jackie's voice had no envy. "That kind of attitude won't get you far. You're only here until the end of this war anyway, yeah? Speaking of which, isn't Lauren supposed to be homeschooling you? How's that going to work now?"

"I can study over the internet. We can video chat and get it done."

"How convenient," Jackie said. "Tell me, what do you want to be when you turn eighteen?"

"You might laugh since it's not exactly typical, but I want to start my own business."

"There's nothing wrong with that," Jackie said. "Like mother, like daughter it appears. I assume you didn't mean this business we're in."

"I meant more like a brick-and-mortar business. It doesn't have to be a physical location. Startup companies use the internet more and more nowadays. I want to be my own boss. I was thinking of taking business classes in college to prepare me more."

"Keep hold of that dream, and clutch it tight to your chest. It's liable to dissolve in the next few weeks, depending on how this war goes. Never lose sight of it, and never change it because of someone like your brother. He has his own dreams, along with Bernard."

"You say that, but I'm going to do everything I can to keep him safe."

"That's what I'm worried about," Jackie said. "I'm worried you'll focus so much on that, you'll give up on your own desires. Loving your family and protecting them is fine, but not when it affects your own future. Roger's choosing a dark path like all of us did. I'd like to see you take a different one. He's pissed on his mother's dream. That makes you her last hope."

"No pressure," Crystal said with sarcasm.

"I heard my name just now." Roger appeared from a nearby hallway leading to Chris's room. "I assume it was to trash on me."

"I was just telling her not to give up her dreams because of her idiot brother. You're liable to drag her down with you."

"You aim for the jugular, don't you?" Roger asked. He narrowed his eyes at Jackie, who gave him a momentary glance before looking away. "You leave family out of this."

"Or what? You run to mommy dearest? What's wrong with telling the truth? After all, according to your sister, virtues are important to us, apparently. If we can save kids, we may as well always tell the truth. Soothing sweet lies would be the antithesis of that."

"You're still pissed about that? Yikes," Roger said. "I guess the rumors were true about you."

"What are those? Choose your next words carefully."

"Or what? You're going to threaten the boss's son to win a pissing contest?" Roger didn't back down from the unspoken threat. He planted his feet.

"You're brave. I'll give you that. That's about all I'll give you. Intelligence isn't quite where it should be, though."

"You want to say that again, bitch?" Roger took a step forward before his sister jumped up and stopped him.

"I call it as I see it. It was stupid to endanger the both of us for some Russian brat."

"At least I still have a conscience and know killing kids is wrong. You sit there and stew on that, Miss High and

Mighty. I'll take being an idiot over a soulless, morally corrupt automaton." Roger stomped off and slammed the door to his and Bernard's room.

"It's been a long time since someone spoke to me like that." Jackie finished assembling the weapon and pulled back the slide with a click. "Even longer since they didn't get their asses kicked for doing it."

"He wasn't wrong, though," Crystal said.

"No, he wasn't," Jackie said. "That's the only reason I didn't get up and kick his ass."

"Not because of my mother and father?"

"I'd take the corporal punishment if he was wrong and just kicking up a dirt storm to piss me off, but, infuriatingly, he was right." She looked at where Roger had come from. "Come out here. You never were as sneaky or slick as you believed you were, old man."

Chris appeared from behind the corner with a nervous smile. "How long did you know?"

"After Roger ran to his room," Jackie said. "How much of that did you hear?"

"I may have procrastinated my report and wanted to hear what you would say. So, pretty much all of it. You know I'd have stepped in if you'd lost your head."

"Trying to play protector to both of us again? You need to learn the same lesson as Roger with that attitude."

"My mama always told me I was kind of dumb." Chris laughed loudly and sat on the far end of the couch behind Jackie, on the opposite end from Crystal.

"Sometimes people are wrong," Jackie said. "I just wish it wasn't us this time."

"I'm getting the feeling we are the ones in the wrong here, even though I know we aren't," Chris said.

"You want to dictate your report, and I can type it?"

Crystal asked. "It'd be no trouble."

"Don't offer to do his work for him," Jackie said. "You'll never stop doing it if you go down that road. He needs to do his own shit."

"Always the taskmaster, keeping me on the straight and narrow. You're the long-lost daughter I never had."

"Cut the bullshit and work, old timer," Jackie said, never turning around.

"What is dictation anyway?" he asked.

"It's where you talk, and the computer writes it down automatically, so you don't have to type."

"That's a thing?"

"Obviously it's a thing," Crystal said, as if explaining the sky was in fact blue. "It's a matter of setting up the voice to text software and configuring the speech recognition to your voice. I can set it up tomorrow if you'd like, but it'd take some effort to get it up and running. You'd have to read paragraphs to get the AI used to your voice so it can recognize what you're saying."

"Sounds like work," Chris said.

"Sometimes I wonder how you ever got to your rank," Jackie said. "You're lazy as hell."

"Only sometimes," Chris said. "Yeah, put it on my desktop if it's not too much trouble. You can walk me through the intricacies later."

"I know I'm not technically a syndicate member, so my word means nothing," Crystal said. "I'll tell you two for reference - Roger does not do well with hostility. You want to change his behavior? Be nicer. You attract more flies with honey than vinegar. If you treat him with respect, he'll be like a little puppy wanting more head pats."

"Did you just compare your brother to a puppy?" Chris asked. "I think he'd be insulted."

"Think about it," Crystal said. "His goal in life is to become a respected member of the Morris Syndicate. What do you think will happen? He's eighteen years old and hates being disrespected. I know how his mind works."

"That's not in my toolbox," Jackie said. "I give swift kicks in the asses when they're needed. Coddling does not help."

"There's a difference between coddling and straight up antagonizing," Chris said. "Point taken though, kid."

"I know you didn't yell at him, so someone had to," Jackie said. "God knows what you two talked about while you were supposed to be bitching at him. We couldn't hear you, so I knew you weren't doing your job."

"That bitching was for my sake?" Chris asked.

"He needed yelling at. The kid needs to learn there are consequences to his actions, and not everybody will like what he chooses."

"Sounds like tough love to me," Chris said.

"It's the only kind I know…"

7

"What's the word?" Roger asked. He gripped the towel draped over his shoulders in each hand. He stood a few feet away from the furniture, not wanting it to become wet after his having taken a shower.

"I'll tell everybody once we're all assembled. Where's Bernard?" Chris asked from one end of the sofa with Crystal on the other end. "He should be here."

"He's washing his hair, but he'll be out soon," Roger said. "I had dibs on the first shower this morning."

"I'm amazed you two could agree on who went first," Crystal said.

"Rock, paper, scissors is an amazing thing," Roger said. He brought the towel up to his hair and rubbed back and forth. Walking away from the living room, he opened a nearby door and tossed the towel into a large white basket before closing it. He came back and sat between his sister and Chris on the couch, daring to momentarily glance at Jackie to find she was not watching him, but the tv. He counted his lucky stars and directed his attention toward the television as well.

"Looks like the kid survived." Jackie broke the uncomfortable silence. "At least that's according to the news. It was a tragedy that his dad was shot. He was a single father. Some pundits would argue it'd have proven kinder to let him die swiftly than to be put in the foster system."

"Must we start this philosophical argument again?"

"I'm just saying. You wanted the kid to live, and he did. Aren't you just ecstatic?"

"What are you two arguing about?" Bernard closed the door behind him. His hair was sopping wet, and he had on his casual clothes consisting of shorts and a t-shirt - a far cry from his normally formal suit. He wandered into the room and took the only remaining chair, the second recliner. "Is this still about the kid? Or was it about the promise you made to me yesterday evening?"

"I didn't promise you anything," Jackie said.

"I don't know," Chris said. "We all heard it last night. Something about ..." He was cut off via a glare from Jackie. Finally in his long life, he'd learned to keep quiet. "Anyway," he said, clearing his throat, "we've been put on cautionary standby. It's up to us, so long as we're staying productive. We have a choice regarding our agenda unless orders come down from on high again. It says we need to be ready to respond at a moment's notice."

Bernard barely waited for the older man to finish talking before silently raising his hand.

"Yes?" Chris asked. "You could barely wait, huh?"

"I had an idea about what could keep us busy," the young black-haired man said, "but I'll let you finish."

"I appreciate the enthusiasm to get us more work. Who wants a break anyway? It's not like we can collect in this neighborhood with the police curiously poking around. Too much shit has happened during the last seventy-two hours.

They're probably shitting themselves, trying to figure out what's happening."

"Lazing about is not an option regardless," Jackie said. "You know that fact. We have a few options. One is we hit the Russians again. Two is we work on more illicit money-making methods online. The third is we research our enemies."

"Research is a dangerous business in war," Chris said. "Necessary, but risky, depending on how you go about it. Physical surveillance is a death wish in this political climate on the streets. Digital is just about as useless."

"What's this about the online money-making thing?" Crystal asked.

"I have known different units to sell the surplus they have on the dark web. It's easy money to send up the chain and look like we're busy. I assume that's what our fearless leader will choose. It would require us to have some guns we're willing to part with. I'm familiar with the packaging and shipping protocols, so it's possible."

"I am not selling mine," Roger said.

"Nor I," Bernard said. "I'm not swimming in hardware. I only have the two weapons."

"While I do, it's not enough quantity to sell tons of inventory. How much do they go for there?"

"Depends on the make, model, and if you sell any additional modifications," Jackie said. "I know groups that supplement their income by buying syndicate hardware cheaper from the armory and then sell it online. That's not an option, since we wouldn't possess inventory for longer than a day on the merchant sites. Most of them you need a certain amount of inventory to set up shop."

"You know a lot about this online market idea," Roger said. "You're sure it was just friends of yours?"

"They told me about it," she said. "I researched more into it and even considered taking advantage shortly before this war. Now, what is this idea you had?"

"Why not go after one of the Russian's weapon storehouses? They're hitting ours. Why not return the favor? There's one that we haven't hit yet. Why not resupply the syndicate with our own weapons the Russians stole?"

"Hitting a weapons storehouse?" Chris asked. "You think that's workable with a small group, in war no less?"

"Sure," Bernard said. "If we use our brains a little, I don't see why not. I'm not suggesting we bust down the doors and go in shooting. I'm not stupid. We can use a little technology and sophistication. In fact, I have ideas that will make retrieving our rightful weapons little more than a minor inconvenience. Better yet, it wouldn't cause noise, and it'd get rid of any guards on the inside."

"That sounds too good to be true," Jackie said, shaking her head. "A weapon cache won't be lightly guarded, and the Russians won't make it easy."

"Not of their own volition, they won't," Bernard said. "Who said we would leave it up to them? A little aerosolized anesthetic, scouting, digital research to get the floor layout, and a moving truck or van is all we'd need. Wait, I forgot the backup van nearby in case. It's just to be safe. It's not a lot of moving parts."

"You want to knock off a pharmaceutical company before we knock off a Russian outpost?" Jackie asked.

"That's the beauty of it," Bernard said with a snap of his fingers. "We wouldn't need to expose ourselves to obtain the drugs, because we already have some of it at the mansion. We'd just have to request some."

"You think we have the stuff already?" Roger asked. "Isn't anesthetics like medical grade stuff they have in hospitals?"

"Of course they do," Bernard said. "We've both seen over the years what happens if one of the syndicate catches a bullet or gets stabbed. We have our own doctor on call, yeah? I know that requires surgery."

"There's no guarantee they'd part with it," Chris said. He grabbed the nearby tv remote and muted it. "We're in a war. They're not going to be eager to hand out medical supplies to perfectly healthy us."

"They will when we explain that it'll gain us crates of automatic rifles, ammunition, and modifications that have been stolen from us. Look, man. Think of this." Bernard leaned forward. "If we do it this way, we don't have to kill anyone. We don't have to fire a single shot. We'd just put the drugs into their ventilation system, get gas masks, and go in once they're all unconscious. You can't detect the stuff, so they'd pass out before noticing anything. It's a brilliant plan, if I say so myself."

"How do you know the location to hit?" Jackie asked. "Oleg never was one to freely give away his group's venues."

"I have my ways," Bernard said. "It's not all about running and gunning. Sometimes it's about gathering information."

"Someone told you," Jackie said. "Don't pass this off as entirely your idea."

"Someone sounds jealous that it wasn't her idea," Chris said. "A huge weapons find would help us tremendously. Now, would this anesthetic kill them?"

"I'd imagine in a high enough concentration, yes," Crystal said. "If he's talking about the same surgical drugs we had back home, it says online that it can be fatal in elevated dosages."

"You know what stuff we have back home?" Roger asked.

"A girl gets bored and wanders around sometimes when

she's cooped up in there. Besides, we've both visited folks who get wounded. You're telling me you never once looked at the damned room? Some boxes had the chemical name printed in full view."

"We get the floor plan, we get the chemical, and then we just somehow dump it into their ventilation system with nobody noticing?" Jackie asked. "You don't think they'd notice someone climbing up their building?"

"Not if their attention is pulled somewhere else. Supposing if we were in the middle of a deadly gang war and the syndicate was hitting different locations. The best part is we're aware syndicate operations are happening at all times of the day. We wouldn't even have to directly coordinate. We'd just have to pick our moment," Bernard said. "Besides, even if that didn't work, we'd have a method to transport it upstairs that I guarantee they wouldn't see or search for."

"You're not talking about drones?" Crystal asked. "One of those tanks would push it for the weight limit. Drone tech has come a long way in the past twenty years for us private enthusiasts, but it'd teeter on the upper limit."

"They made limits to be tested."

"I like the idea of waltzing into a Russian storehouse and stealing everything while they're out of it." Chris reached up and rubbed his stubbled chin. "It'd be a nice, quick, and easy way to help the war effort for not a lot of work or risk, if we're careful."

"You're not actually considering this half-baked plan, are you?" Jackie asked. "It's a pie in the sky dream."

"I like pie," Roger said. "Who doesn't?"

"The kid's right," Chris said. "What's our first step in this?"

"We need to recon the storehouse, and I know the

perfect method to scout without approaching close," Bernard said. "Crystal, how far is the range on a drone that you control?"

"Most toy drones only fly twenty to one hundred yards, but we're not talking about toys. One of my higher end models can fly two to five miles and still make a round trip. How far away is this place, anyway?"

"I know the perfect rooftop we can prepare this from then," Bernard said. "It's an abandoned building over-looking Oleg's territory on technically neutral ground. We'd still need vigilance, but we wouldn't be poking the prover-bial Russian bear, so to speak."

"Let's make this happen," Chris said.

"I guess I should get on with the requisitioning of the gas and one of my top end drones then. They're back inside the mansion."

"I'll send our plans to your mom then, shall I?" Chris asked. "I'll also requisition two transport vehicles, one for the stealing and one to stash nearby beforehand. If the worst happens, we switch vehicles for safety and burn the first. Safety first is our motto, after all."

Meanwhile, in Russian territory...

"The job is finished," a gangster taller than Artyom said. "What is needed next?"

"Very good," Artyom said. "Did you get the weapons, Mikhail?"

"Of course," Mikhail said. He pointed at his men extracting and carrying crates from the back of a van. "They're right there. It was full of them. I think they were trying to move them when we got there."

"They're smart, but slow," Artyom said. "That's why I

mentioned earlier that speed was of paramount importance and, like the professional you are, you took advantage."

"A quick coordinated assault brought them to their knees, choking on their own blood within ten seconds of the breach," Mikhail said.

"I have no doubt of that. Come with me. I want to show you something." He led the man to a smaller room. It had a bulletin board with tons of papers assembled haphazardly. A huge map was in the middle of it with some X's drawn in red marker. Other parts on the map had red circles around them. "Look here," he said, pointing at one of the red circles. He grabbed a nearby red marker and crossed it out. "That's another of their supply houses raided and looted."

"What are these?" Mikhail asked, pointing toward the green marker circles.

"That's where they've retaliated. I wanted some difference in color for clarity's sake. They've hit us quite a few times, as you can see."

"There are many more red circles compared to green."

"That's the beauty of the plan. We're hitting them far more. At this rate, this war will end in our favor. We cannot allow them a chance to breathe and recover. The locations they've struck us at were not all tactically sound." He poked one green circle. "This was a restaurant that we had no weapons at, beyond their personal arms. They burned it down and killed everyone inside except for one child. While it's a tragedy, we still have a net gain. I'm certain they felt satisfied killing our personnel, sure, but not much else was accomplished."

"It appears we're running out of red circles," Mikhail said, his eyes flittering around the map. Most of the red circles were marked, with a minority still circled.

"When that number hits zero, their entire operation will

be well and truly destroyed. They won't have weapons enough to sell, and thus they won't be able to pay their roster. The syndicate will crumble under the weight of their own deserters."

"We'd need to kill their leadership before it's truly over," Mikhail said. "I assumed assassination was why I was sent here - not to play soldier."

"We'll get there in due time. Once we've exhausted their personnel supply, we can make our big move. Right now, their leadership is holed up in a veritable bunker. While a direct assault could work, with the amount of manpower they have, they could hold fast. This is a game of death by one hundred cuts. It's my favorite type of game. Watching our opponents get weaker as they stagger around the battle-field before they fall over always gave me a sick sense of pleasure."

"I am seeing why Oleg picked you as his second in command. This is a battle plan a general would devise, not a gangster."

"Sometimes a military mind is needed for criminal ventures. He knew that when he recruited me decades ago. Why, I remember when you joined us. You were just a young, snot-nosed kid who wanted to feed his family."

"You remember that?" Mikhail asked. "Even I remember little from back then. Legions of dead bodies stand between that time-period and now. I had forgotten."

"You were keen to prove yourself worthy. I was relatively new to the group and had just met Oleg. You were quite the hothead."

"It helps to use hatred when your job is to kill. That's the big lesson I learned. It helps with the inevitable self-reflection. Once you give up on being a virtuous human, you don't care what suffering you inflict anymore. That was from you, if I recall correctly."

"In war, there's no etiquette," Artyom said. "There is only one exception."

"Children," both men said in unison.

"I'm glad you remember. That is an unforgivable line that no soldier or assassin should cross."

"It's the code I live by," Mikhail said. "Not that it comes up often. They don't send me after kids."

"It seems our enemies share that shred of moral fiber," Artyom said. "You will continue going after every single one of these properties. Your next job is this one," he tapped his finger on one of them. His finger moved and tapped at every location. "I have personnel assigned here, there, and here already. We keep the pressure mounting, and keep them guessing where we're going to attack next. We may suffer casualties, but if we accept that and just gain more than they do, we'll win eventually."

"Is it true what they say about the syndicate's leader?" Mikhail asked. "Is it true it's run by a woman?"

Artyom looked over at Mikhail. "Yes, it is. Why? Do not underestimate her. She's the spawn of the late great Daniel Morris."

"Damn," Mikhail said. "I was hoping to meet Daniel Morris himself one day. He's dead?"

"He sure is. However, who killed him is a bit of a mystery."

"We don't know?"

"The official story is a stray bullet caught him during the last raid of the war with the cartel nearly twenty years ago. I was there that day," Artyom said. Memories flashed back to that hellish landscape. "I don't believe it personally. I suspect foul play."

"You think she knocked off her own father?"

"I don't see why she wouldn't. That's just my personal theory, though. It's irrelevant to this war. My point is, I know just how far Mrs. Morris is willing to go, so we're jumping farther. That's not a problem for us."

"Does she have children?"

"She does," Artyom said. "Why? You want to meet them too? She has a son who turned eighteen recently and a seventeen-year-old daughter. The daughter is off limits. She's not a combat personnel. The son, however, is free game."

"Wasn't that the one you kept alive?"

"I should've known that rumor would make the rounds. Yes, I did," Artyom said. "I was still hoping to avoid this senseless war. It's rumored they were the ones who burned down the restaurant. The story of a lone teenager rushing in to save that kid from the burning building caught one of their faces before the feed went out. It sure looked like Rachel's son to me."

"You saw that feed?"

"All feeds route off site. I simply pulled up that building's CCTV. It appears when one pays it forward, the universe keeps it in motion. I saved him - he saved one of our own sons."

"You may regret keeping him and Elizabeth Morris's kid alive. Shall I kill them?"

"For now, you focus on the businesses. There may come a time later when we need to draw out their leadership and their sons will serve our purposes perfectly. Two eighteen-year-old boys love getting themselves in trouble, as we both know."

"I understand," Mikhail said.

8

"As soon as I put out one fire, three spring up," Rachel said. Her hair was disheveled, and it looked like she hadn't showered since this war broke out. She looked over stacks of papers all over her desk. She had pinned a map on the wall beside her desk with marks all over it.

"They're going for an overwhelming stratagem," Elizabeth said. "Whoever is in charge of their battle plan knows how to keep us off balance."

"We're ceding ground on the south side of the city." Warren walked over to the map and crossed an X through another of their properties. "Word came in that we lost another storehouse."

"Shit," Rachel said.

"We have, however, seized some arms from two more Russian properties during the night." Ben walked over and seized the pen from Warren. He circled two nearby buildings near the one he crossed out. "The south front is not lost, just teetering."

"We're losing men every day," Rachel said. "We can't keep this up forever. I didn't think Oleg had hordes of manpower at his disposal. Many of them I've never seen before."

"If he was smart," Warren said, "he probably received more troops from Russia before starting this war. That's why he's trying to make this a numbers game. It would corroborate what the prisoner told us yesterday. He came from Mother Russia a few days ago."

"The slimy bastard planned this out," Rachel said. "What are our options, tactically speaking?"

"We can either go for maximum casualties, or we can play for the guns," Warren said. "Those are two options I see. They have the numbers advantage, but we are killing more than them. They're focusing more on weapons and taking away our income. If we take away their ability by slaughtering more, we'll win long term."

"That's assuming they aren't receiving more by plane every day. The Russian mafia's leadership is sending them over," Elizabeth said. "No doubt because they're aiding Oleg in taking over this city so he can send more cash back their way. Going solely for body count is not a smart idea."

"Then we're left with cutting the head off the Russian serpent," Ben said. "If we killed Oleg, would that stop this war?"

"Artyom would probably inherit the title," Elizabeth said.

"That dude is creepy as fuck. I don't care what anyone says." Warren shivered. "He's too damned calm."

"He's also extremely loyal," Rachel said. "There's no guarantee that'd end the war. It could spark a blood feud if he's as close to Oleg as we think."

"Blood feud's already started, sweetheart," Elizabeth said. "It's just a matter of how much of it is spilled."

"The prisoner mentioned one name yesterday," Warren said. "Mikhail," he said. "Who is Mikhail?"

"I had Lee try to find intel, but the name belongs to a ghost," Rachel said. "All he could put together was that he's an assassin of sorts. Not quite just an assassin. He gets whatever job done that they give him."

"If they have an ace waiting, then we require a trump card of our own," Rachel said. "Let us talk to this prisoner. I want a word with him personally. Maybe I can pry intel out of him you couldn't."

"I promise, boss," Warren said, "I was not gentle with him."

"I am aware, but this needs a woman's touch. Who knows what else he knows?" She stood up from behind the desk and marched toward the exit, with Warren and Ben following.

"The guy didn't strike me as the brains of the operation," Warren said as they exited the main office. "He's just a grunt."

"Possibly, but even grunts hear things they aren't supposed to. Who knows if it could be important. What did you do to him?"

"Nothing major," Warren said. "Some punches to the gut, assorted shallow cuts to get the blood flowing, and bruises."

"Perfect," she said, leading the two employees downstairs to the first floor. "Escalation will be our friend here." She held up a hand and removed the black leather glove that was almost always covering it to reveal the mutilation she suffered long ago. "If he's squeamish and simple, as you mentioned, my act will go over like a house on fire. It's been a long time since I questioned captives, but it's like riding a bike, my old man used to say. You never forget how to inflict fear."

The group reached the ground floor and opened a nearby door, heading even further down. Concrete was below, along with a low moaning sound that escalated into full on screaming. Rachel removed her other glove and shoved her hands in her tight dress pants.

"Just let me leave already!" the male voice said. "I told you everything you wanted to know. You promised you'd let me go."

"You promised to let him go?"

"He doesn't need to know it was a lie," Warren whispered back. "It gave him motivation to talk."

"Good work," Rachel said as they reached the bottom. "I'll make use of that." She saw the man tied up to a chair along with a lone guard keeping watch on him.

"Be quiet," the guard's female voice said before putting duct tape over his mouth.

Rachel came up behind the guard. "At ease. Wait a minute." She reexamined the guard's face. "Lauren? You're on guard duty down here?"

"A girl's got to find something productive to occupy her free time. Home schooling over video conference doesn't soak up much of the day. Besides, it lets me have some quiet time whenever this jackass stays quiet."

"You can head upstairs. We've got this," Rachel said. "We need to find out if our guest knows anything else about his employers he'd like to share before we make his life even worse. Oh, and check with Lee. We had two unique requisitions this morning. You can deliver those, but be careful."

"Sounds like a plan, boss. Have fun, everybody." Lauren brushed past Rachel and headed up the stairs.

Rachel turned to the tied-up prisoner. His arms were

tied to the arms of the chair, his legs tied to the chair's legs. She approached and got within a few feet. She leaned down. "Did you enjoy a pleasant sleep last night?"

The man attempted to communicate, but it was unintelligible.

"Didn't your mother ever teach you not to mumble?" Rachel took her normal hand out of her pocket and gripped the duct tape. She ripped it off, which was accompanied by a grunt of pain.

"Oh, you brought the psycho back here," he said. "I told him what he wanted. Why am I still here?"

"You have a name, buddy? It's impolite to ask things without introducing yourself first. My name is Rachel Morris. What's yours?"

"Alexei," he said.

"I'm guessing that sounds more masculine in the Russian dialect, because it doesn't in English. Now enough about that." She stood up straight and looked down at him. Her face was one of indifference and her tone matched that. "You told my associate what he wanted to know. You're going to answer my questions before you have a hope of leaving. Am I understood? Now, be a smart boy or you won't enjoy the dire consequences."

"What do you want to know?"

"How refreshing, having someone eager to please when I question them. It's rare, wouldn't you say so, darling?" she asked Ben, never looking back.

Ben walked up beside her. "They usually have more fight in them," he said. "This one must be a coward."

"Cowards have their uses, dear husband." Rachel took the hand out of her pocket and rested it on Ben's chest. She noticed her prisoner looking at her hand. His widening eyes told her all she needed to know. She unconsciously licked her lips, and she had a devilish smile. "Are you looking at something, my dear guest?" She held up her four fingered hand. "Oh, did this shock you? Too bad," her voice changed. "It's not nice to make a lady feel self-conscious. You never know what they'll do. Fetch me a tourniquet, baby."

"I don't envy you," Ben said, keeping his cool while looking at the petrified man. Meandering over to the table nearby, he picked up a sturdy piece of wire along with some tools, including a wire cutter, shears, pliers, and a knife. He laid them out on the miniature rolling table beside his wife. "Do I want to know your plans, dear?"

"That all depends on if he tells me something relevant. If not, I'll leave him to Warren back there." Her gaze never left the tied-up prisoner's eyes. "Now tell me something, quick for your sake. I am told you mentioned a Mikhail yesterday."

"Yes," the man said. "What about him?"

"Who is he?"

"You don't know the Ghost of Moscow?"

"Fancy title," she said, clearly not sounding impressed with her monotone voice. "What's he known for, since you're a part of his fan club?"

"He's a problem solver. The higher ups send him when they need something done. They say he's never failed a mission to date."

"I'm sure the legends also say he doesn't piss either, but I'm more interested in his skills. How capable is he?"

"Better than your best member," he said without pause or thought. "I guarantee."

"Guarantee, huh? Where is he?"

"You expect me to know? I'm not privy to his schedule."

"That disappoints me," Rachel said. She picked up the pliers from the table. "Where are Artyom and Oleg then?

Surely you know where your bosses are holing up during this war."

"I'm just a soldier. They don't tell me anything."

"Just where to strike and whom to kill viciously," Rachel said. "You know we have the camera feeds from every store-house leading to us, right? We know you and Mikhail were on a squad together. You must know where he was heading next. Lie to me again, and we will share something in common."

"All I know is where we were supposed to deliver after taking the guns. It's the mechanic's shop on Park Drive. I told your man where yesterday. I'm new to the country, Ms. Morris. It's not like Oleg gave me the detailed breakdown of where all his properties are. You'd know more than I would since you've been here longer. Please, ask me a question I can answer, and I'd be happy to."

"You're saying the last known location of Mikhail was where you told him yesterday?"

"That's right."

She turned around. "Isn't that where Chris's email said they were going to strike?"

"The anesthetic request?" Warren asked. "I believe it was."

"Did you tell them?"

"The only people I told were you, your husband, and Elizabeth, since she was here watching the interrogation."

"I guess we know who the leaker was," Ben muttered. "What's her angle here?"

"Loyalty issues?" the prisoner asked.

Rachel gave him an annoyed look before delivering a backhand to his head. "Be quiet. Only speak when spoken to." She leaned in close to Ben and whispered in his ear. "Send Lauren with them. I want to know the entire story."

"We're not going to step in and cancel the operation they're planning?" he asked. "If this Mikhail was last seen there, they could land in real trouble."

"Have you no faith in them?" Rachel asked. "Not in the foolish, reckless kids, but Chris and Jackie? They've come up with a plan that involves sedatives. Logic would dictate it's not as dangerous as going in with guns blazing. Now make sure you catch Lauren before she leaves. At least send her a message if she's already gone. That girl was always prompt. It's a blessing and a curse. Now as for you..." She returned her attention to their captive.

Ben rushed to the steps and ran upstairs, exiting the basement.

Rachel gestured Warren over. "I want you to bring me Elizabeth after we're done here. I want to see what she's planning. That woman is scheming during her old age."

"Yes, ma'am."

"As for you," Rachel paced in a circle around the chair that was bolted securely to the floor. "What was the next job?"

"You think they give us a schedule? This is more like the military. We're told the day of what we're doing and where we're headed. I assume it's for operational security for moments like this."

"How convenient," she said. "For them, I mean. It's quite unfortunate for you. You'd better give me something good."

"I heard Mikhail say something about meeting with Artyom. I assume he's the one he's reporting to."

"You report to who?" she asked.

"Mikhail. I came over with him on his hand-picked team."

"It seems he's not an excellent judge of character,"

Warren said, "what with picking a cowardly rat who squeals at the slightest provocation."

"What use is loyalty if I'm dead? You said you'd let me go, so I'm seizing that opportunity is all. It has nothing to do with loyalty."

"So we see," Warren said. "You're an embarrassment to your group."

"Now let's not be discourteous hosts, Mr. Davis." She stopped on the man's right side, knelt on one knee, and placed the man's pinky finger between the cold pliers. "Let's switch the rules a bit. You answer or you lose some weight."

"I already told you I'm willing to answer. None of this is necessary."

"Yet you claim ignorance on many things we ask. It's a good excuse for not talking," she said. "This will quickly jog your memory. Trust me, I know." she held up her hand for him to gawk at. "I leave Mr. Davis for the down and dirty process of it, though. I have an image to uphold, so I can't be seen covered in blood."

"With great pleasure, boss," Warren said. He took her place and gripped the dirty pliers tight using both hands, ready to squeeze.

"This is the last stretch. Survive this and you leave alive." Rachel stepped back a few yards and moved to his front. "Now, is Mikhail here to assassinate me, my children, or my officers?"

"Not to my knowledge. Only he or Artyom would know. If he was, though, you'd already be dead."

"Right. You're his team member - of course you'd say that. Next question," she said. "How many soldiers accompanied you and Mikhail?"

"I'd guess around seventy," he said. "We were forced to charter a private jet to enter the country on the down low."

"Which means the losses Oleg's recently faced are temporary. Smart man, calling reinforcements before he ambushes us. It shows premeditation. None of this info is new, but having direct numbers is nice. Time for the last question before we let you run home to daddy Mikhail. Did you honestly think you're getting out of this alive?"

"What?"

"Do it." Rachel turned around and walked for the stairs as unimaginable, horrific screams erupted behind her. She headed upstairs and slammed the door behind her. "You." She snapped her fingers, causing a nearby syndicate member to stop in his tracks.

"Yes, Ms. Morris?"

"Go downstairs and help Mr. Davis with his duties. That's an order."

The junior member got near the door and heard muffled screams. He looked back at her.

"What are you waiting for? Get down there. You should be thankful you're doing that rather than going off to war."

"Yes, ma'am." He opened the basement and for a moment the panicked, frantic screams rang crystal clear before the door closed again. She made her way back up to her office to find Ben and Elizabeth already waiting for her.

"Lauren has been informed," Ben said as soon as she entered her office.

"Good," she said. "Now as for you, old lady." She looked at the aging gangster heiress. "You leaked the address our guest told us to your son, didn't you?"

"Dear me," Elizabeth said. "Whatever gave you that idea?" She brought a hand up to her chest.

"Cut the act," Rachel said. "I already know you did. We didn't know of that property and then magically the next day our son's team sends a report that they're hitting it while requesting a big tank of anesthetic? When coincidences pile up like that, they become evidence."

"So what if I did?"

"That's where Mikhail was last spotted. Did you even know that?"

"It's one man," Elizabeth said in a dismissive tone.

"One man called the 'Ghost of Moscow'," Ben said.

"Titles always aim to make their target sound more important than they really are," Elizabeth said. "Besides, I viewed that report, same as you. They have a plan that will ignore anyone inside. Hell, if we wanted to, we could order them to slit their throats while they're out from the gas. We'll get weapons back, kill a bunch of Russians, and our sons will get some experience and fame."

"I sent Lauren over to oversee this shit show. Even I know there's no sense trying to stop my son when he's set his mind on something. She should at least keep them safe."

"Lauren? Does that woman possess combat training?"

"She can hold her own. Don't jump over my head with their team again."

"Turning into an overprotective mama bear, niece? The boys need to learn their own lessons. I learned that by watching your father grow up. They're stubborn as mules, but they will pleasantly surprise you, I find."

"You're playing games with your son and our son's life," Ben said with a growl. "Not to mention that Crystal is accompanying them." He moved over to Elizabeth and gripped her by the neck. "You're lucky I don't..."

"Enough. Quiet before you say or do something you'll regret."

Ben let her go and backed off.

"You two are such worrywarts." Elizabeth rubbed her neck with a glare toward Ben. "This will end the war faster."

"Don't pretend that's your agenda," Rachel said. "You must think I'm dense or totally distracted to not see your game here."

"Whatever are you talking about?"

"It will not work," she said. "Ben is my next inheritor, should something happen to me."

"Sometimes it's not up to the current boss to decide. It's the will of the people. Your husband has enjoyed life in the ivory tower for the past eighteen years. You think they'll choose Ben or one of the soldiers out there, risking their lives?"

"This is on you if it goes wrong, and trust that I will enjoy taking it out on you if that happens."

"I'm quaking in my boots," she said. "After all these years locked in this gilded cage, dying would break the boredom."

9

"This is the place." Roger turned into the parking lot of the mall. "Why are we transferring the anesthesia in a crowded location? It seems counterintuitive. Isn't anesthesia illegal?"

"Don't act suspicious and nobody will bat an eye, dude," Bernard said from the passenger seat. "When are you getting a new car? This thing's over twenty years old."

"It's my mother's old car, thank you. It's not flashy like yours, but she's reliable."

"Whatever you say," Bernard said. "There she is." He pointed out the front windshield of the car. "Park over there next to her."

"Yes, boss," Roger sarcastically said. He pulled the car into the nearby parking space. They could see Lauren smoking a cigarette, leaning against her own car beside them. The pair got out.

"Long time no see," Roger said.

"It's always nice to see the two troublemaking Morris boys again." Lauren exhaled a large puff of smoke into the air above them, then tossed the near spent death stick to the black asphalt below and snuffed it out. She gave each of them a hug. "I've got a surprise," she said.

"A pleasant surprise or a bad one?" Bernard asked. "We've had our fill of nasty surprises lately."

"Yeah, I heard about the Artyom incident. Sorry you had to see that on one of your first jobs," she said. "First thing's first though. Let's complete our assignment. You've secured room for the tank?"

"This baby has a large trunk," Roger said. "It should fit if the specifications we were given were correct." He opened his car's trunk while Lauren did the same.

"This is it?" Bernard asked.

"You wanted it, not me," she said. "Is something wrong?"

"I'm hoping it will be enough."

"The thing's half as big as the nitrous oxide tanks you see in the dentists' offices. If it's found lacking, then nothing will work," Roger said. "Come on. Let's stow it inside and get it out of the public's sight. We don't need looky-loos."

The two young men hefted the large, awkwardly shaped cylinder out of its confines and moved it over to Roger's trunk. They lowered it into the compartment and shut it.

"There," Roger said, placing a hand on his lower back and stretching. "Now, what was this surprise you mentioned earlier? Surely you didn't mean the gas itself?"

"If I've told you once, I've told you a thousand times, Roger, don't call me Shirley. Now, I have your sister's drone in the back of my car. I doubt it can fit in your little trunk."

"I see you still harbor hopes of leaving the syndicate and becoming a stand-up comedian. Don't quit your day job," Bernard said. "Now spit it out. We're on the clock here."

"You're always in such a rush," Lauren said. "You need to relax, or you'll have high blood pressure when you're older.

Anyway, I've stalled long enough. I got a text from your father." She pointed at Roger.

"Okay," Roger said. "And?" he asked.

"Turns out mama bear didn't like where you were going after she found where your friend got his information."

"Where did you get that info, anyway?" Roger turned and asked his best friend. "Didn't you say it was from a deal you did before?"

"Is that what he said?" Lauren asked.

"Make your point already," Bernard said. "We're burning daylight here. I don't enjoy being out in the open when we're locked in a war."

"We both know you got that info from your mother. She's the only person who had access to privileged information that would send it to you. The only others who knew were Davis, Ben, and Rachel. She's trying to give you guys a job that rallies the troops and makes a name for yourselves, isn't she?"

"I don't pretend to know my mother's motives. When she calls and tells me about a juicy target, though, I don't ask questions."

"Maybe you should," Lauren said, her tone turning serious. "Fame is not worth it if it gets you killed."

"Folks apparently don't have faith in our plan," Bernard said with a smug grin. He gave a gentle nudge with his elbow to Roger's side. "We got that other job done, and still they doubt our ability."

"Burning down a building is a far sight different from what you're proposing. I heard about the needless complication that occurred during that fiasco. Your partner in crime had a fun time playing hero."

"There won't be innocents in their storehouse," Roger said.

"That you know of," Lauren said. "What if one of their single dads brought his kid in there? You planning to rush in and get yourself killed if children are present?"

"If you know about that, it must be common knowledge," Roger said.

"Things rarely stay a secret with gossip. Everybody wanted to hear about the boss's kid's first job. Most of the grunts loved the tale. They thought it heroic, but there is another group that thinks it was dumb and reckless."

"They are welcome to their opinion. Is this an indictment of my moral past choices, or was there a point to today's surprise?" Roger asked.

"They sent me to join this merry little band of yours and make sure you two don't get yourselves killed," Lauren said. "Isn't that just great? You get to work with your teacher. Most students only dream of this moment."

"Aren't we just the luckiest?" Bernard asked, clearly being sarcastic.

"Don't be a jackass, Mr. Morris."

"Don't call me that," Bernard said.

"You don't want me calling you Bernie. How can I distinguish you two then? Would you rather I call you by your full name, Bernard? You're both Mr. Morris."

"Do Chris and Jackie know?" Roger asked.

"They will when we return. My luggage will be sent over in due time. I'll manage with what I packed in my car until they're delivered. We can't send syndicate men, so they're using the postal service."

"You don't want to fight," Roger said. "I can see it in your eyes."

"Do I wish to give up the cushy job of home-schooling unruly teenagers for the glorious life of a soldier on the streets in life and death battles daily? No, I do not," she said.

"We don't always receive what we want, something you two spoiled brats need to learn."

"Is that all?" Bernard asked. "We need to return and prepare for the next phase of this job. Standing around jawing all day isn't helping."

"You always were rude," Lauren said. "You need to respect your elders more."

"Well, you're not old yet," Bernard said. "Now follow us. We'll lead you back to the apartment. We'll have to double back a few times to be safe."

"Sounds like a plan," she said.

That night...

"I don't think I've ever seen a syndicate member use one of these before," Lauren inspected the high-tech piece of flying technology. "You think we're safe up here?"

"As safe as we expected," Chris said. He had a rifle slung over his shoulder and was monitoring the street below. "We're in neutral ground, so I wouldn't call it safe; but I doubt the Russians would make a move. They'd piss off too many street level gangs."

"I notice we're still here," Jackie said. "I guess we don't mind pissing them off."

"We're just flying a drone around," Crystal said while performing a last-minute inspection of the drone.

"The roof of an abandoned business building is hardly subtle, but no one's here tonight, I suppose," Lauren said. "Let's hurry and get this done."

"Just a minute. I'm just doing last-minute checks." Crystal finished her inspection and moved over to the brief-case she'd brought. It contained a headset that covered her eyes and two controls to fit in either hand.

"That looks like a VR headset," Roger said.

"It allows me to see what the drone sees in 4k resolution at sixty frames a second," she said, "while recording the footage so we can study it later. It's the very latest in reconnaissance technology. Everybody take a few steps back." She grabbed the headset and put it on. She felt around for the controls until she felt them in her palm.

"There you go," Roger said, placing them in her hands.

"Thanks," she said. "Now, back up from the drone. It needs clearance to take off."

Roger backed off and stood next to Bernard a few feet away.

"Don't just stand there, kids," Jackie said. "Watch the other directions of the building. We're not getting ambushed tonight. You can rest on your laurels after we get back to the apartment."

"Yes, ma'am," Bernard said. He and his friend took the remaining two sides that weren't being guarded by Chris and Jackie. They had their handguns out and ready.

Lauren gave Crystal some room. "Alright, whenever you're ready."

Crystal pressed a button on the remote control in her right hand. The drone lit up and a whirring sound showed it was working just fine. "Take off is always the trickiest part. Give me a minute. Landing is much easier."

"Take your time," Chris said. "We only get one shot at this, and we can't waste it due to pilot error."

"This is quite the ingenious plan, after hearing the fine details," Lauren said.

"Don't let them hear that," Jackie said. "Those boys don't need an ego boost."

"I'm their educator. We're supposed to boost our students' confidence."

"Not anymore. You're in the trenches now, so act like it."

"You're a kind of wet blanket, aren't you, Jackie?" Lauren stuck her tongue out in a childish display. "No one likes a jerk."

"Kiss my black ass," Jackie said.

"Can I have quiet, please?" Crystal asked in a meek voice. "I need to concentrate."

"Sorry. My bad," Jackie said.

The drone wobbled a bit as it ascended a few feet in the air vertically. "Steady," Crystal said, willing herself to control the machine. "Just a few feet and we're ready." The drone rose higher until it was well above their heads. It zipped toward the cityscape without delay.

"I will never tire of this feeling," Crystal said with a wide smile. "It's the best feeling - flying around the city like this."

"You feel like you're flying, huh?" Bernard asked. "Neat toy."

"That device isn't a toy," Roger said. "She got mom to buy her the expensive ones. They're usually upwards of two to ten thousand. How much was this model, sis?"

"Ten thousand," she said. "I had to be positive the model could sustain the weight needed."

"Weight?" Lauren asked. "What weight could it need to carry?"

"She thinks it'll carry the tank up to the top of the warehouse," Roger said. "I'm inclined to believe her. With drones, she knows her stuff. It's been an obsession for her since her early teens."

"Why try to drag that heavy tank up a ladder, right?" Crystal looked down while her thumb pressed downward on the control pad. "Hold on. Are you guys seeing this?"

"Lauren's the only one over there with you," Bernard said. "Ask her."

"I see the feed on your laptop, yes," she said. "This is the place? Hm, it looks big. It could house a lot of weapons. I see ventilation shafts coming out from the top of the place. It should fit the bill for what we want."

"How tall is the building?" Jackie asked. "We'll need a ladder if there's not one already affixed there."

"I'm circling the building now from a distance and looking," Crystal said.

The screen near her feet showed the enormous building from a few dozen yards away. It slowly listed to the right, gently circling the building.

"Can this zoom anymore?" Lauren asked.

"Give me a second. Sudden camera changes make me nauseous when piloting this. Anything you observe on that screen is what I'm viewing. There we are."

The screen zoomed in on the warehouse's sides. Lauren leaned in. "I'm not seeing any ladders on it."

"They probably removed it if there was one," Chris said. "I would too. No sense leaving a tactical weak spot for your operation like that. That means we'll need to bring our own ladder. How tall is the thing?"

"It looks like it's two stories," Lauren said. "Wait," she said. The drone approached the warehouse, now encroaching closer than a mere twenty yards. The details were now clear. "We're too close. One of them could see."

"You think people look upward? I thought I'd secure us a look inside and see what we're looking at. We may see inventory they have or how many personnel are inside." Crystal saw a Russian through the window. He was looking right through the window toward them, but showed no signs of having seen the flying device. He turned and kept walking, calm as can be.

"Which won't do us much good if they see our drone and fortify the warehouse," Lauren said. "Back it off now."

"Fine," Crystal said. "Have it your way. I got some footage of the inside through one of their windows. We can study that later with a fine-tooth comb. Is there anything else we need before I bring this baby back?"

"Count how many cars are parked in the lot," Lauren said. "It'd give us a more precise estimate of how many personnel are present than looking through a window, and it's a lot safer. After that we're done."

"Yeah, sure," Crystal was obviously disappointed, judging by her deflated voice. "Here," she said. She backed the drone off and continued circling around the building. This time she angled the camera downward so they could view the surrounding parking lot.

"Looks like at least a dozen cars there," she said.

"That won't matter with the gas in there. It just means more Russians we can take out in one fell stroke," Bernard said.

"I'm heading back now."

"Good, I'm getting cold out here," Jackie said.

"You could be going through menopause. I hear that makes you cranky," Lauren said. "That and temperature swings."

"You're lucky you are friends with the boss, or I'd beat the shit out of you."

Later that night in the warehouse...

"What is it?" Mikhail asked. "I know you didn't bother me for nothing. No one is that stupid."

"Sir, I think I saw something earlier."

"You saw something?" Mikhail asked. "Can you be any more vague?"

"I was patrolling the second-floor catwalks, and I looked out the window. I thought I saw something hovering outside. It couldn't have been a helicopter since we'd have heard, but then I thought it could be a drone recording footage."

"Are you positive you spotted a drone?" Mikhail asked. "Who am I kidding? Of course you are if you're coming to me with news. There are two options," he said. He hefted himself upward out of the office chair and moved to the guard. He led him outside the cramped office and into the spacious main room of the warehouse. "Show me where it was, specifically," he said with authority.

"Yes, sir," the grunt said. "Follow me." He led him up a nearby flight of steps and onto the walkway above. He walked across the metal grated catwalk toward the side of the building and pointed upward at a large rectangular window. "It came from there, sir. I realize it may have been someone just playing with a drone for fun and all, but I don't believe in coincidences in war."

"A smart outlook," Mikhail said. "If it was there, it was a nosy civilian or a scouting mission. Nobody would be dumb enough to charge into this fortified building without prior knowledge of what's waiting inside."

"You think we're going to be hit here, sir?"

"I don't know," Mikhail said. "That is a possibility. Resume your watch. Thank you for bringing this to my attention. I have to call Artyom and see what he thinks. I know I want to prepare, but he's the one in charge."

"Yes, sir," the grunt said. He performed an about face and continued his monotonous patrol.

Mikhail went back to his office and picked up the landline on his desk. He picked up the piece of paper that Artyom gave him, which contained the phone number to contact him. He input the number and waited.

"Yeah?" Artyom asked.

"It's me," Mikhail said. "I just received a rather odd report from a guard. He saw a drone flying around, poking its nose where it shouldn't. I think we're going to get hit here soon."

"Your location would be..." Artyom paused for a good minute. "It'd be an inconvenience to put it lightly. I assume you desire to preemptively take care of the attacker. You desire to set up an ambush then and want permission?"

"You are the commanding officer."

Artyom grunted over the line. "Take a majority of your manpower outside and set them up where you see fit. We can't take everyone out, or they'll see that it's a setup. We need cheese to bait the trap. I'll leave it to you where you and your men post up while waiting. Just keep five men inside. That's the minimum number to guard a place that size that they'd expect. Once the trap springs, eliminate them all. We cannot lose that warehouse or what's in there. We can't move the merchandise inside for the time being. Every movement with guns is a coin flip. Our best bet is to prevent the theft."

"I understand. Catch the rats in the cage and eliminate the vermin."

"Thank you for bringing this to my attention. I trust you to get this done. Now, if you'll excuse me, I have other matters to attend to."

"May luck ever favor you," Mikhail said before hanging up. "Son of a bitch," he said. "Parry, counter, riposte - war never changes." He walked to the main room and yelled.

"Everybody get down here right now. We've got something happening."

Within a minute he could hear footsteps on metal grates, concrete, and panting as he saw men running down the stairs and over to him. He waited for them all to assemble into a circle around him before he started.

"Gentlemen, thanks to an especially observant guard among you, we have been tipped off that we're going to get hit here soon." He heard grumbling coming from the men surrounding him. "Quiet!" He silenced them with a single word. "Don't view this news as dangerous or scary. Think of it as an opportunity for us to wipe out Syndicate members dumb enough to enter our territory. Here's how we'll prepare..."

10

Lauren, Roger, Bernard, and Crystal were the only folks still awake after their scouting trip. Jackie and Chris had already turned in for the night, leaving them awake.

"We should totally be in bed ourselves," Lauren said. "You realize this, yes?"

"I need to implement these modifications before tomorrow as a safety net," Crystal said.

"What is it you're putting on there, anyway?"

"Something Mother ensured I didn't have access to until now. This is an attachable mini-gun."

"Christ," Bernard said. "That looks small for a traditional mini-gun, though."

"It's drone sized," she said. "It has a smaller ammunition capacity, but I'm hopefully not going to need this killing machine. I think Mom got these for the tech division anyway, so us techies feel useful if shit hits the fan. Why limit us to sitting with our computers when we can kill from behind the screen?"

"You three differ totally from our school sessions, even just a few years ago," Lauren said. "I imagined none of you getting involved in this business - well, except for Bernard here that is. His mama always wanted that for him, for God knows what reason."

"It's my birthright," he said.

"That's not brag worthy," Lauren said. "Speaking of your mother, rumor is Rachel is pissed at her."

"Why is that?" Roger asked.

"Turns out she got that warehouse's location from a captured prisoner. The prisoner also mentioned, after Elizabeth gave the location to you, that it was the last seen location of the so called 'Ghost of Moscow'."

"What the hell is that fancy title?" Bernard asked. "Some operator of their group or something? He sounds like he needs taken down a peg."

"We might end up doing that if this job goes off without a hitch. They say he's never lost a fight, he's never failed in an operation, and he always gets the job done." Lauren looked down at her trembling hands. "It makes me nervous that we're going near it, if I'm honest."

"I'm surprised Mother hasn't sent a platoon to drag us away if she knows that much." Roger rolled his eyes. He lifted a leg and sat it on his other, reclining into the seat.

"I imagine that was her first response. My bet is Elizabeth is the only reason she hasn't. She's had to sell this unique plan of yours as safe. For her sake, your plan had better work safely."

"What's that supposed to mean?" Bernard asked. He pounded one of his fists into his other open hand.

"Nothing," Lauren said, looking away. "It means nothing."

"It better mean nothing," Bernard said. "She's nothing but loyal. She's just giving us our chance to prove ourselves from their overprotectiveness. We're grown ass men, for God's sake. Everyone's been treating us like we're children."

"I can hardly blame a mother for trying to make sure her babies are safe during a gang war," Lauren said. "Truthfully, I wish you three weren't out here in this war-zone either. I watched you grow up, and I shudder to even imagine one of you dying because of this foolishness."

"That will not happen," Bernard said. "We will not die so easily."

"Said every grunt entrenched inside a war zone before he died through no fault of his own - alone, deep in the trenches," she said. "Battle does not respect your perseverance. It doesn't care about your plans. The sturdiest, most stubborn of men will die from a bullet through their skull. I've seen too many die over the years."

"Aren't you a regular ray of sunshine?" Crystal asked, still tinkering with the drone's attachment. "If I can fit this behemoth, I can attach the towing attachment and gun simultaneously. The box carrying the belt of cartridges weighs more than I thought."

"Towing attachment?"

"It's basically a fancy word for a small platform below where we can place the canister that is tied to the four support beams so it doesn't fall off. Whoever goes upstairs on the roof will need to cut or untie them, but it's a small price to pay to ensure it reaches where it needs to."

"Mother is not one to make rash decisions of life or death," Roger said.

"I don't know how you presume to know her intentions," Lauren said. "I've witnessed her rise to power in this syndicate and know how ruthless she can be. Not that it's a bad thing. She's mom to you two and cousin to you, Bernard. It's hard to set aside family bias and see someone for who they really are."

"You're saying my mother is a different person than I know her to be?" Roger asked.

"Aren't you a different person than I thought you were? You used to just be rambunctious teenagers, playing pranks and learning from me. Now you're hardened syndicate members. You've inadvertently proved my point."

"I know my mother. She may be annoyed with Auntie Elizabeth," Roger said. "She'll just lecture her for a bit and never let her forget it."

"It's done," Crystal said, throwing her arms up in celebration. She got up from the floor, revealing its splendor for the rest to see.

"Where's the platform?" Bernard asked.

"It lowers when it's hovering. It can't come out now and I'm not activating it inside the apartment for safety reasons. The focal point I was referring to was the gun attachment. It was harder to install than I gave it credit for."

Sure enough, the drone had a mini-gun pointing forward on its front. A belt of bullets was fed into it from a nearby box tucked away above it.

Bernard got off the chair and knelt beside it. He rested a hand on the barrel. "It's steady and secured. The last question is, does it fire?"

"That's a question we'll hopefully not have to find out," Crystal said, "but it's ready in case we do. It's fed with bullets from a compartment behind the main body. It only carries five hundred rounds, so it'll go quickly if I'm not careful. Technically, it could hold more rounds, but if it's towing a canister, I need to keep the weight down to be safe."

"If your mother saw this, she'd weep," Lauren said. "Seeing her daughter prepare a weapon of this caliber. She never wanted you to fire a weapon, never mind this monstrosity."

"Only to keep all of you alive. Remember, I won't be with you all on the ground. I'll be a safe five minutes away all by my lonesome. This is my only way to really help beyond digital means."

"Mother can eat soap if she doesn't like it," Roger said, coming closer to inspect the thing. He placed a hand on Crystal's head, which she batted away nigh instantaneously. "It looks to me like you did good."

"Don't treat me like I'm five years old still," she whined.

"Yes, yes," he said dismissively. "You're a big girl now. I know. Can't a guy dote on his little sister every so often?"

"We should hit the bed now," Bernard said. "No sense staying up longer. It'll just drain us of needed energy for tomorrow night. I'm hitting the sack, and I urge the rest of you to do the same." He headed towards his and Roger's bedroom and disappeared inside.

"Yeah, I'll be right behind you," Roger said.

"Then get out of my room. I'm sleeping on the couch," Lauren said. "Crystal, you realize we're going to have to buy another bed and put it in your room? I am not sleeping here long term."

"I don't have a problem," she said. "It might be cramped, but it'd be better than sleeping on that sofa."

Everyone said their goodnights and headed for their room. Roger closed the door behind him to see Bernard already in his bed, covered in blankets. He changed in the dark interior out of his formal suit and into something more suited for bed before climbing into his resting place. He placed his hands behind his head and stared at the drab ceiling. Before long, he heard snoring nearby.

He's asleep already, he thought. *I envy that ability to fall asleep quickly.* He wasn't sure how much time passed as the next day's events played in his mind. He pictured the entire operation from start to finish. Sometimes his mind threw him curve balls and something went wrong. While he was in the middle of his daydreaming, he heard a slight creaking. He looked toward the nearby bedroom door to notice light sneaking in through the crack. He closed his eyes and stayed still.

"Are you awake?" a female voice asked. He could tell it was his little sister, Crystal. The door closed and for a second, he believed she had left when he gave no verbal answer. Instead, he felt something getting into bed with him. *A habit she never broke when she was nervous or scared,* he thought. *It happened after the massacre and every night since. I have to get her help. This can't go on forever.*

She got under the covers and snuggled up next to him. She buried her face in his side and he could feel her body shake. He could feel a wet spot forming on his side. *Fuck it,* he thought. He acted like he was waking up.

"Hm?" he grunted. "Crystal?" he whispered. "Is that you?"

"Maybe," she said, matching his quiet voice.

"What's wrong? Why are you upset?"

"I just got to thinking about tomorrow," she said. "What if Lauren was correct and something horrible happens?"

He wrapped one arm around her shoulders and hugged her. "Don't go thinking like that. It helps nothing. Alright?"

"I can't help it. What if Mom's correct and we never should've been involved in Syndicate business?"

"You trust your big brother, yeah? Then trust Bernard and my plan. It's a foolproof one. We won't even have to fire a gun since they'll all be asleep, thanks to a certain drone obsessed girl. You're the reason we'll be fine. I have faith in your abilities. Now have some faith in ours."

"It's hard to. I still have nightmares of watching those Syndicate members dying in front of us. The gunshots and the way they fell is burned into my memory, and I don't want you to join them. I don't want to imagine you not being alive one day because of a single avoidable bullet."

"I don't plan on joining them for a long time, Sis," Roger said. "We all have our time to die, but mine is not soon."

"You don't know that," she said, holding him tighter.

Roger looked over at Bernard, who was still snoring, so he was pretty sure he was asleep. He knew he'd never let either of them live this down if he caught them. He looked back at the ceiling. "I know we've done our homework this time. That's what I know. If you do the prep, plans work. Isn't that what Lauren taught us in school? You trust her wisdom, yeah? We've done just that. Worrying won't help anyone. We need you in tiptop shape tomorrow. You need your sleep."

He didn't hear a response, but noticed her body had stopped shuddering. *Oh, don't tell me,* he thought. *Shit, she's asleep.* He reached over with his free hand to the night table and grabbed his phone. He set an alarm to vibrate before he knew Bernard's would go off. *At least I can move her out of here before he wakes. If she can sleep peacefully here tonight, then it'll benefit all of us. I guess I'll let her stay.*

11

"Everything's set," Crystal said over the call. "I'm ready to deliver the payload whenever you tell me to."

"Give it a minute," Chris said. He was behind the wheel of a van they'd received from the syndicate, which they used to transport guns. It looked like a moving van without the decals on the outside. He, Jackie, Roger, Lauren, and Bernard were all inside. "We need to decide who's climbing up to the roof to hook the drugs into their ventilation system. We've got the ladder. Are there any volunteers? Surely you won't volunteer the old man?"

"I can do it," Roger said.

"No, I'll go," Bernard said.

"Such eager volunteers," Chris said. "Who's faster between the pair of you?"

"Bernard is," Crystal said. "Don't listen to my pigheaded brother. He knows he's slightly slower than him."

"Bull," Roger said.

"Don't be mad at the facts, buddy," Bernard said. He poked Roger in the arm. "I'll be right back. Don't go anywhere."

"Now I'll keep watch for any outside patrols while you approach. Listen to me if you want to be safe," Crystal said. "Can everyone hear me before you head out?"

"Communications check," Chris said.

"Check," Roger said.

"Heard," Bernard said.

"You're all fine to me," Jackie said.

"I'm here," Lauren said.

"Alright, let me get in position," Crystal said. "Stand by."

Roger looked over at his side toward his longtime best friend. The two older members up front were putting on their gas masks. Bernard himself was not doing so yet.

Bernard looked over at Roger. "Hurry, man. Put on your mask. You don't want to forget when you head inside. You'll pass out quick, and then we're screwed."

Roger reached down to the gas mask on his lap. He held the mask up to his face. "Yeah, I'm aware," he said. "Just stay calm over there, Sis," he said. "No pressure or anything."

"Your concern is noted," Crystal said.

"Look there," Chris pointed out the windshield. A drone could be seen flying toward their destination. "Also, stop distracting our ace pilot. She's the crux of this scheme of ours working."

"Mute your microphone before putting all that pressure on me; but lucky for you, I thrive under it."

"It looks like it." Jackie watched the small device take its position directly over the warehouse, about forty feet above it.

"Alright. Now I need someone to reach the roof and remove this canister."

"That's my cue," Bernard said. He filed the gas mask away in the backpack he had in his lap before throwing it over his shoulder.

"Sounds like I'll carry the damned ladder then," Roger said, stuffing his inside his coat. "I'm going too, since I was always better at tying knots than you."

"I'll be fine."

"That wasn't part of the plan," Jackie said.

"One more man might help keep you out of trouble. Having another pair of boots on the ground should help keep their partner safe," Chris said. "I'll allow it. You two had better be careful, or it's our asses when we explain this to your mothers."

"Your concern is duly noted," Bernard said. "Come on, brother. Let's get this done."

Both young men exited the van. They moved to the back and threw open the rear doors of the vehicle. Roger entered and picked up a very tall ladder that was folded up inside. He got back outside while Bernard closed the doors behind him.

"Follow me," Bernard said to his friend towing the climbing tool.

To the common eye, the pair looked conspicuous, but they weren't doing anything illegal yet. They weaved in alleys and winded around buildings before crossing. They received odd stares from stopped drivers who witnessed the pair crossing the street, but that was all that came of it.

"Hold up," Bernard said, stopping him and Roger in a nearby alley. They saw the warehouse, but it was a hundred feet away.

"Problems?" Chris asked.

"I've spotted guards patrolling the south side," Crystal said.

"That's why I said hold," Bernard said.

"How the hell did you spot guards from here?" Roger asked.

"I'm dialed in. What can I say? Not heaving that ladder around affords me the luxury of focusing on our surroundings. Thanks for that," Bernard said. "Now come on, pack mule. Carry your weight before I sell you."

"Hee-haw." Roger did his best impression of a donkey.

"What a pair of jackasses," Jackie said. "Stop treating this like a game and be serious."

"You'll place the ladder on the south side," Crystal said. "That's the side closest to you, if you're where I believe you are."

"Yes, we are on the south side. The patrol went behind some larger trucks. Tell us when we can move."

"You're good to go now. Get moving. Go fast and stay low."

Roger and Bernard got out of the space between buildings and ran as fast as they could toward the warehouse. Bernard climbed over the waist high chain-link fence and turned around to take the ladder to allow Roger to follow suit. He handed the ladder to Roger and ran once his friend was clear of the impediment.

"Hold up behind that nearby truck. Quick!" Crystal said.

Bernard and Roger ducked behind a large semi-truck. Roger was careful to not allow the ladder to poke around the vehicle and give their position away. They could hear footsteps growing nearer and some Russian being spoken. They couldn't understand the language, but they could infer by their tone that neither was keen on being outside this late.

"Trust me when I tell you, you need to make your move now. There are two patrols. Go now. Get up there and don't delay, or the second group will catch you."

Both young men turned the corner and rushed ahead.

Roger looked left and spotted the patrol that had just

passed them facing away. They were a fair distance away, but his sister had jumped the gun by sending them, in his opinion. *Not the time or place to complain. They'd hear me,* he thought.

Bernard led the pair through the sparse parking lot. They saw assorted vehicles other than the large eighteen wheelers scattered among the lot. They got closer to the warehouse, now within twenty feet. Bernard weaved around a van sitting near the giant garage doors near the building's front. He reached the brick exterior of the building and turned. He waved Roger over. "Hurry, man. We're on a timer," he said in a quiet voice.

"I'm going as fast as I can," Roger said, while carrying the ladder. He got it off his shoulder and Bernard helped him get it extended and leaned against the building. He held the ladder and nodded to Bernard. "You go first. I'll hold it."

"Got it," Bernard said, climbing on the tool. Every step echoed in the quiet surroundings as Bernard ascended toward the roof.

Roger angled his neck up and watched his friend eventually reach the top and climb over before disappearing out of sight. He started his own climb. He'd never climbed a ladder faster in his life, he was pretty sure.

"I hope you're almost up there," Crystal said. "The next group will be there inside twenty seconds."

Roger was halfway up the ladder. "I'll be up there. As soon as I'm up, Bernard, you'll pull the ladder up behind me."

"I got you, brother. Now hurry down there. If I'd known you'd take this long climbing, I'd never have let you come along."

"Screw off." Roger looked at the approaching rooftop

and saw Bernard peeking over and down at him. He moved each arm and leg with purpose, taking care not to go too fast, as he'd seen men fall off ladders around the mansion when he grew up. He remembered one fool who'd fallen off the roof of the small house they were building for Elizabeth years ago and the sound of the crack when he met the grass below.

"You got maybe ten seconds and they're turning the corner," Crystal said. "Hurry, Brother, please."

"I'm going as fast as I can." Roger was within the last ten rungs and kept his pace. He reached the top of the ladder and climbed over the crest before falling unceremoniously onto the roof in an uncoordinated pile. Bernard leaned over the edge, pulling up the ladder. He got to his feet and rushed over, helping his friend pull up the only evidence that they were there. It was not an entirely silent process, however. They had the ladder halfway up when they saw the next pair of Russian patrols turn a corner and come into view down below.

"Hold it," Bernard whispered to his friend standing right beside him. Both men felt their shaking hands gripping the ladder. The ladder was above the eye level of the guards below. Both teenagers held their breath as the group approached where the ladder was but mere moments ago.

The group below paused underneath where the ladder hung precariously above. One took out a pack of cigarettes before handing one to his partner in crime and lighting up both cigarettes with his lighter. They spoke more Russian before continuing to pace forward with their cigarettes in one hand, side by side.

They watched the pair turn the corner before pulling the ladder up with renewed vigor. When the climbing implement was clear of the roof top side, they gently laid it down on the large open area they found themselves standing on.

"You two nearly gave me a heart attack," Crystal said.

"Was it that close?" Chris asked. "We can't see crap back here."

"Close? Yes. In fact, they didn't even get the ladder fully onto the roof before the Russians were standing below with it suspended above them. One look skyward, and they'd have been easily spotted."

"You two are regular daredevils. You know what they say. Fortune favors the bold, so let's not waste this opportunity."

Roger decided he'd drag the ladder back to the edge of the roof, near to where they came from.

"There are two ventilation shafts that appear similar," Crystal said. "Find which one's blowing air and which one is sucking air. You want the latter, obviously."

"It's pretty obvious which is which." Bernard saw one expelling what looked like white smoke into the night sky above. The other had nothing exiting. He moved toward it and stuck his hand near the exit. He felt no air pushing against his hand. "Found it. Now to get the anesthetic ready. You can deliver it whenever you're ready."

Roger finished getting the pair's escape method ready and jogged over to his friend before looking up at the sky. "Everything alright over there?"

"Just picking my moment. Keep your britches on," Crystal said.

The men watched the drone above descend and gently touch down a few feet away from their position before the engine shut off immediately.

Bernard unsheathed the knife at his side and got to a knee. He cut the restraints holding the canister on the small platform affixed to the bottom of the drone before taking it off. He didn't forget to take the associated tubes they'd gathered before that were taped to the undercarriage of the drone.

"You got the tubes too?" Crystal asked. "I can't see crap except for Brother's knees and your hair while you're getting stuff off it."

"It's a little unnerving having this gun pointing right at me," Bernard said, carefully peeling the tape off. He grabbed the accessories they'd need to deliver the gas into the warehouse and stood up. "Alright, we're good." He tossed a tube to Roger. "Help me set this up. It'll go faster."

Roger caught it and turned around. He reached into his pocket with a gloved hand and pulled out a roll of industrial tape. He stuck a length of the cord to the vent's exterior, making sure it was secure before feeding the tube downward into the vent, deeper and deeper until the tubing was out of slack. "It's in there. Now to hook it up," he said.

"We'll also need to do something about the patrols outside," Bernard said. "There are four guards, and the team can't approach until they're gone."

"You leave that part to us," Chris said. "We can't let you kids do everything here, now can we? We're making our approach now and will tell you when the guards have been dealt with. Do not turn on the gas until I order."

"I guess we get a few minutes break then." Roger sat down near the vent and watched Bernard connect the tubing he set up to the tank of anesthetic.

"I think that's it. Let me make sure it's connected good and tight. I don't want to nap because of a damned loose tube."

"You should wear your mask before you turn on the gas," Crystal said in a meek voice. "It's pretty obvious, really."

"So sue me. I don't think of everything right off the bat," Bernard said. "It'll be as you say." Bernard took off the backpack over his shoulders and placed it on the roof. He undid the zipper and rifled through it until he found the gas mask. He placed it over his face. "Come over here, lazybones."

"You need me to tie the straps around back?" Roger asked. He got to work, making sure that the mask was air tight before he secured it to his friend's face. He backed off a few feet before reaching into his coat and pulling out his own mask. "Watch how it's done for next time."

"God damn," Bernard said, his voice muffled by the mask. He reached up to the eye part of the mask and rubbed. "This thing fogs up easy. I hate wearing this."

"You'll love it when we don't all pass out in there," Roger said with his hands behind his head, tying the straps. "It's only for like ten minutes. Tough it out."

The nearby drone started up its engine and took flight once again.

"You two are good here. Let me help the other two. Where are you two now?" Crystal asked.

"Near the south side," Jackie said. "We parked the van nearby and are on foot. We have to do this quietly. You understand that. Right, old man?"

"I'll be like a ninja losing his virginity, subtle and quiet."

"Always classy I see," Jackie said. "Now be quiet," she said.

The two young Syndicate members moved toward the side of the rooftop and stepped over the extended ladder. They looked down and saw two figures outside the chainlink fence they'd climbed over just earlier.

The first climbed the fence with relative ease while her partner was slower, but still quick by civilian's standards.

"You've lost a step, you old coot," Jackie said.

"I can still show you a thing or two, sister," Chris said. "I'll kill the guard on our right. You have the left. Alright? Once we have them under control, we're going to switch positions to the corner. Use your knife on this one. Which side will they be coming from?"

"Your right," Crystal said. "As of right now, the east side."

"Got it," Chris said.

"Get ready down there." The drone listed rightward and peered down the side of the building. "The first set of patrols is approaching soon."

Both figures reached down to their hips and pulled out something - the boys couldn't tell what. They assumed it was their knives but couldn't see from here. They watched the patrols below take a wider angle compared to before, not staying beside the warehouse, but now in the middle of the parking lot.

The guards passed the truck their partners were hiding behind. They saw the pair skulk out from behind it toward their targets. Their progress was aided as the group paused again and talked. They couldn't hear from here but could guess they were talking as one guard was very animated when he spoke, using his hands to stress every Russian word.

Roger and Bernard watched the two older operators get closer. The bird's-eye view of it all happening gave a cinematic, if surreal, feeling to the whole situation. It quickly amplified the surreal sensation as they saw both wrap an arm around their assigned target's throat while the knife hand got ready. They saw them slit their throats. Thick ropes of crimson blood shot out of their throats with every heartbeat of their dying bodies. The blood did not stop; the spurts became weaker and weaker, shooting out the front of their necks while each held them in place.

Jackie's target broke free and fell forward onto the asphalt below. The blood shooting out had weakened him, and all he could do was roll over and try to reach for his weapon. She was too quick for him, however, and she stepped on his arm. She knelt and stabbed him another half dozen times in the chest to finish him. Chris's faded off with no extra fight, slumping against him before he tossed him to the ground like a sack of potatoes. "Let's move and get ready for the next group."

The pair moved to the nearby corner that Crystal had directed them to. "Same plan," Chris said. "I've got the big one. You get the small one. I'd hate for you to break a nail."

"I'm going to smack you later."

The pair waited to ambush their next targets. This one went like clockwork, if clockwork was a chaotic, bloody mess. Both grabbed their targets as soon as they passed the threshold of the corner. Chris utilized their forward momentum and used his left hand to secure his victim's arm. He pulled him closer while he used his right to stab his throat over and over. Blood shot out, staining his suit. His victim didn't even have a chance at grabbing for his weapon. He was too busy trying to fend off the attacks unsuccessfully and trying to scream.

Jackie, meanwhile, chose a more elegant solution than Chris's brute force method. She grabbed her target's arm and yanked it toward her while her other hand shot out at the same time. She took the knife out of his throat and tossed the knife to the ground before grabbing his arm reaching for the firearm on his belt line. "Just let it happen," she cooed. "Go to sleep. It won't be as bad that way. Listen to my soothing voice, baby boy, and sleep," she said.

Bernard's eyes widened as he noted the night and day difference in their methods. While Chris used his brawn to physically impose his will on his prey, Jackie was like water. Using motion, momentum, and her own advantages until her target lowered to the ground and stopped moving.

"Now I'm covered in blood," Jackie complained. "You know how hard it is to get blood out of clothes? Of course you wouldn't. You don't do your own laundry."

"Stop complaining," Chris said. "Turn on the gas, boys. We're heading back to the van and coming back. Get your gas masks on if you haven't already and get back to ground level afterward. That's an order."

"Yes, sir," Bernard said. He ran back to the canister and twisted the wheel at the top, listening till he heard hissing after his motion. He opened the valve further, eliciting a louder hiss. "That should be good. Get the ladder ready, buddy."

"Already on it," Roger said, leaning down and grabbing the ladder. He awkwardly got it over the edge of the roof and carefully lowered it gently little by little until he felt the bottom hit the black top below. He gingerly got onto the ladder and saw his friend approach as he lowered himself down. "Did I ever mention I hate heights?" he asked while looking down.

"Not until now," Bernard said. "That should give you more reason to hurry. You're slow as a grandma driving to church on a Sunday, dude."

Roger saw Bernard's foot was only a rung above his hands and changed his climbing method to something he'd seen on television before. *Fuck it,* he thought. *I have gloves on. It should work well, right?* He grabbed both sides of the ladder and took his legs off the ladder. This resulted in him sliding down the ladder at an accelerated pace. He was thankful he had the gloves on, seeing as he could feel the heat building in his hands as he slid down. He reached the bottom and backed away, giving his friend space.

"That was a neat trick," Bernard said. "You need to teach me that sometime." He looked over and saw the van pulling into the parking lot. He waved them over. "Now we play the waiting game. How long for this drug to affect our targets?"

Lauren spoke up. "According to the internet, it depends on the concentration. My concern is how we'll know it's worked."

"That part's easy," Crystal said. The drone lowered until it was eye level with the two young men. She turned the hovering device to look at the incoming vehicle containing the rest of the ground team.

The van stopped nearby and backed until its rear doors were directly in front of the giant garage doors. It came to a full stop, the front and sliding door opening. Chris hopped out and the boys could see Lauren in the driver's seat. She gave them a small wave. "I bet you boys never expected to see your long-time teacher on a job with you when you were kids."

"I can't say I ever imagined it, no," Roger said. He watched Chris and Jackie put on their respective gas masks as they talked. "I guess I always imagined you being more on the backend than on the front lines."

"If I had my way, I'd have stayed home teaching," Lauren said, "along with you two. Your mothers trusted me to keep you out of trouble, and here I am doing the same thing. Except instead of chasing you around and disarming your pranks, I'm your driver for the evening. How times change."

"Let's skip the trip down memory lane," Bernard said. He checked his watch. "Can you see if the drugs worked?"

"Give me a second." The drone hovering above moved toward the window from the previous night and peered inside. "It looks like they're affected, but they're still conscious. Some are trying to run for the door, but it's already too late. They're out on their feet. I'd give it a minute or two to make sure they're truly asleep."

Jackie wasn't paying attention to the small group, choosing instead to watch their surroundings as best she could. Chris was doing similar, except on the opposite side while the group talked.

"Don't be so nervous," Lauren said, looking Roger in the eye. "I've been on tons of these operations. You two did great earlier. All we need to do is pack the goods inside the truck, and we're heading home. You two will have to help me move a new bed in tomorrow morning, okay?"

"Yeah sure," Roger said. "You got it."

"I think the last guard inside just fell, and he isn't moving," Crystal said. "Everyone get your masks on. I only have about ten minutes of charge left. I'd like to fly this back before the juice empties."

"Alright, chatty Cathy," Jackie said. "Put the damned mask on. No more time for stalling," she said. "Come here and help. You want to talk, work to balance it." She slung the rifle over her shoulder using the attached strap and made for the garage door. She saw the two teenagers get ready. "On three," she said. "One." she gripped the bottom of the garage handle on her side. "Two, three," she said. The three grunted and threw the large gate up. They backed to the side to allow the van clearance.

Lauren backed the van into the large open warehouse. She saw everyone else file inside before shutting the door behind them. "Alright." She climbed out of the driver's seat and hopped down to the ground below. "Let's get this baby loaded and leave before they know what hit them."

"I'll get the Russians." Bernard reached down and

extracted his knife from its sheathe. "You guys get the guns loaded up. I don't want one of these bastards surviving the night."

"Jackie, you're with me." Chris walked over to a stack of crates piled on top of each other about chest high. "Roger, you and your teacher can start over there." He pointed across the room, where another bunch of crates were visible. Many of them had Morris Syndicate markings on the boxes, showing they were once theirs.

"Come on, dear pupil," Lauren tugged on his arm, pulling him over toward their assigned pile. "You'd better not be physically weaker, or I'll never let you live this down."

"As if that'd happen," Roger said. "You only weigh, what, like a hundred pounds?"

She stopped on the other side of the nearby pile and gripped the bottom of the heavy rectangular wooden crate. "Come on," she said. She saw Roger get his grip but lifted first, almost causing Roger to lose his grip. "Don't lose to a girl now. What would your sister think?"

Roger got it under control and helped her carry it back toward the car. He could see Chris and Jackie were having no troubles at all. "Come on," he said. "We can load more than they can. I bet you," he said.

"The hell you can," Chris said. "Come on, Jackie, let's show these young so and sos who's their superiors."

"Is their juvenile streak rubbing off on you?" Jackie asked. "Fine, just so we can be done faster," she said.

Bernard wasn't paying attention to either of the groups or their childish games. He approached the nearest downed guard laying nearby. He lowered himself to the ground and thrust the blade point below the man's ear and dragged the blade across his jawline all the way to his other ear.

"Christ, kid," Chris said, glancing over as the pair moved back to the pile of crates. "Don't you think that's overkill?"

"Nothing wrong with inflicting a little fear. Not to mention, what I'm doing is a gang trademark of a local street gang. Why not point the authorities toward them?" Once he was done dragging the blade, he grabbed the now loose skin and yanked it from his neck all the way up over the man's face and laid the slack skin down, leaving his bare neck and red face visible. He got up and moved to the next victim as soon as he finished.

"That boy ain't right," Chris mumbled.

Bernard continued his work. He was glad he'd researched history's most gruesome postmortem mutilations. He'd read they'd inspired more than fear, they inspired terror. While his newfound method wasn't nearly as gruesome as his favorite, the blood eagle, it should get the job done.

"Where did you get the idea?" Roger asked as he and Lauren moved another crate toward the van.

"Looks like something the Vikings would have done if you ask me," Lauren said. "I don't know that the Russian Mafia will scare as easily as Norwegian civilians centuries ago, though."

"It's the effort that counts," Bernard said with another project done. "I doubt the Russians will call the cops, but the rank and file are more easily scared than the ones we've seen in a while. Bonus points if someone calls the police, since they'll think it was those hood rats that hit them, not us."

"You're not wrong," Roger said with a wince. "That's just fucked up. I'm not even going to lie. Now hurry and help us move these. The quicker we're gone, the better. Now hurry, butcher of the Russian warehouse. Pull your weight and stop playing with your dolls."

Bernard kept at his work unabated by the verbal jabs from the others. "I want them to think twice before attacking us," Bernard said. "I may be a savage, but I want the Russians to know. Their soldiers will think twice."

"Leave him," Lauren said. "We both know once he's set his mind to something, he's stubborn as a mule." She and Roger lifted another crate into the van's rear and pushed it as far into the cabin as they could manage before moving out of Jackie and Chris's way.

"We're up to four crates now," Chris said. "How many boxes do you think we should grab before we vamoose?"

"As many as our van can carry if you ask me," Jackie said. "Many of these crates display our markings on the crate. No sense shying away after we did the prep."

"That's probably another six," Chris said. "Hurry, Bernard. Another body would speed this up."

"I'm going as fast as I can manage," Bernard said while finishing the mutilation of another dead body. "You're going to thank me when they see this. I wouldn't be surprised if the Russians lose dozens of men after seeing this spectacle."

"What was it called when a person thinks they're more important than they are, teacher?" Roger asked, picking up another crate full of guns.

"Delusions of grandeur," Lauren said. "At least you're a hard worker and not playing arts and crafts like your partner in crime." She glanced over with a wince. "That's not a display a normal human should witness." She looked away and back at Roger. "This just exemplifies what I always said during class."

"What's that?" Chris asked with a chuckle. "I'm dying to hear this."

"That Roger here and his sister were the sane students."

"I resent that," Bernard said. "I always received the same grades. How's that make them better, exactly?"

"When I said to write a paper, they wrote a paper immediately. You complained, procrastinated, and played until a day before the deadline. Usually, you dragged them into your schemes too."

"I can't deny that," Bernard said. "I always said work smarter, not harder."

"It was nice to witness students listening, and then there was this jerk, Bernard," Lauren said.

"Those eight hours every single day always seemed obnoxiously long," Roger said. "You never got mad at our dumb questions though."

"Nothing to get mad at when one of your students is trying to learn. It's when they're slacking off that I got pissed."

"She's looking at me, isn't she?" Bernard asked. He finished the last body, put his knife away, and ran back to join the group.

"How nice of you to join us, spawn of Elizabeth," Lauren said.

"Why do you always call me that?" Bernard asked. He reached the pair and helped them move faster.

"You're both Mr. Morris, so I had to get creative. Don't tell me you don't like the pet name."

"It's demeaning," Bernard said as the group moved ahead of Chris and Jackie's group in boxes delivered. "It's like I'm not an adult."

"Oh shush," Lauren said. "You know I didn't mean it like that," she said. "You need to lighten up, or you'll never get a girlfriend, young man. That goes for the pair of you. Trust me when I tell you, women covet a man with a sense of humor."

"I'm not sure all women share your sense of taste," Bernard said.

"How scandalous to imply that," Lauren said. "You're more like the children I never had. I watched you all grow up, after all."

"God knows we spent more time with you than our own parents," Roger said.

"Running a syndicate doesn't leave a lot of time to play mom and dad," Jackie said. "You two know they love you, right?"

"She has a heart after all," Bernard said, carrying a crate by himself. "Mark the date down, boys."

"We have a problem approaching," Crystal said.

"Elaborate further," Chris said.

"There is a van approaching the warehouse. Now it could be nothing, but they're heading straight for you. Wait," she said. "I take that back. There are two vans approaching. One from your front, and one from the back."

"This was a setup," Jackie said. "I knew we never should have taken this job."

"Calm yourself, woman," Chris said. "Roger, Bernard, I want you two to post up near the back entrance. Jackie and I will go hold the line in the front."

"What about me?" Lauren asked.

"What about you? Pick somewhere to be and start shooting."

"I'm with the boys then," Lauren said. "I'll keep the both of you safe. Just stay near me and you'll be fine." She and Roger tossed the last crate in the back alongside Jackie and Chris, and the group scattered.

Roger and Lauren took refuge behind an especially large

shipping crate in front of the rear entrance. They had another crate in behind them, effectively blocking any fire from Jackie and Chris's side. Bernard took cover across the room between two crates himself, blocking fire from his front and back. He couldn't see where Jackie and Chris went, but they weren't in sight anymore from his position.

"How close are they?" Chris asked.

"Within a block," she said. "I estimate they'll be there within two minutes."

"Get ready, boys and girls. This will be bloody, nasty, and scary. Hold your line, keep each other alive, and we'll all pull through together."

Roger took out his revolver and inspected it. He flipped the chambers open and saw the six bullets nestled within. His hand was shaking. He could feel the adrenaline rushing through his blood. Lauren's hand rested on his forearm. He looked over with wide eyes.

"I'm right here," she whispered. "Stick with me, and you both will be fine. I never let you two get yourselves hurt, and I'm not starting tonight."

"I'm fine," Roger said.

"Yes, you are," she said with a sad smile. "That goes for you too, son of Elizabeth."

"I don't need coddling and neither does he."

"So independent," she said with sarcasm in her voice. "I guess I did a good job as a teacher then. They grow up so fast."

"Zip it," Chris said. "Keep the chatter to a minimum. We'll need to communicate during this firefight, and hearing won't be easy inside this warehouse."

"Understood," she said. She pulled out her own semi-automatic pistol from her belt line and moved her left hand to Roger's shoulder. She locked eyes with him and patted his shoulder.

Crystal interrupted the relatively touching scene. "They're in the parking lot and getting out now. It looks like they're circling around both sides of the warehouse and are trying a pincer attack."

"That's usually a KGB tactic. Guess Russia's organized crime took a page from their book. Once those doors open, unleash hell. Don't give them a chance to speak or even get inside. The more ground we give up, the likelier it is that we'll get flanked, and that's a death sentence. Take turns reloading and always keep lead flying toward those damned doors. Is that understood?"

Everybody indicated their understanding before the line fell silent. The atmosphere was stifling. The fogging of everyone's masks didn't help matters.

"At least if they get inside, they'll be woozy," Jackie said. "That should help."

"A ray of sunshine emerges during almost every storm," Chris said.

"They are preparing to enter," Crystal said. "Shall I shoot from here?"

"Negative," Chris said. "They'd turn and shoot that out of the sky in a heartbeat. You can after the shooting starts if you like. An ambush play will provide more use out of that flying contraption. Use your best judgement. Fly it inside during the chaos. Try not to shoot it if you see it coming in, everyone."

"No kidding," Bernard muttered to himself, not over the call.

The sound of screeching metal met their prepared ears as the nearest door opened. The dead silence didn't last long. Gunfire erupted in the enormous building, and it didn't stop. Roger watched Lauren scoot toward the other side of the shipping crate and lean around the side with her gun pointed toward the warehouse's rear door. He did the same on his side. He could see Bernard himself already aiming.

The back door flew open with incoherent Russian orders being yelled.

He squeezed the trigger and the first man trying to enter fell flat on his face. He writhed on the ground. Roger lowered his aim and fired another round into the man before raising his aim. He kept count of how many he had left in the chamber, a technique Chris himself had taught him years ago.

He kept firing, but the men were no longer trying to run into the kill zone. They were too busy taking cover on the outside of the door. Roger counted to six and ducked back behind cover. He remembered the words of his father. *Seven seconds, that's slow.* Even with the ringing in his ears, he could still hear his father's words. He'd finished reloading before he even realized it. He saw Bernard duck behind cover and so he covered him. Roger kept firing, keeping the lead flying downrange. He hit one man who tried to lean into the doorway. The victim was too slow as the shot connected with his torso. He fell backwards and rolled to the side, out of sight.

"I'm going in the front," Crystal said.

No one bothered to acknowledge the sentence, too busy fighting for their lives. Truthfully, no one could even hear the timid voice in the ensuing chaos.

Roger kept firing until he reached six in his mind again. He had the unique perspective of being able to see the front while he reloaded from his vantage point. Their attackers had gained a foothold just inside the warehouse. Their cover wasn't the best, being only waist-high boxes, but they were stubbornly holding their ground. He reloaded using another speed loader while he saw the drone flying in above the men near the front. It stayed high out of their sight and turned around. He saw the mini gun spin up before returning his attention to the task at hand.

Amid the hail of gunfire, a new sound made itself known. Rapid fire didn't describe the veritable cloud of projectiles now raining down on the other side of the Russian arms warehouse. If anyone could hear anything, they'd have heard the splintering of wood as the crate withered under the storm of death raining down on them, along with tortured screams, gurgles, and panicked Russian orders.

He could see the ones lucky enough not to spring new holes under his sister's assault running in the open, trying desperately to reach more substantial cover. They tried to shoot up at the drone. He could even see a few sparks of said bullets hitting their target, but it stayed afloat and firing.

He got back to firing when he saw his two partners reloading once again. When he peeked around the corner, he could see another body on his side laying on the one he'd hit earlier.

"We can't sit in here forever." Jackie could barely be heard. "The police will be here within ten minutes."

"You suggest we all make a run for the van in open ground right now?" Chris yelled back. "I'd rather be in prison than six feet under."

"That seems to be our choices, doesn't it?"

Roger kept his aim where their target's heads were popping out. As soon as he saw the armored body and helmet clad head pop out, he fired. The helmet jerked, causing his target's neck to violently snap backward. He fell backward and did not move. "We've got more targets," he yelled, trying to be heard over the cacophony. "Then I think we're clear."

All gunfire momentarily stopped as everyone met the ever-familiar ringing in their ears.

"The front is clear," Jackie said. "Crystal, head around the back outside and finish the Russian assholes," she said.

"I'm on it," she said. The drone exited the large garage and set about circling the building.

Roger kept firing and doing his thing when he heard the voice of his sister.

"Get behind cover in there now."

He did not hesitate to follow the order as the blasting started anew outside, along with more screams of pain, agony, and death.

"I think that's all of them," Crystal said.

"Everybody run for our van now," Chris said. "That's an order, dammit!"

Roger, Bernard, and Lauren didn't wait to be told again. They broke out of their cover and sprinted toward the vehicle with all their might. Lauren hopped in the driver's seat while Chris hopped in the passenger's. Roger, Bernard, and Jackie squeezed into what little space remained in the backseat and slammed the door shut.

"Get us out of here," Chris said.

"I'm already on it." Lauren had the engine started already and hit the gas. It was bumpy, exiting the warehouse as the van trampled dead bodies and a few surviving Russians during their exit. They finally reached the road, and everyone breathed a collective sigh of relief.

Their peace was broken in a single moment, as it often is on a pitched battlefield. A single gunshot rang out. The windshield had a bullet hole appear, cracking and splintering it, causing it to web outwards and making it hard to see.

"Sniper!" Chris saw Lauren slumping forward on the wheel. He reached over and grabbed the wheel and turned onto a nearby different street. "Get her out of this seat. I can't drive this way."

"Son of a bitch," Jackie said. "Boys, lift her up and get her back here.

Roger and Bernard reached forward and got her out of the front seat while Jackie took Chris's place in the passenger seat.

"This can't be real," Roger said. He and Bernard helped set her body where Jackie was originally. Her head was no longer in one solid piece. The sniper was precise. She was hit dead center in the forehead.

"God damn," Bernard said.

"Her head's almost gone," Roger said.

"Large caliber rounds inflict that on human anatomy," Chris said.

Another shot rang out, and another bullet hole appeared in the van's windshield. This one missed its mark because of Chris's erratic driving. An indentation appeared in the seat in front of Roger, showing the bullet had lost its kinetic energy and had found its new home in the seat.

They turned onto another street.

"Where the fuck is he?" Chris asked.

"I think he's atop the building where we set up during the scouting night," Jackie said. "It's the tallest building nearby, with quick access to the ground floor to peel out quickly."

"If that's the case, we're in the clear, but we can't lollygag here. We need to switch these vans and get rid of this one. It's only a block or two and we're set."

"We're going to need to leave Lauren inside," Jackie said.

"What?" Roger asked.

"Kid, we left that van in a factory parking lot. Now it's not likely we'll be spotted by anybody, but I'm not taking that chance. We can't be moving a dead body in public. Besides," her voice fell, "we can't leave this evidence for the police to find. We must burn all of it, and that includes her and her gear."

"She's a human being," Roger said. "She deserves a proper burial, damn you."

"We don't always get what we deserve, kid," Chris said. "You need to learn that soon." He pulled up to the van they'd placed there earlier in the day. "Look alive. As soon as I back us up, everyone's getting out and transferring the crates to our new van. Jackie, I leave torching this van to you. Make sure you get all her gear. We can't risk any tech leading back to us, and that includes her phone, etc."

"I'll get it done, old man," she said, her voice having lost its usual demeanor.

"Good." He put the car in park. "Now get to work."

Everyone, minus Lauren and Jackie, got out and got to work transferring their ill-gotten spoils. While they worked, Jackie reached into the back and pulled out the container of gasoline, then worked dousing the vehicle liberally.

"Crystal," Chris said. "You're moving, yes?"

"I got the drone filed away and I'm out already, yes. Why? Did something happen?"

Nobody wanted to answer, not even Chris. "Uh," he said, "yeah, we'll tell you once we get back. Now make sure you aren't followed, and return to our apartment. Be careful, and don't speed. Don't draw any unneeded attention."

"I may only have a probationary driver's license, but I'll

be fine. I'm more worried about what the hell happened that you won't tell me."

"Do not talk and drive," Roger said. "He said we'll tell you later, and he meant later."

"Geez," she said. "Alright then. You're welcome for saving all your asses by the way. I'm leaving this call if you're going to be like that." A click indicated she'd left the call, and it was only their immediate group.

"I can't believe this," Roger said. He transported the final gun crate into the back of the new van.

Chris took him by the shoulders and guided him into the back. He pushed him inside. "No time to mourn, kid. We need to leave this immediate area before cops spread out after they arrive at our little operation site." He waved Bernard inside after him and slid the door shut with a loud thud.

Bernard saw his friend looking toward the back of the cabin, toward the vehicle where their teacher's body rested. "Are you alright?" he asked.

"Not right now," Roger said.

"Right, just keep it together, man. You know I've never been competent with this kind of emotional thing."

"Yeah," Roger said, his voice distant.

The front doors both slammed shut and the smell of smoke met the pair's nostrils.

"That's everything," Jackie said. She tossed the small pile of clothes and devices over to Chris. "Stow those and we're off."

"Back to the apartment?" Bernard asked.

"Negative," Chris said. "Roger, get your sister back on the line and apologize. Jackie, get us back to the mansion."

"Yes, sir," Jackie said, starting the engine.

Roger pulled out his phone and texted his sister. "I'm

sorry about snapping at you earlier. Get back on the call. Our leader wants to tell you something," it read. He didn't have to wait long to receive a text back. "Damn it," he said out loud. "She's probably texting and driving to reply that fast."

"She knows what she's doing," Bernard said. "Your sister is tougher than she looks."

"Fine, but you owe me," the text message read.

A tone sounded in the earpiece.

"I'm here," Crystal said.

"You make up with your brother already?" Chris asked.

"Let's say yes," she said. "Why am I back on this call?"

"Head to the mansion. We're reporting to your mother directly, and it wouldn't do for only one of you to be there when we deliver the news."

"News of the guns we got?" she asked.

"Did you not tell her?" Chris asked.

"Tell me what?"

Chris paused, trying to find the correct words. Everyone in the cabin knew there were none that would shield the young tech enthusiast from the reality of her longtime teacher and friend burning in a van with half her head blown off - all because they couldn't risk keeping her carcass with them to provide a proper funeral.

"Well?" Crystal asked. "I'm parked while talking for safety, and I'd like to get driving again. I'd rather not give my brother a stroke by talking and driving again, so I'm in a fast food parking lot with the engine running."

"We'll tell you there," Chris said. "Drive safe."

"Whatever," Crystal said

"Now, to deliver these guns to your mother," Chris said.

12

"Make sure you tell them to expect an attack. Send reinforcements before that happens." Rachel slammed the phone down. She looked up at the large double doors when she heard a knock. "Come in," she said.

They opened. Roger, Bernard, Crystal, Chris, and Jackie stepped inside and lined up in front of the large desk.

Bernard looked over to where his mother would normally stand to see the spot unusually empty.

Rachel followed his line of sight and preempted the inevitable question. "You're wondering where your mother is, I take it? She is in her home outside. I confined her to her quarters after her latest stunt." She raised an eyebrow and inspected the group. "Where's Lauren?"

Ben studied the group's faces. "She didn't make it, did she?"

"She headed back to the apartment," Crystal said. "Didn't she?"

"No," Chris said.

Rachel looked up at her husband. "Get her out of here."

Ben nodded and moved over to his daughter. "Come on, sweetheart. I'll explain everything."

"She's just running late." Crystal allowed her father to grab her hand and guide her out of the room. "Right, Dad?" The pair exited the room and closed the door, muffling Crystal's unfortunate questions.

Rachel waited a few moments to allow her daughter and husband to gain distance. "You all didn't even tell her?"

"With all due respect, ma'am," Chris said, "after the night we've endured, there wasn't a good chance."

"There never is," Rachel said. "How did it happen?"

"Sniper fire," Chris said. "We were making our grand escape after a minor complication. Everyone was in the van heading out. Lauren pulled onto the road, and it happened in a flash. A hole appeared in the windshield. It hit her in the head. We're lucky I regained control of the wheel and got us out with no further casualties."

"This was probably Mikhail's doing," Rachel's somber voice said. "This was why I didn't relish you going near that infernal warehouse. Elizabeth went behind my back, though, and that's what led to Lauren dying. I can't blame you, Bernard. You received a text from a top brass giving you a location, and you jumped on it. It showed initiative, but every action has far-reaching consequences that we rarely can see."

"May I ask a question, ma'am?" Bernard asked.

"I am pissed at your mother, if that's the question. She'll be fine. She's just learning that I don't appreciate when she puts my son and daughter at risk. Here, it cost my best friend."

"How long will she be in solitary?"

"That depends on a variety of factors," Rachel said. "Do not concern yourself with your mother. She can handle herself. Moving on to the partial success of this mission, how many gun crates did you acquire?"

"We're just going to gloss over her death that easily?" Roger asked.

Bernard looked over at his friend and shook his head.

"I am not glossing over anything," Rachel said, plainly annoyed. "Sitting all night crying will not bring her back. She died doing her job. I'm respecting her wishes by addressing it. She was your teacher, but she was my friend, Son. Do not interrupt me again."

Roger did as he was told and stayed quiet. He proverbially bit his tongue as his mother moved a stack of papers to the side of her desk and stood up.

"I'm sorry. He's been on edge ever since it happened," Chris said.

"You do not have to apologize on his behalf," Rachel said. "I saw that look in the mirror over a decade ago. Once upon a time, I was as disrespectful to my father as he is. Do you know where the sniper shot originated?"

"Our best guess is the rooftop we scouted from the previous night. The angles line up and it's the highest area that has easy access to the ground and a ladder nearby. I'm betting he fired the shots, immediately entered whatever car he'd stowed nearby, and left before the police came."

"Speaking of police, I'm sure they're going to have a fun time with the body of Lauren." Rachel's voice lost a bit of its luster when talking about her friend's corpse. "What did you do with it?"

"We left it in the original vehicle. When we moved the guns to the new one, we removed her clothes, electronics, and jewelry."

"All our vehicles have the VIN tags taken care of already. If you took everything else off her, they'll just consider her a

Jane Doe in an unfortunate situation in a bad part of town. She deserved better for her service. Unfortunately, as my son is no doubt learning in that obstinate skull, there was a good reason I didn't want him to join this bloody life. You will watch as people you know and love die in brutal fashion." She saw her son glaring at her. "Unfortunately, he wants vengeance. A mother can read those hate-filled eyes. I know because I possessed the same feeling burning in my gut years ago."

"As would I," Bernard said.

"You're all not going after him," Rachel said. "Not again. I don't want any of you anywhere near Mikhail. I won't risk another Lauren happening. Not with my boys and daughter. Call it favoritism if you like. What are you smiling about?" she asked her son. "Wait, don't tell me. You're thinking you and your little friend will sneak off and do it anyway. Right?"

"Whatever are you talking about?" Roger asked.

"Don't try to lie to your mother. It's what I would have done when I was your age. The young always think themselves invincible. You've all got a reality check tonight. No one's truly safe from a bullet to the head. For now, deliver the crates to the armory downstairs. Our supplies were running low, and they need refilling. Turns out having everyone grab what they need really drains the stocks. Thankfully, you all pulled through, barring tragedy."

"Can we at least try to find the guy?" Roger asked. "That's all. We wouldn't even go after him. We want the guy to pay for his actions."

"It would also Cripple Artyom and Oleg if they lost a field commander," Bernard said. "Can't forget that."

"You two would be terrible car salesmen," Rachel said. Her gaze lingered on her son. "You wish to find him and that's it? Why do I not believe that? Why would I believe you'd follow orders and not engage? I know our bloodline. We love our revenge."

She was interrupted by the door opening and Ben coming back inside the room. He took his place by the desk. A noticeable wet spot stained his coat, about where Crystal's head would have been. "I'm sorry about that," he said. "What did I miss?"

"We'd still be getting our revenge," Roger said. "We would tell you where he is, and you could send someone you believe could get the job done. That way, we'd be doing our part in getting that bastard dead."

Rachel walked to the enormous window behind her desk and turned her back to the group. She stood beside Ben and pulled the curtain to the side.

Ben leaned close to Rachel and whispered something the group couldn't hear from where they were.

She responded in kind. She faced Ben and looked into his eyes. "You're sure?"

"Yes," Ben said.

"Alright then, boys," she said, turning back to the window. "Have it your way. You can find this Mikhail, and you will send the location to me. Your father will take care of this."

"Dad?" Roger looked over at his stoic father's face. "You're sending him?"

"What about it?" Ben asked.

"I just didn't expect that," Roger said. "You're always at Mother's side, keeping her safe. I don't remember you ever leaving the place and killing someone."

"You would not remember," Ben said. "I remember a time this type of assignment was commonplace. I am not afraid of getting my hands dirty."

"You bet your ass he can manage," Warren said. "This

man is nearly as deadly as me, and that's saying something. With your dad on the job, I have full confidence this so called 'Ghost of Moscow' will be dead."

"Your father has seen far more field experience and has dealt with many more lethal situations than you," Rachel said. "You could learn from him."

"I'd love to. Why not take us along, Father?" Roger asked. "You know Bernard and I are quick learners."

"Nice try," Ben said. "That's a hard no."

"Damn."

"I could assist your husband, ma'am," Chris said. "Not to change the subject, but we know I possess more experience than Ben in killing and assassination. Having backup is never a bad thing, and I'd watch his back with my life."

Rachel stood side by side with Ben and didn't turn. She asked him something incoherent from this distance. He gave her a similarly quiet answer. "That depends," she said. "If your group is not busy, I wouldn't be against the idea. You're one of our best, Chris. I would like you to accompany Ben, but I do not want to drag you from work your team's planning."

"With all due respect, this would take an hour. I can make time without sacrificing any jobs we're planning on."

"No, I want you focused on keeping your team safe. This war has taken a toll on both organizations, even if Oleg doesn't admit it. We're both hurting. Honestly, I don't see this conflict going on a lot longer. Both sides are searching for a coup de grâce."

"Police are stepping up their patrols lately, with so many shootings and killings happening," Warren said. "That's bad for business, no matter how you slice it."

"Yes," Rachel said. "I'd imagine the street gangs are unhappy because of this side effect of our little war. I have gotten complaints. Not that those pissants matter, but I am aware of their annoyance." Turning around and facing the group, she circled around her desk and sat on the front, near the group. "There will be a small vigil tomorrow morning at six a.m. for Lauren. Attendance is not mandatory, but I would appreciate it. You are all dismissed. Stay the night here. It's late to drive back to your apartment. Also, feel free to use any resources here that are still available in tracking down Mikhail. If you'll excuse me, I have to comfort my daughter. Roger, Son, I'd recommend you join me. She needs all of us right now."

"Yeah, of course," he said.

"As for the rest of you, you're dismissed."

"Wait up for me before you head for your mother, dude," Roger said. "I'll go with you and see if she's alright."

Rachel frowned at the remark but said nothing else.

"Right on," Bernard said. "Take as long as you need. Your sister comes before my mom being annoyed. I'll be waiting in the living room, catching up with gossip floating around the joint.

"Come with me then if you're finished. Where is she, dear?"

"She's in her old room," Ben said.

"Did you tell her?"

"I did."

"It had to be done," Rachel said. She passed Roger and headed toward the doors. "Don't stand around, you two. Let's get over there."

Roger turned around and felt his father brush past him before continuing along behind his parents.

Later, in Crystal's old room...

Ben and Rachel had already left the room once their daughter stopped crying just a short while ago, but Roger stayed after they left. "I'm sorry for yelling at you tonight."

"You already said that in the text." She sniffed, trying to not allow her runny nose to run rampant after her sobbing. "Was that why you were so short?"

"Yeah. I had just moved her darn near headless body out of the front seat and to the back. I had to sit next to her until we reached the backup vehicle. It's still no excuse for yelling at you. I thought you were texting and driving. We'd just lost Lauren. I didn't want you getting hurt."

"Yeah," she said. "Was it quick for her at least?"

"It happened in a flash. She was there one second and gone the next," Roger said, trying to keep his composure. "It hurt having to watch her body get enveloped in the flames of the van."

"I imagine so," she said. She leaned into her brother's side and felt his arm snake around her shoulders and give a gentle squeeze.

"That's not the only reason you're upset," Roger said. "I can tell. You did a good job tonight."

"I killed over half a dozen men," she said. "It may have been the drone, but I was the one controlling it. That counts, I'm pretty sure. Seeing their bodies fall back and hearing their moans of agony felt almost like a video game, but I knew deep down it wasn't. Those men won't go home to their families and loved ones again because of me."

"You also kept me, Bernard, Jackie, and Chris alive because of it. Without you, we'd have been pinned down and either died or been caught by police. You were the hero of the night."

"Stop trying to make me feel better. It's not going to happen."

"I know," he said. "Believe me, I know nothing will make us feel better right now. I have news that's the closest thing, though."

"What's that?" she wiped her nose.

"We're tasked with finding the guy who shot her," he said.

"Oh great," she sarcastically said. "Just what I want to do."

"I figured you would," Roger said. "You'd have a hand in finding the bastard who killed Lauren. Without the location, mother can't send someone to kill him."

"It won't be us, I take it?" she asked.

"No," Roger said. "It won't be us. She's sending someone more experienced."

"Who?"

"Father is being sent to kill Mikhail once we secure his location."

"No," she said. "Why him and not Mr. Davis or Chris or someone else? Why another family member of ours?"

"He's experienced in being boots on the ground according to Mother, and she trusts he can do it."

"I can't find Mikhail only to lose father too because of my actions. I can't bear that burden. If he dies, it'd be my fault."

"Not if your dependable brother's plan works," he said.

"What does that mean?"

"I wouldn't let him die."

"You're planning on sneaking off and helping him against orders?" she asked.

"This is going to happen. It's already decided. No one is going to blame a son if he follows his father and tries to keep him from dying. I'd need backup though, but it's our best chance. She has already assigned him to kill this

Mikhail. Now we can either help him or let him do it on his own. I don't know about you, but I prefer to keep him alive. If you don't help find him, Lee will. I doubt he'll tell me where this sharpshooter is to help him, so we need you to take this job, for Dad's sake."

"You promise I won't have to kill anyone else?"

"You know I can't promise that," he said. "Just help us find this guy, and we'll take care of the rest."

She got up from the bed and walked to her desktop perched on her desk in the room's corner. She sat down in the office chair and turned the device on. "Yeah, I can do that. I'll check if Lee has any ideas on how we can track Mikhail."

"You think he'll let you take point?"

"That guy does the bare minimum. If he can pass a job to someone else, he will. He'd consider teaching me any skills I need to be far better than doing it himself." She typed on the keyboard as she spoke. "Stories say he was never the same after a job nearly two decades ago."

Roger looked at his sister and saw her barely holding back the tears she was just shedding. "You don't always have to be emotionally strong. Crying is a part of human nature."

"I'm all cried out tonight. It solves nothing anyway. If I want Father to be safe, I must try," she said. "Just promise me you'll stay safe and keep him safe."

"You know I can't promise that. I can only do my best."

"I know. While I wish it was different, I've learned that lesson over the past week. Nothing ever is guaranteed. We can only play the odds."

Later in the lobby...

"There he is," Bernard rose from his chair. "Later, boys. We have work to start."

The group of Syndicate members sitting nearby each gave their goodbyes as Bernard left and walked to Roger, who was descending the nearby stairs. "What's with you?" he asked. "Is your sister alright?"

"She'll help us find this bastard," Roger said. He walked with Bernard toward the front door. "I had to do some convincing, but she's onboard with making sure this guy ends up dead."

"Good." Bernard grit his teeth and balled his fists at his sides. "He deserves a dirt nap after killing Lauren. Truthfully, I didn't have any ideas about how we'd find this guy if we didn't have electronic wizardry. You know I'm hopeless with machines, but they're useful."

"Just like the stories of my grandfather, your uncle," Roger said. "Mother said he was hopeless with machines. You inherited that from him. Whereas me and my sister took more from my mother and her mother before her, Tanya."

"Enough of the family-tree history lesson." Bernard pushed the door open and stepped out into the night air. "Let's ask Mom about this dumb bullshit. I don't see why your mom put her in solitary, though. All she did was try to help us."

"I see why," Roger said. "It resulted in Lauren dying."

"She couldn't have known that would happen."

"Maybe you're right, but that's why I believe." Roger turned the house's corner and the modestly sized cottage came into their view. A lone guard stood perched outside the front door, keeping watch. "Armed watch too? Mom didn't mention that."

"Leave this to me," Bernard said. He led them over to the

guard.

"Yes?" the guard asked.

"We're going inside," Roger said.

"Ms. Morris is supposed to be here in solitary," he said.

"Not anymore," Bernard said. "We're going to talk to her for a few minutes. Don't worry. Can't a kid see his mama around here?"

"This is explicit orders from Mrs. Morris," he said. "She said, and I quote, 'No one is to see her until I say different'."

"I am Rachel's kid, and this is Elizabeth's kid," Roger said. He jabbed a finger toward Bernard. "I'm guessing you must be new?"

"Yes, sir," the baby-faced young guard said. His eyes were shifting between the pair, and his lip was slightly quivering at the situation he found himself in.

"Look, new guy." Bernard took a step toward the guard with an amiable voice. "We don't want to get you in trouble, alright? We're just wanting to ask the advisor to the boss a question about stratagem, so we can end this war with the Russians as soon as possible. Don't get in our way. Just let us slip in, and we won't tell anyone if you don't want us to. You'll appear like the good soldier. We end this war quicker, and we all return to normal operations that much sooner. It's a win-win for everybody, don't you see? Besides," he reached into his back pocket and pulled out his wallet. He took out a hundred-dollar bill and stuffed it into the guard's jacket pocket. "We all could use a little more scratch, yeah?"

"What am I supposed to do? Boss says no, and the boss's kids say yes? Listen, if anyone asks, you were never here. Alright? I can't afford to have anyone know this happened."

"We're discrete," Roger said. "No one will know besides us. See? Now, was that so hard?"

"Hurry inside, please," the guard said, stepping to the

side. He swiveled his head, looking for the patrols he'd witnessed pass hundreds of times over the day.

The pair didn't wait for further instruction and got inside quickly.

"I'm home!" Bernard yelled in the small building's foyer or what passed for one.

The entrance room wasn't spacious, but it served its purpose, containing a coat and shoes rack along with a welcome mat. Roger followed Bernard through the clean, slightly cramped, but still luxurious inside.

"Bernard?" Elizabeth's voice came from nearby. "I'm in the living room. Come see your aging mother."

Roger followed his friend into a cozy room with a sofa and a large television. He saw the gray-haired older woman had her back to them. She looked over her shoulder. "Oh, little Roger is with you too. What a pleasant surprise. How did your last assignment go?" She saw their faces fall. "That bad, huh?"

"Not exactly," Bernard said. "We received a load of our guns back, and we killed a lot of Russians, but we had a snag of sorts."

"That is a phrase I've heard many times in my time." Elizabeth got up and met her son halfway to the couch and gave him a warm embrace. "What happened, baby? Please take a seat. I'll get you some coffee or tea if you prefer. It's one of the few luxuries your mother allows me in here."

"I'm sorry she put you in here," Roger said.

"It's not your fault, sweetie." Elizabeth waved off the apology. "I know you two did everything you could on your job, but she got a fly up her ass. She never told me about what or why I'm confined."

"Really? Roger asked.

"Yeah, she got some email and then immediately

confined me to quarters. I have no clue why," Elizabeth said. "Did you want coffee or tea?"

"Please, allow me to prepare it," Roger said. "It's where it always is?"

"You're a regular sweetheart." Elizabeth allowed her son to lead her back to her seat. "Could you get me some tea while you're at it?"

"Sure thing," Roger said. He exited the room, leaving the mother and son alone.

Elizabeth pulled Bernard down and whispered in his ear. "I lied," she said. "I know Lauren bit the bullet during that last operation. Got to play the doddering old grandma type, right?"

"That's quite underhanded, Ma," Bernard said. "Anyway, how are you doing out here?"

"That big-headed fool stuck me out here out of vengeance," she whispered, making sure Roger wasn't within earshot. "How did she die, anyway?"

"Sniper shot got her while we were in the car making our daring escape," Bernard said. "We almost all made it out."

"That's this life," Elizabeth said. "Our lives are at the whims of the roll of a die sometimes." She placed a hand over Bernard's hand, which was on his knee. "I'm so glad you weren't harmed. I worried the whole time you were out there, you know. It's odd. I don't remember doing that much before you."

"Roger and Crystal are taking it very hard," Bernard said.

"You've been respectful to Rachel, Chris, and Jackie then?" Elizabeth asked.

"Mostly. I had to retort a few times directed toward Jackie, but that was just friendly ribbing. You know how it is. I haven't been an asshole, if that's what you're asking."

"Good, you must keep up appearances."

Roger poked his head around the nearby corner. "Which kind of tea would you like? I forgot to ask."

"Green tea will do just fine, sweetie. Thank you again. Oh, and don't forget to put a tablespoon of honey in it. You know your Auntie Elizabeth likes it sweet."

"Sure thing, Aunt Elizabeth. It'll be a few minutes."

"Take your time, sweet boy," Elizabeth said. She waited until she heard the steps head away before continuing. Her honey covered veneer disappeared, replaced by a deadly serious tone. "Now, what's your next job?"

"We're to track this Mikhail, but we're under strict orders to not attack him. We all suspect he was the sniper who killed Lauren. He's a crack shot."

"How boring," Elizabeth said. "That won't earn you much respect from the boys. Who is supposed to kill him?"

"According to Rachel, we find him and then she sends her husband out to kill him."

"That's smart," Elizabeth said. "You two do the legwork, while her second in command gets all the glory. She knows what she's doing for all her faults. She knows the men and women will only follow someone they trust and like. Killing one of the enemies' elite units will inspire just that."

"Disobeying orders wouldn't, Mother, if that's what you're about to suggest," Bernard said. "It'd make me look like a wild card that can't follow orders."

"Wild cards are fun though, dear," Elizabeth said, squeezing Bernard's hand. "Your uncle and his friend were wild cards, and they rose through the ranks, if you catch my drift."

"You're not proposing what I think you are?"

"You are going to find this shit stain, and then you'll scout it," she said with a sly smile, "to see if your intel's valid.

After all, you can't send the second in command in to assassinate this Mikhail if you're not even sure he's there. Due diligence is important. If it happens you see an opportunity, however, then you take your shot."

"Shouldn't we at least report it to Ben before we go?" Bernard asked. "We'd look like proper renegades if we didn't," he said.

"Having two independent parties there to kill the same target is dangerous," Elizabeth said.

"It would be a mark on my name if I disobey orders though, even if Roger insists on it," he said.

"True. Here's what you do then, Son," she said. "You two will report where Mikhail is, but then you try. But be careful. You don't want Ben seeing you there, so you'd have to be subtle. If you pull that off, it takes the wind out of her man's sails on being the next inheritor of the syndicate while filling yours. The rank and file love a hero who killed someone who's been killing them in droves. You two would be considered heroes. Combine that with your lineage, and you'd be two steps closer to being the next in line."

"Tea and coffee is ready," Roger said, entering the room holding a tray with three fresh cups on it. He carefully made his way over to the coffee table in front of them and placed it down. He slid over one cup toward Elizabeth. "Here's your tea." He moved a different one toward Bernard. "This one's for you. I know you love your coffee black, you savage." He picked up the last cup and sipped quietly. "This one's mine." He sat down in a nearby chair across from the pair. "What were you two whispering about? Is it about mom's detaining you? I can handle trash talking about my parents, you know."

"Oh, you don't want to hear about such things," Elizabeth said. "Now, how did that last job go?"

"Not too good, Auntie," Roger said. "We got the guns and killed a lot of Russians, but we lost Lauren during the escape."

"Oh, sweetie, I'm sorry you had to see that," she said in a soft voice. "How did it happen?"

"She got her head blown almost clean off," Roger said. "We had to get her body out of the driver's seat quickly, or we'd have all crashed."

"It was bad, Ma," Bernard said. "I don't know if I'll be able to wear those pants again. I think I got brain matter on them. It still makes me sick to even think of it."

"I still can't really believe she's dead," Roger said, staring down at the carpeted floor.

"Oh no," Elizabeth said. "I'm sorry you two had to see that. I know she'd never have wanted that for either of you. You know Lauren loved the both of you, right? She spent so many hours teaching all of you. I bet she imagined you both as the children she never had. She'd tell me that occasionally when we talked. It was always something about you boys and Crystal. She'd complain about how busy you kept her, but she always had that little smile while she did."

"Yeah," Roger said. He said nothing else and kept his gaze fixed on the coffee table's legs.

"I'm sorry for reminding you of such a traumatic event. Just know she loved you both. I have no doubt of that."

"I know," Roger said.

"It wasn't right, Mom," Bernard said. "We suspect that fucker Mikhail is behind it. It had to be him," he said. "We didn't see him inside at all."

"He was probably posted up on a nearby building and bailed after the second shot," Roger said. "What a coward's way of killing someone."

"She didn't deserve that," Elizabeth said.

"We're tasked with tracking down that waste of life." Roger's voice was filling with hatred and determination. "Mother forbade us from killing him, though."

Elizabeth saw Roger's free hand balling into a fist and his teeth clenching after the statement. "Now why would she do that?"

"She's sending Father," he said. "I guess she doesn't trust us enough to get the job done."

"Have you read the famous inspirational quote regarding inaction, 'All it takes for evil to triumph is for good men to do nothing'?" she asked.

"A few times," Roger said. "Why?"

"Don't do nothing, boys," Elizabeth said. "You know this Mikhail character is an evil man. Do what you know to be right."

"Pardon?" Roger looked up at her. "You think we should do it anyway? What about following orders?"

"Following orders is fine, but let me tell you a story, Roger," she cleared her throat. "Years ago, when I was a young gangster, there was another young man named Roger and one named Daniel. You two probably know these names. One night I was called by Daniel. Or at least," she said, "that's what it showed on my cell. Roger escorted me there and shielded me from the brunt of the bomb they'd planted to kill me. He ended up in the hospital ward afterward."

"I remember this story," Bernard said.

"Then be quiet and let your friend hear it. I know he hasn't," Elizabeth said. "After this, Roger and Daniel had a tough decision. Their orders from Bernard, whom I named you after," she poked her son in the side, "were to remain under the radar and let him handle the retaliation. However, they did not follow that order. They went to a nearby Irish bar who we were at war with and who they suspected set the bomb. They blew it up, using the ovens in the back and the gas lines. You know what happened to them?"

"They got in trouble?" Roger asked.

"No such thing," Elizabeth said. "While I and Father were pissed, the rest of the family viewed them as heroes. Even if my father wanted to discipline them, he'd have been fighting the will of his own roster. Sometimes it's not completely about the will of the boss. The will of the soldiers matters regarding decisions. If you were to kill this Ghost of Moscow, the rank and file would shield you from repercussions, and it would elevate you."

"I guess that makes sense, but we've been ordered to tell Father, and he'll take care of it," Roger said.

"Tell him," Elizabeth said with a shrug. "Just be sure you're the operatives who arrive first and take that burden off his weary shoulders, if you understand my meaning." She took a sip from the cup. "Ah, that honey is just the thing I needed. If this syndicate business doesn't work, you'd be fantastic at a coffee shop."

"Gee, thanks," Roger said, with a hint of humor in his voice. "I've got Crystal talking to Lee. We're allowed to track him, so that shouldn't raise alarm bells. He can give her insight into how we can track this so-called ghost."

"That man?" Elizabeth scoffed. "He's a fool. He's good at his job, but he's a fool through and through. Don't trust him with anything resembling a secret. That's my advice."

"Noted," Bernard said. "Are you doing alright out here, Ma? I know you love work, and I don't think you get any done here."

"She didn't want my counsel, so she shall get none. That's her loss and your two's gain, right? I am considering this a vacation. I get to catch up with my soap operas and relax, instead of standing all day and throwing my two cents in. It's probably better for my back this way, if I'm honest. Though I will admit, I miss working. I live for it. She'll cool off after a week or two. Don't you two worry. I'll be back advising her before you know it and keeping us on track."

"Alright, Mom." Bernard upended his coffee mug and chugged the rest of the contents before putting it back on the tray. "If you ever need anything, you know you can call either of us."

"Dear," Elizabeth said, "she took away my cell. I couldn't call you if I wanted. When she said solitary, she meant alone. You aren't supposed to be here. How did you deal with the guard stationed outside?"

"We convinced him it'd be in his best interest to not report our visit," Bernard said.

"The kid's a bit of a wuss," Elizabeth said. "Still, make sure he's not going to run to someone squealing. We can't have you two getting demerits right before such an important task. Right?"

"We'll make double sure to be safe," Roger said, finishing his beverage. "Sorry to visit suddenly, but we wanted to confirm you're alright," he said.

"That's thoughtful," Elizabeth said. "It's been decades since someone has been so thoughtful. I see why she named you after him, if I'm honest."

"Mom?"

"You don't look like him per se', but you are polite. That's a rare quality around here."

"I'm not that polite," Roger said. "It's only toward people who deserve it, and I'm more than a little stubborn toward my parents."

"Just like him." Elizabeth's eyes glassed over, falling into daydreams of her onetime love that shared the young man's name. "He left his parents to join us, you know. They kicked him out and outlawed him from that house. Too bad about his sister, though. She died too early."

"Excuse me?" Roger asked.

"Nothing," Elizabeth said. "Ignore this old lady's ramblings of love long past."

"Love?" Roger asked.

"I don't want to hear this," Bernard said.

"Yes, your mother was not the only lady to love Roger," Elizabeth said. "I was the only girl he was interested in. He didn't even consider your mother, if I'm being honest. She was young, and he was an upstanding man. Well," she said, "as virtuous as us gangsters can be."

"Okay." Bernard got up. "We should leave before anyone gets curious about where we are, buddy," he said. "If your mom found out we were here, she would be pissed."

"Sorry to cut this visit so short, Auntie." Roger stood and moved to Bernard's side. "We don't get to talk as often as we should."

"Don't worry about that, sweet boy. You just remember what I said. If you two do that, you'll get your vengeance, fame among the men, and your mother won't be able to do crap. Just make sure you two succeed. If you fail, even I won't have pull to get you freed of the confinement she'd likely put you two under. So be extra careful, boys. Please."

"We won't make you worry, Ma," Bernard said. "Now rest up and leave it to us."

"My boy," Elizabeth said, getting up and wrapping her arms around Bernard. "You two have grown up so fast. Now go out and make me proud."

Meanwhile, in Lee's tech room...

"Your eyes look red and puffy," Lee said.

"Did you hear what I said?" Crystal asked. "You're going to help me find this guy."

"I thought your little group was off the Mikhail chase," Lee said. He reached up and scratched his clean-shaven head. "Especially after your minor incident with the drone. It's all over the net. Apparently some kid filmed out his window using his phone and recorded the whole incident a few miles away."

"I did what I had to. They would have all died if I hadn't."

"Damn, sorry to hear that," Lee said. "I had to kill a guy once, you know," he said. "It involved me taking control of his car and driving him onto some nearby train tracks. It was not a pleasant sight, and it fucked me up for years. You should talk to somebody about that. Your mother would probably be a smart start. I know she's dealt with what you have. You know what you shouldn't do? What you're proposing. It will not help; it's going to make it worse."

"You are not my father, and I have my mother's permission to hunt this guy down, but not to kill him. You are going to help me find this jerk. Then we inform Father so he can kill him, not us. So don't worry about that."

"If that's what the brass wants," Lee swiveled around in the chair, "that's what they shall get. Now, this will take a while. My only idea is to find some traffic camera footage. That will take time to comb through. If you want to help and make it faster, I could use the help. If not, I'll get it as soon as I can."

"How will you accomplish that?" she asked. "Traffic cameras feed into a government building or the police department, don't they?"

"Are you that interested? Remote intrusion isn't something that can be done unless you're trained. We need to grab the footage around that area. To manage that, I'll break some local laws. Now, as far as the work you'd do - it'd involve searching through multiple video files and finding Mikhail. It's time intensive and mind numbing, but that's how we'll piece together where he is. Are you up for it?"

"Anything to find this guy," she said.

"Take a seat and wait a while. I'll get the files, but I have to set up my safety nets first. This isn't something you take chances regarding." He grabbed a USB stick and stuck it into the desktop on the desk beside him.

Crystal watched him navigate the various program windows. She took a seat at the desktop beside his and placed her purse on the table beside its keyboard. She wiped her eyes and saw some makeup that had run earlier when her father pulled her aside. *He didn't even mention that I must look a mess,* she thought. She unzipped her purse and reached inside.

"It never feels better, I'm sorry to inform you," Lee said, not looking at her.

"What's that?"

"Nothing," Lee said. "I'm just talking to myself. They have deployed most of my department across town to different teams of personnel. I'm the only one left here. Look at this barren office," he said.

Crystal looked at the two additional long tables filled with up-to-date desktops placed atop. The room was dark and cool. "Yeah, it is empty in here besides us, come to think of it."

"They're all doing what you're doing, helping the boots on the ground, and here I am," he said. "This is the first thing I've done since this war started, other than watching our network security."

"We can't have them cracking into our network, though. It's a necessary job."

"Maybe," he said. "Alright, now be quiet for a moment. I need total concentration," he said. He gazed at the screen and watched the monitor intently.

She pulled out some wipes from her bag and cleaned herself up as best she could before tossing the spent remains in the trash bin under the desk by her seat. She pulled out her phone and saw that she had an unread message from her brother. *Are you alright? You can't be after tonight. Can we head there? We just finished up with Aunt Elizabeth,* she read in her mind.

She typed with her thumbs the response. "I'll be right out. Don't barge in here. He's in the middle of something delicate. Be right out." She stood up from the seat without warning. "I should return in a couple of minutes."

"I'll be here," Lee said.

She didn't verbally answer, as she could see he was still working. Taking her purse, she left the room, emerging back into the mansion's familiar hallways. She looked to her left and saw Roger and Bernard coming around the corner.

Roger rushed ahead of Bernard and walked up to his sister. "Hey," he said in a soft voice. "Are you okay?"

"Not really," she said, keeping her composure with a deep breath.

"Aw, come on," Bernard said. "That kind of face doesn't suit you. Where's the happy-go-lucky little sister I know?"

"Replaced by one who killed multiple gangsters just earlier," she said. "Can we please change the subject right now? I just pulled myself together earlier, and I don't want to break in the middle of the hallway."

"Fair enough," Roger said. "How did it go with Lee?"

"He's working on finding the guy already," she said. "He

said I'd have to help search through a bunch of recordings to help him find where Mikhail went. If we can use the city traffic cameras and follow his car, we'll know where he is. We're lucky he knows how to do this, because I don't," she said.

"Why not try to learn?" Bernard asked. "Could be a useful skill to have."

"Because I don't want to break into whatever the hell office that houses all that surveillance footage. I'm good with computers, but not radically skilled. Not like my grandma was, at least according to the stories."

"You're my little sister," Roger said. "I bet if you put your mind to it, you'd surpass even Tanya. You just need to try."

"Possibly, but not tonight," she said.

"I understand," Roger said. "Sorry, we're just antsy ourselves right now. Let's find privacy and head to my prior bedroom."

"We're going to mine if we're going anywhere," Crystal said. "Come on." She led the boys through the lower floor and up the stairs to the second story. She reached her hand out and traced along the wall toward the familiar room from her childhood, now seemingly a distant memory in the forefront of her mind. "Home sweet home," she said. She threw open the door and stepped inside.

"It's been a while since I've been in here," Roger said, stepping through behind his sister. "I remember it being pinker."

"It hasn't been pink since I was like seven years old," she said, walking over to a large dresser housing an enormous mirror and assorted makeup sitting atop. She got to work fixing her makeup as the boys looked around. "Shows how often you come around."

"It's not like we weren't hanging with you every day. It

was just usually in one of our rooms," Roger said.

Crystal's room had posters from assorted video games hanging at odd angles above her bed. In front of it was the standard 4k television and assorted game consoles tucked underneath. Her personal desktop would've sat atop the nearby desk in the room's corner if it hadn't been moved already.

"It's a welcome change to enter a room where the dirty laundry isn't laying on the ground," Roger said. "What do you think?"

"Don't blame me. The laundry lady always gets me the basket late. I have to put them somewhere," Bernard said. He leaned back against the door. "Seems like a nerdy motif, but it's your room, nerd."

"You two will help me with this video job," she said, finishing up the touch-ups. She moved over to her bed and sat down before laying back. "With four sets of eyes, it'll be done four times as fast, and we want this guy gone quick, right?"

"The sooner he's dead, the sooner people stop dying," Roger said.

"The sooner we get back to making money," Bernard said. "Yeah, I'm down to help if you can explain to me how to do it."

"Good," she said. She raised an arm and draped it over her eyes. "What are we doing after we find the guy, exactly?"

"Official orders are to tell your father," Bernard said.

"Since when have you two done anything that you've been told?" she asked. "I'm guessing you're not going to do that after our talk earlier."

"That's right," Roger said.

"You'd best tell me why I should go along with this half-cocked plan."

13

Ben took off his formal coat and tossed it in the nearby basket at the foot of the king-sized bed. He looked over at his wife, who'd just stripped down to her bra and panties before she sat on the bed. He had on a pair of shorts and climbed in next to her. "You seem tense," he said, crawling over to her. He placed his hands on her shoulder and massaged.

"It's this damned war, and this latest plan isn't sitting right with me," she said, leaning into him. "It's been a while since you entered the field, honey," she said.

"Is that what you're worried about?" he whispered into her ear in a husky voice. He kept his ministrations up as she melted into him. "I can handle it, baby."

"I know you can," she said. "It doesn't make it any easier to send the love of your life after a psycho sniper. Anything could happen out there; you know that."

"You're sending me because you trust I can get it done and to keep our boy out of trouble, I assume. I'm not objecting; hell, I basically volunteered. Now, try to get some rest tonight. You deserve it after the unending number of calls.

All those orders to different teams. You've stood over a map of the city for the last few days. That's not good for your shoulders, neck, or anything, probably."

"You haven't changed much since I first met you, you know," she said. "Oh," she moaned. "That's the spot."

"Yes, that's filled with tension. Let me see if I can fix these nervous knots." He concentrated his efforts on the firmer region of her shoulder.

"You're always taking care of me, even to this day. You're going out and risking your life to hunt Mikhail. I feel bad," she said. "You were supposed to get a cushy desk job keeping me safe as a stay-at-home bodyguard. You weren't supposed to be risking your life doing stuff like this again."

"We didn't expect this war with the Russians. This Mikhail is breaking our backs with how effective he is. It's my sworn duty to end his rampage, and I aim to do just that for you and the entire syndicate. The fact that I'm able to run my hands all over the most beautiful woman is an enormous added perk."

"You have become a sweet talker over the years, darling." She turned around, stopping the massage. She got onto her knees and delivered a quick peck on his lips. "I almost miss the stuttering young gangster that was too afraid to talk back. It was cute, I'll admit."

"I've grown up since then, I'm proud to say." Ben moved his hands from her shoulders to her face. His right hand cupped her soft cheek while his left moved to the back of Rachel's blonde head. "You've matured a lot since then too, you know, in all the best ways. You still have your youthful beauty yet possess experience to deal with this war without missing a beat."

"I'd say I've missed a few beats this time, sweetness." She reached up and laid a hand on his right arm, cradling her face. "Like when this war started. I knew we were getting too sweet of a deal. I knew Oleg had been bitching about prices, and analyzing it, I see those verbal jabs were his losing patience. If I'd been more attentive, none of this would have happened. So many people would still be alive."

"Don't blame yourself for everything," Ben said. He let his arms fall and leaned in. He wrapped his arms around her light frame and pulled her close to his chest. "Nobody is perfect, not even you. We're all doing our best. The men trust your judgement, and so do I."

"The men trust you and Warren more than me," she said.

"Nonsense."

"You think so?"

"You've led us for nearly twenty years. I know I'm right. Now get that self-doubting malarkey out of your beautiful head. That won't help anybody right now. You can lean on me anytime you want, like right now. The rank and file need the strong, confident leader that I know you are. You can be weak in front of me. You don't need to show strength all the time. Let your proverbial hair down around me. It's alright."

"Sometimes I think you spoil me when it's supposed to be the other way around. Wasn't that what I promised you all those years ago?"

"A husband is supposed to care for his worrying wife, and I take that sacred duty even more serious than that of your bodyguard. I love you, and I want you happy. It makes me sad when I see you doubt yourself."

"You're too good for me." She returned the hug and nestled her face into his chest before taking a deep breath of his scent.

"You take your time," Ben said. He rubbed her back, and

the pair settled into a silence that gave them a few blissful moments of peace in their normally chaotic lives.

Eventually the tender moment ended like all pleasant times in life. She pulled away from his warm, comforting embrace. "I don't relish you hunting that nutjob," she said with a wipe of her eyes.

"We both know if I didn't, Roger and Bernard would rush to kill him. They're young and dumb. They'd be in far more danger. I know how young men think. You think you're invincible until you don't. That car crash taught me the value of being careful. They haven't had that event, and I don't want them to nearly die learning it."

"What will we do?" Rachel asked. "We know Roger is royally pissed about Lauren. I saw the same fire burning in his eyes that reminded me of when the original Roger died. He's not letting this go, I can tell."

"There is one simple way of doing it without being overly invasive," he said.

"Do tell," she said.

"We bug Roger's and Bernard's cars. That way, I'd see them if they're trying to butt in on my job. I'm bringing Lee on my assassination attempt, and he'd make sure they turn around."

"That would probably work," Rachel said. "Well, better than my original idea of trying to lock them in their rooms."

"We both know they'd break out if we did that. They're ingenious in their disobedience. We'd probably end up with a guard that saw nothing and no camera footage. At least this way, they won't even suspect they're already caught. The car driving itself back home would give away that they're caught, but it's the best idea I have."

"I like it," Rachel said. "We'll do that."

"I'll take two bugs and plant them on the bottom of the

cars tomorrow morning before the vigil," Ben said, pulling out his phone and setting the alarm for four thirty a.m. "That should wake me before the early morning vigil and still have time to bug their cars without them noticing. If any patrols spot me, I'll see that they don't get too curious or chatty with the boys."

"Good." Rachel got under the covers. "Now come over here. I want my husband."

Ben finished setting the alarm and placed it on the night table at his side before crawling over to his wife's open arms. "Yes, ma'am..."

The next morning...

A small group composed of Rachel, Ben, Roger, Bernard, Crystal, Chris, and Jackie was all that showed at this unheard of time for a mourning vigil. They all stood in front of a large photo of Lauren. It showed her years ago when the three teenagers were all small children. Various other kids of syndicate members were in the picture too, all smiling for the official class photo. Roger, Bernard, and Crystal were all near her with beaming smiles while she smiled at the camera. It was hard to see the picture since it was still relatively dark, illuminated only by the nearby light affixed above the door to the mansion and the various candles the participants were holding.

Rachel stepped forward and cleared her throat. "I appreciate you all coming out this morning at such an early hour. I realize the hour is not typical for a vigil, but we're not typical."

The group nodded and grumbled various affirmations.

"Now," Rachel said, "we're gathered here today to send off a dear friend, a loving teacher, and a dependable woman who touched all our lives in her unique way as only she could. She was never afraid to speak her mind. She knew more than most, and she was braver than our strongest. I know I and others will miss her dearly now that she's gone. However, having said all that, she knew that life wasn't easy, especially the one we've chosen. She faced that choice with courage, knowing the potential consequences. Even knowing that, she gave life her all - first being boots on the ground, then educating our children. She gave every bit of her being to those kids." She stepped back toward the circle of attendees. "Would anyone else like to say something?"

Roger took a step forward to find himself beaten to the punch by Chris.

"I would, ma'am, if that's alright," he said.

"Go right ahead," she said.

He cleared his throat before starting. "I am ashamed to say I wasn't her closest friend, but I knew her well. Recently, she was assigned to my team. Lauren fit the description you just heard to a T," he said. "She never complained or worried. I knew her to calm us down when we needed it in dire times. She died saving the rest of my team from her fate, and she died a hero. Although she didn't need to be the soul in the driver's seat, she jumped inside without thinking. She didn't deserve a bullet through the head. It should have been me. I'm old." He tried to force a chuckle. "I'm nearing the end of my prime if I haven't reached it already. It happened in front of me. I've seen folks die in war all my life, but this one doesn't sit right with me when I was sitting right there." He reached up and wiped just below his eye.

Jackie stepped forward and brought him back, ending the impromptu speech.

"Anyone else?" Rachel asked.

"Yes." Roger stepped ahead and took his spot. "She was

my, and many others, teacher for over a decade. She was lax on disciplining us, if I'm honest, not out of incompetence or any such nonsense. I believe it was because she loved all of us so much she couldn't bring herself to scold us often. She was always there to encourage you if you were unsure of yourself during a project. She was always happy to talk after class or tutor you."

Bernard silently stepped forward and stood near his friend, nodding along with every point he made.

"She never made me feel dumb for answering a question wrong, even if I was admittedly. She was the perfect teacher by my approximation, as she had the patience of a saint to put up with us hell raisers. We pranked her nigh on every day for a month at one point. She simply took it in stride. I guess my point in this long rambling diatribe is that she'll be missed by many. You know," Roger said, "when I was younger I heard the saying 'You don't know what you have until you lose it'. I now know the true meaning behind those words. Be thankful for what you have before it's too late. That's what I've learned out of this." He stepped back into the crowd with Bernard, opening the spot for anyone else.

"Anyone else?" Rachel asked. "Do not be shy."

"I suppose I should." Jackie took her turn. "I didn't know her all that well, if I'm honest. We bickered and bantered a little before the job. I never knew Lauren as a teacher or friend, only a colleague. While her sense of humor didn't gel with me, I cannot deny her work ethic. She took her job seriously, and that demands the highest respect from me, if nothing else. I regret I didn't know her as well as I should've. She didn't hesitate to do her job when the metal met the meat. That says a lot. You can tell the mettle of a person by how they react to guns firing around them, and she passed with flying colors. She was reassuring to the younger talent and kept them calm, no doubt attributed to the relationship she'd built with them over her teaching career. This syndicate is now lesser for her loss. That is all I have to say."

"Ben or Bernard? You have anything before we draw this vigil to a close?" Rachel asked.

"I think everything's been said," Bernard said. "I'd be repeating at this point if I tried to convey my feelings."

Ben quietly shook his head.

"Alright then." Rachel stepped forward next to the picture. "That draws this vigil to a close. Unfortunately, we do not have her body because of circumstances. There will be a ceremonial funeral held after this war ends. Check your emails every day. The date of her funeral will be sent once this war dies down." She turned and placed a shaking hand on the heartwarming picture. Her voice turned quiet. "I'll miss you, old friend." Her voice returned to the louder one from before. "That is all. I thank you all for coming and paying your respects. Be careful out there, everyone. You are dismissed," she said.

Jackie led Chris back inside the mansion, holding onto his arm, leaving just the teenagers and their parents, minus Elizabeth.

"That was a beautiful speech, Son," Ben said.

"Thanks, Dad. I was telling the truth is all."

"You've always been the better orator," Bernard said. "I figured I'd let you speak since I'd have just butchered it and looked like a fool. She deserved better than my bumbling."

"You've been quiet, dear," Rachel said, looking at Crystal. "Are you alright?"

"I'm tired and sad. Forgive my being quiet. I was awake all night poring over traffic camera footage while looking for the mean son of a bitch that killed her."

"You need rest, sweetie," Ben said. "Go take a nap real quick."

"I can't. The longer it takes to find him, the longer her killer is out there."

"Look, we'll find Lee and convince him to teach us how to do it," Roger said. "You need a break, judging by how tired you are. We'll take care of it. Alright?"

"Of course," Bernard said.

"If you say so," she said. "I could use a good sleep." She headed back inside the mansion with that abrupt exit.

"As for you two," Rachel said. "You're not planning anything else, are you?"

"Only thing we're planning is to find this bastard," Roger said.

"You're sure?" Ben asked.

"Yes."

"Alright then," Ben said. "You two should head inside and learn about computers. You want my advice? Make some extra strong coffee before you head inside. Lee will need it, and he loves it black. That'll earn you points with Lee. If that fails, just tell him I ordered you there."

"We'll do just that," Bernard said. "Come on, buddy. Let's not waste any time." He patted Roger's arm and walked over toward the door with Roger following.

Ben and Rachel watched the pair exit inside.

"I don't trust that story one ounce," Ben said.

"As you shouldn't," Rachel said. "They're eighteen-year-old pissed off boys. They're up to something. I know I would have been at their age."

"You thought things through compared to our son," he said, grabbing her hand.

"You know you're not supposed to show public displays of affection when we're on duty, sweetness."

"I don't see anyone else here. Do you?" Ben asked, giving it a squeeze. "You looked like you could use a little reassurance after that heart-warming speech earlier. I'm so proud of you. I'm sorry about losing her, but I'll make it right. That bastard who killed her will die by my hand. I promise you that."

"You just be careful," she said, leaning into him and giving him a hug. "I can't lose you too."

"You know me," he said, looking down and planting a kiss on her forehead. "I'm always careful."

"Just don't take any unnecessary risks. Did you accomplish what we talked about last night?"

"I awoke extra early and planted it. Those boys won't be going anywhere without us knowing where. I made sure of it. So stop worrying about that. I'll take care of them. Just leave it all to me. Have I ever let you down before?"

"Never," she said. "That's why I wanted you. I know I can trust my big, powerful man."

"Good," Ben said. "Let's hope Lee and the boys find him soon. We can't have this guy going around freely doing as he pleases for much longer."

14

"We've been driving around all day," Bernard said. He had his leg propped up against the glove compartment and was slouched in his seat. "Are we sure regarding our intel?"

"I saw it with my own eyes," Crystal said. "The car we watched him enter headed out of town in this direction. Our best method of finding him is to investigate every house in the immediate area looking for his car. It's time consuming, but it's our only lead. Now stop complaining, and get ready. We're almost at the next house." She looked out at the golden, dying rays of the sun filtering through the thick forest.

"It was a black van, right?" Roger asked.

"For the tenth time today, affirmative," Crystal said. "A black van with no discernable markings is what he drove after firing his shots."

"I'm going to pull up a suitable distance away behind these trees. If it is him, we don't need him knowing we're here. You know," he said, "just in case."

"Something tells me this house will prove similar,"

Bernard said. "It'll be some poor sap or couple living out here. Who'd even choose to live outside the city? I love living in it far more."

"Some prefer the simpler life," Crystal said. "There's nothing wrong with that."

"Let's see what we've found." Roger put the car in park off the road. "Come on." He unbuckled his seat belt and got out of the car, along with his sister and friend.

"I need to stretch my legs." Crystal did some stretches while the boys walked toward the nearby house through the tree line. Roger's phone buzzed in his pocket. He fished it out as they walked. "Who the hell?"

Bernard leaned over. "Unknown caller, huh? Could be one of us. I'd answer it."

"You shouldn't have that phone if you want anonymity," Crystal said. "They could track you here."

"Too late now," Roger said. He answered it. "Who is this?"

"Imagine my surprise to see your car heading out into the woods. Put me on speakerphone, and make sure it's low for God's sake."

Roger knew better than to argue and did as his father ordered. He reached a hand out and stopped Bernard from continuing on as they stopped in their tracks. "You're on."

"Stop immediately what you're doing."

"With all due respect, sir," Bernard said, "we don't know this is his base. We haven't seen if his car's there or not. We didn't want to waste your time driving to this place."

"How thoughtful." Ben's voice was laced with sarcasm. "The fact you two are walking up to the target's suspected house armed and sneaking through the woods is supposed to fill me with confidence, is it? Move back to the car right now. That is an order."

"Just one minute," Bernard said. He stepped closer to the tree in front of him and peeked around.

"That was not a suggestion."

"This is our place alright," Bernard said, ducking behind cover. "That's his van."

"Then report back here on the double or I don't care who your mothers are, I'm going to confine you to your old quarters as soon as we're back."

"We're on our way back," Roger said. A strange electronic sound sounded after his words.

"Yes, so Lee tells me."

"Lee's out of the mansion?" Crystal asked.

"How nice of you to join the call, sweetheart," Ben said. "Next time introduce yourself. It's rude to lurk like that."

"Sorry, Dad."

"I see your car," Ben said. "Are the keys still in there?"

"Yeah, Dad," Crystal said.

"Good, we're moving your car. Who drove? Whoever drove has no sense of subtlety. If he exited the property, he'd know something was strange considering where you parked. This is straight amateur hour here." The sound of a door opening and closing shut with a thud reached their ears.

"Hi, Dad."

"You have explaining to do, so don't act friendly, Daughter. You should've known better than to help these two knucklehead delinquents," Ben said as the sound of the engine reached their ears. "Are you two almost back?"

"We're here," Roger said, stepping through the brush and emerging near the road. He could see his father sitting in the front seat, waving for him to get in. He looked back and saw Lee climbing into the car his father had come in. They climbed into the back seat next to Crystal.

"We're moving this. You don't go after the target in broad

daylight, boys. What were you thinking?" He started the engine and turned them around on the sparsely populated road. It wasn't difficult to turn around. He saw Lee following him in the rear-view mirror.

"I keep telling you, we simply wanted to confirm Mikhail was here," Roger said.

"You keep saying it, and I keep finding it hard to believe, Son. This wouldn't be your first incident. You've snuck out before repeatedly. I'm wondering, what was your grand plan?"

"To alert you and return to our apartment," Bernard said. "I'm being honest here."

"They are, Dad," Crystal said. "We were here scouting the joint."

"Uh huh," Ben said. He pulled over out of sight onto a small dirt path. He turned off the beaten path into a clearing before turning the car around to exit the forest clearing easily. "Now we're out of sight from prying eyes. You're sure he's in there?"

"It was the same car," Bernard said. "I saw it with my own eyes. You saw it too, right Roger?"

"It looked similar," he said.

"Alright then," Ben said. "What do you two have on you, weapon wise?"

"Huh?" Roger asked. "I've got my revolver on me."

"I have my semi-auto," Bernard said.

"Alright, here's what's going to happen," Ben said. "I know you two are crazy about doing this, so you're going to help me."

"We are?" Roger asked. "Why?"

"Because everybody knows you two idiots were planning on doing this before you informed me. At least this way I'll keep you two alive and out of harm's way. You two are going to drive this back to your apartment and gather your rifles, tactical vests, the helmets to match, and night vision goggles for at least three - if you're not wearing the vests already, which you'd better be. I also need you to get that fancy drone of your sisters. I have some ideas that could prove useful here."

"You want the gun thing, too?" Roger asked.

"No," Ben said. "It won't be needed. We can spare our operators the burden of more blood on their hands. I'm the one getting my hands dirty, not her. Crystal, you're with me. Let's allow the boys to deliver their cargo, and we'll review our plans for tonight."

"To be safe, boys," she gripped the car handle, "get my giant box of modifications and bring my tool box. It's in my room in the closet. It should give us some versatility in what we can do."

"You heard her," Ben said. The father and daughter exited the car and watched as the boys climbed into the front seats.

Ben guided his daughter over toward the one Lee was in and sat on the hood of the car. The pair watched the boys start the engine and pull out. "I'm lucky I intervened in time before they alerted him."

Lee exited the car and slammed the door shut. "I'd say. If there's a time for you to use your drone, this is it. You could have flown above the house. Nobody would've noticed."

"Call it an oversight," Crystal said. "You know how little sleep I had. We were searching for that damned car."

"Oversight she says," Lee said.

"Enough. This is getting us nowhere. I have my rifle in my trunk. I'll find a location to set up camp tonight."

"You're going to shoot him through the window?"

Crystal asked. She tilted her head. "How's that going to work? You'd never know which room's his."

"No, that'd be a fool's errand," Ben said. "One fact I know about this life is how paranoid you become. This ghost's been working for decades, just like me. I'm going to use that to my advantage. Your brother and his ambitious friend want to help. They'll get to safely."

"I'm lost," she said. "How are they going to help and remain safe?"

"Trust your father. I've been doing this for years. Now help me find a spot. Lee, pull the local map up on your laptop and pinpoint the house."

"It'll be a minute." He opened the back door of the remaining car and reached inside. He retrieved the laptop and placed it atop the car so he could work standing.

"Hey, wait a minute." Crystal elbowed Lee out of the way. "You put something on their car."

"Did I?"

"It sure looks like it," Crystal said, pointing at the screen. "Those are not motherboard serial numbers. That looks more like an external device, judging by the name."

"Maybe I did," Ben said. "I've had enough senseless death, and we both know your brother and his friend are hotheads at the best of times. A father does what he must to keep his young safe. That includes you and your brother, young lady. It's a hundred years too early to fool your father. I know about sneaking, and those young idiots aren't slick."

"Yeah, you got us." Crystal let Lee get back to work and watched his progress. "The boys weren't planning on attacking him, truly."

"Let's say I believe that then," Ben said.

"You're not serious," Lee said.

"It seems a moot point now," Ben said. "You are not to speak to Mrs. Morris about tonight. Am I clear, Lee?"

"I understand, but if she asks me, you know I can't lie."

"Just allow me to report this. I'll get it taken care of. Where's the damned map?" He hurried and stood beside Lee.

All three huddled around the small device. Lee zoomed in on the already downloaded map. "Here it is. Keep your britches on."

"Alright," Ben said. "It looks like there's tree cover around the entire rear of the house along with the north side. Is there a closer view available?"

"Not until the boys return with that infernal drone," Lee said. "This is a public map, sir," he said. "Minor details in the middle of nowhere aren't there. The best I can manage is this top-down view of the premises, blurry as it is."

"Alright then." He studied the pixelated picture with a rub of his chin. "How long do you believe it'll take them to report back?"

"I don't know," Crystal said. "Maybe twenty minutes is my guess. It depends on how bad the traffic is."

"We'll wait," Ben said. "We'll properly handle this our first attempt."

Two hours later...

"Now would prove an excellent chance to send the drone," Lee said. "Surely he's returned by now. If not, what's it hurt to check again?"

"I've got the night vision camera working for it." Crystal wiped her brow free from the sweat and looked down at her handiwork. "What do you think?"

Everyone looked down at the drone sitting a close distance away in the clearing.

"Let's test the feed first," Lee said. "Here we are." A window popped up on the screen showing their green tinted surroundings. A small window in the monitor's corner showed the drone's view. Text appeared in the corner stating 'Night vision mode activated'.

"It's working," the bald man said. "Find if there's a rear exit. We can't have him running out the back without our knowing."

"That, and we need to count cars parked nearby. If it's just him, that's a different beast than if he has company with him. Just make sure you keep it very high. We can't have them hearing its sound or seeing its flashing red light.

"I know, Dad. I've done this before." Crystal grabbed the remote controllers and gripped them tight. She reached up and pulled the goggles down over her eyes. "Wish me luck," she said. She piloted the device up and over the nearby tree line before it disappeared out of view.

Everyone gathered around the laptop feed to see what it found. They waited as it flew over the forest between them, making conversation.

"Why did you have us retrieve the helmets, anyway?" Roger asked. He tapped the side of his tactical helmet. "I didn't think we'd be doing anything dangerous. Isn't that what you want?"

"That depends on what intel we discover," Ben said. "Have patience and trust your sister's recon ability. We'll get all we need to make the plan and carry it out. Now be quiet." He pointed at the screen. "She's almost there."

The screen showed the tree line ending and open land coming into view. It rapidly gained altitude before getting too close to the edge of the tree line and angled its view downward.

"Here we go. Get ready," Crystal said. She pressed her thumb forward, and the drone flew forward. The house they were seeking came into focus. "Let me zoom so we can view how many vehicles are sitting there and if our target's home." She pressed another button on the remote while the drone was hovering in place. "There we are," she said.

The camera zoomed in on a bird's-eye view of the place.

"I'm not seeing his van," Roger said. "There're lots of cars parked already."

"Oleg's no doubt using one of his properties as a bunkhouse for his recent arrivals," Ben said. "It's what we'd do. Look to the right."

The camera shifted slightly to the right to reveal another car turning off the nearby two lane road. It got into the already crowded driveway and backed in.

"That looks like our man," Bernard said.

"Wait and see if he matches the description of our guy," Ben said. "More than Mikhail probably owns the same car. We are near a major metropolitan area, at least for Ohio anyway."

The camera zoomed in further. The graph with a minus symbol and a plus sign showed the zoom was as powerful as technologically possible, seeing as it was positioned far right brushing against the plus sign.

"That's him alright," Lee said.

"I think you're right," Ben said. "Try to secure a decent view of exactly how many cars there are. It should help gauge how many men he has inside."

The camera shifted back toward the front of the house, showing two aisles of cars in front of the garage.

"I'm counting at least six in the front," Crystal said. "There're more parked behind the joint."

"I definitely see one parked around to the side as well," Roger said, pointing toward the screen to illustrate his point.

"He's riding deep in there," Ben said. "Alright, this can work."

"It can?" Crystal asked.

"Sure it can. Move that drone toward the back of the flophouse. Is there a rear exit? If it has a dirt bike or four-wheeler parked nearby, we need to be aware he'll escape during any attempt we make and plan accordingly."

"I never thought of that," Roger said.

"Hence why they sent me, Son, and not you two," Ben said. "A step ahead is a step behind. Be three steps ahead, and that means anticipating the moves of your prey before you even make your move. It's a lot easier to cut them off in the planning stage than it is to improvise after it's started."

"I see a car, but no dirt bikes or four-wheelers. It appears old and beat-up, but I can't see it clearly," Crystal said. "Is there anything else we need to know before we make our final plans?"

"Circle around the place and we'll search," Ben said. "Take a close look, everyone. The smallest detail could be key in our plans."

Everyone crowded closer around the lone laptop atop the car, trying to get a better view of the cozy house in the country.

"It has a lot of windows," Roger said.

"I see the nearest neighbor is a long distance away," Bernard said. "Looks like they're already in bed too, judging by the lights being off."

"The police response time here would be at least twenty

minutes," Lee said. "The Toledo PD would be the ones responding, I'm pretty sure."

"There's a dirt path leading away from the house and deeper into the tree line," Crystal said. "Do you see it? It's behind the car out back. It's not large. I don't think a car could fit on it."

"We have no method of knowing what's inside the garage. It might house a bike ready to dash toward that path. We need to take that into consideration. I saw it had a back door. A runner could pilot a bike through that garage's rear door and escape out back. We'll take care of that eventuality before we move," Ben said. "We'd also best make sure we bug his car while we have the drop on them. I'll take care of that part."

"What if it has a car alarm, Dad?" Roger asked.

"It's not going to sound off if you attach it to the bottom of the car, Son," Ben said. "It just requires a featherlight touch. Just ask your mother. I'm great with that."

"I wish I didn't hear that," Roger said.

"Me either," Crystal said, audibly disgusted.

"Don't be babies," Ben said. "If you're old enough to sneak out against your parent's wishes, you're old enough to hear about adult things."

"Is this all we need? This drone's batteries are running low," Crystal said.

"Bring it back," Ben said. "I've got everything I need to make a comprehensive plan to cover all our bases."

"Got it. I'm bringing her home," Crystal said. She turned the flying craft around and flew back.

"Now, while she's piloting, let's review. Lee, we have the bugs, right?"

"You told me to bring them, so I did," Lee said.

"Good. There are too many damned cars for me to bug

alone, so I require help. Now, if anything goes wrong during this, you are to retreat immediately. Don't sit waiting for guards to exit. You're taking off in a sprint toward the tree line. That is the condition or you're not getting involved, and it'll just take longer while I do them all myself."

"Place them on the bottom gently, right?" Bernard asked. "We can manage that, sir."

"I should hope so," Ben said. "To be safe, I'll show you two idiots how it's done using this car before we head out, just to be sure. I'll bug the vehicles in the back, and you'll bug the cars parked in the front. That way, even if he escapes inside the car parked behind the home, we'd know where he ran to. The potential bike inside the garage is still a kink in our plan, but unless I break in and look, it's the best we can do. For all I know, that's where they're putting men in sleeping bags, ergo I'm not itching to bust in on a hunch."

"You wouldn't have to anyway, sir," Lee said. "I have something that keeps you outside until you know it's safe inside. It's a simple device that allows you to snake it under the door while you're safely outside. It's lightweight and easy to use."

"Good thinking, but how would I enter?"

"You never learned how to lock pick, Pops?" Roger asked.

"Did you?"

"No, but that wasn't my question."

"I learned a bit, but I'm not confident in my skills," Ben said. "Give me enough time and I could get it."

"Looks like we'll have time, Dad," Crystal said. A faint buzzing sound accompanied her voice. The group looked up and saw the drone descending toward the nearby clearing beside them, before gracefully setting down more like an elegant butterfly than a man-made device.

"I'll make that call when I'm back there. You boys get the two cars, the rest won't be able to leave since they're in the back of the line. I'll bug the cars parked at the side. Once you're finished, you're heading over here," he pointed to the side of the house in the tree line. "I want you behind the biggest, thickest tree you can find. Once you're there, you're going to wait for my signal before popping this entire operation off."

"How you want us to do that?" Bernard asked. "It's a fair question."

"You have rifles, armor, and ammo. How do you think? Use your imagination. Shoot the window; hell, shoot a car. I don't care what you hit. It's all about the noise that will jolt them awake. They'll grab their guns and rush outside, or they'll hole up inside. Now Mikhail will try to make his escape, I'm betting. That's when he'll be most vulnerable, and I'll seize the opportunity. While he's thinking he's slick, leaving his men to die, I'll take him down while he's occupied. Once he's outside, I'll tell you to run. You will run to your car and leave straight away. I'm trying to minimize the lead being flung at you, so your mothers don't kill me. Is that understood?"

"I understand you want us to leave you while you're still near lots of enemies," Roger said. "That's suicide, Father. Where will you be?"

"I'll be back here," Ben said, pointing behind the house. "I aim to put him down while he runs away. Trust me, he will run. He's too important to Oleg, and I know the type. Once you make a name for yourself, you think you're worth more than the rank-and-file troops. He probably views them as expendable."

"That's a lot of assumptions," Lee said. "I also don't like you being back behind the house near a kicked hornet's nest by yourself."

"I didn't know you cared, Lee, buddy," Ben said. "We're thrilled to hear you say that."

"Oh no," Lee said.

"You're going to be over here." He dragged the screen further up to reveal another road behind the trees behind the house. "Lee, you'll be here before anything starts. You can guide me back to you using my phone's GPS because I won't be able to see much in the forest at night."

"I can do that," Lee said. "I don't suppose we have any spare vests, do we?"

"Sure we do, big man," Bernard reached over to the stack of them and tossed one toward him to catch. "Here," he said. "Put that on. I don't know why you're worried. The trees will stop any lead coming your way."

"When this guy's involved, drivers tend to die. Or did you forget?"

"Point taken," Bernard said, his voice deflating.

"Now, Crystal, you're going to be the driver for the boys. We're keeping the cars here, so post up over there." He pointed off toward the direction of the house. "I expect you to be wearing one of those too, for safety's sake."

"It's not a problem," she said. "I got it."

"Good," Ben said. "Are there questions before we get this done tonight?"

"Let me get this straight," Roger said. "We're bugging the cars first off."

"Correct," Ben said. "In case he gets away, we'll know right where he went."

"You're possibly breaking into their garage to bug any motorbikes or four wheelers, in that same vein."

"Yes."

"Then we're moving back this way and hiding behind cover to wait for your signal," Bernard said.

"I see you two were paying attention," Ben said. "That's good."

"On your signal, we rain down hell on that house," Roger said.

"Very good," Ben said. "Then, when I give the order, you two run to your sister inside the car. You all need to leave as soon as you're inside. Lee and I will be fine, I promise. Leave it to your old man, and we'll all get out."

"Alright then," Roger said. "Let's get this done."

15

"I don't hear any car alarms, so I suppose you two are doing well over there?" Ben was nearing the rear of the house, and his voice was low. He hurried across the back-yard and stayed low. He approached the beat-up car and planted the bug on the underside of its carriage.

"The cars are bugged, Father," Roger said. "We're moving back to the assigned position now," he said.

"Good," Ben said. "I've got the one out back set up. I'm going to use this new device and see what's hidden inside the garage." He pulled out the device. It had a square screen and some directional inputs attached to a long, thin black lens at the end. He lowered to a knee beside the door frame and placed the narrow cord looking appendage under. He gazed at the screen and viewed the interior in night vision.

"Is it working, sir?" Lee asked in his ear.

"Perfectly," Ben said. "I see a four-wheeler inside. It'd be perfect for an escape vehicle. I guess I'm going to brush off my lock picking skills that your mother taught me years ago. This could take a while. Get comfortable wherever you're at."

"Did you try the door first, Dad?" Crystal asked. "If it's for escape, there's a good chance they'd keep it unlocked. It's not connected to the house after all."

"Good thinking," Ben said. He stowed the device into the backpack he had over his shoulder and pulled out his handgun, ensuring it was ready to fire just in case. Using his left hand, he gripped the doorknob and twisted. To his relief, it opened. "You were right," he whispered.

The interior was pitch black. Ben reached above his head and pulled the night vision goggles down over his eyes before turning them on. The room bathed in the familiar green shade of the advanced goggles with an electronic hum. He could now plainly see what he was stepping towards. Reaching into his pants pocket, he pulled out another bug to plant on the bike. He planted it and headed back outside, shutting the door as gently as he could manage.

"The bugs are planted," Ben said in a quiet voice. "I'm moving to my position now," he said. He walked, not jogged, trying to keep the noise to a bare minimum near the house. "Standby," he said.

"We're ready and waiting, old man," Roger said. "Waiting on your mark."

"Remember what I mentioned beforehand," Ben said, almost to the tree line behind the house. "Once he's outside of the house, you three are leaving instantly."

"We remember," Bernard said.

"You'd better. I know my son has a penchant for trying to be the hero. That won't fly here."

"It was a small child, Father," Roger said. "You'd have done the same."

"That doesn't make it the right decision, Son," Ben said. "Now be quiet and get ready." He got behind a suitable tree and laid down on the cold dirty ground, trying to make sure he had a good sight line toward the rear doors of the tiny house and the garage. "The only hitch to this plan is if he exits the front. If that happens, I'll adjust and your departure will be delayed, but I don't think a veteran like him will wander into the kill zone without cover. It's hardly worth mentioning."

"If we see him, I assume we have permission to fire?" Bernard asked.

"Yes," Ben said. "Just fire in bursts and prioritize your safety over the kill. Understood?"

"Yes, sir," Bernard said.

Ben placed his backpack to the side and dug around inside of it. He pulled out what looked like binoculars and brought them up to his face. "Looks like I'm about forty yards away." He lowered the lenses and brought his attention to the scope. He adjusted the scope to the appropriate distance. "Zero in your weapons, boys - especially you, Son," Ben said. "You're farther away than I am, so it's doubly important."

"I got it," Roger said. "We're seventy yards away, and we made the adjustments already."

"You tend to forget," Ben said. "Can't have you missing the broad side of a house. Your friend would never let you live that one down."

"Is everyone ready? Once we start, there is no stopping," Ben said. "Keep your cool and stick to the plan."

"We're ready," Roger said.

"Ready for the getaway," Crystal said.

"I'm ready to guide you to my car and get us away clean," Lee said. "I'm in position."

"Good," Ben said. He took a deep breath and looked through the scope leveled at the house's rear exit. "Shoot whenever you're ready, and set this powder keg off in style, boys. Make it convincing so they believe they're under attack. Toss grenades to make a statement. I doubt they'll reach the house at that distance, but the effect's all we need. Panic will be our friend."

"Let's start, buddy," Bernard could be heard.

Ben waited for what seemed like multiple minutes, anticipating carnage before the first shots rang. The ground below him shook from a blast originating from the front of the property. "Let's see what we shake out of the tree tonight."

More firing met his ears. This time the origin seemed closer.

"They're firing from inside," Bernard said. "They're not coming out."

"I wouldn't expect them to," Ben said. "Keep their attention. Do not leave yet. The target hasn't exited the house. If he doesn't, then we can consider leaving. He will leave, especially if I do this," he said.

"I don't like the sound of that plan," Crystal said.

Ben got to his knee and reached down to his belt line to pluck a grenade. He prepped by pulling out the pin and tossing it as hard as he could toward the house. It ended up landing on the top of the house's roof and rolled down out of sight toward the front of the house. "Take cover now. Lumber may come flying your way soon."

A much closer and stronger shockwave came from beneath his feet. Splintering wood and dust shot up into the air. He got his rifle at the ready and pointed it toward the back door. He could hear screams of panic nearby.

"God almighty," Bernard said. "You blew up half the fucking house."

"That should get him moving," Roger said.

More gunfire erupted. It was obviously more than Roger and Bernard shooting now.

"Yep, he was right," Bernard said. "That's got the hornet's nest revved up. Be on the watch back there. He'll make his move soon I bet."

"They're hunkered down inside what remains of the front of the house," Roger said over the blaring gunfire.

Ben didn't answer yet. He had his rifle pointed straight at the back door, just watching and waiting.

"It's been one minute," Lee said. "We have nine minutes at the latest before we should leave."

Ben saw the back door shoot open. Their target wasted no time and sprinted over to the garage. His finger wrapped around the trigger, prepping to squeeze it whenever his target slowed down. He followed him scoped all the way toward the garage door. "He's going for the garage rear exit. You two leave. Hurry before the rank and file decide to get brave."

"You got it, old man," Bernard said. "Good luck," he said. "Come on, buddy. Time to hit the road. We did our part."

"Don't miss," Roger said.

The gunfire continued unabated as the line went quiet.

Mikhail didn't bother stopping to open the door, choosing instead to bash his shoulder into it mid sprint and open it that way. "My only shot is when he first gets outside. He'll have to stroll it out if he exits out the back."

"Two minutes have elapsed," Lee said. "Eight minutes before we need to leave, sir."

"He's taking his sweet time inside that garage."

"Shall I get him out of there?" Crystal asked.

"Negative," Ben said. "It'd take too long to get your drone packed away and escape. Hold on," he said. The door swung open again. "This might be my chance." He tried to slow his racing heart and calm his trembling hands as the adrenaline rushed through him.

"We're leaving then," Crystal said.

Sure enough, the four-wheeler came into view, along with an engine's roar. The rest of Mikhail followed. He had a helmet on and was fully intent on escaping.

Ben exhaled and took aim at his center mass. "Come on," he whispered. "I can't get an angle on his chest from here. I might hit his arm."

"Take that shot, boss," Lee said.

"Fuck," Ben said. He watched as Mikhail began trying to start the stubborn engine. Thankfully, the thing seemed intent on making him work for the privilege. He lined up his shot as best he could from his location on the forest floor. He squeezed the trigger as soon as the roar of the engine overtook the dying amount of gunfire being fired off nearby.

The shot resulted in a glancing blow, seeing as Mikhail was already in motion as the engine roared to life. The projectile ended up connecting, but not where Ben aimed. Instead of a chest shot, it hit him in the side of the abdomen. He rode past Ben and circled around the house, out of Ben's sight.

"No," Ben said, scrambling to his feet. "Fuck."

"We can't stick around, boss," Lee said. "Get back here. Did you at least hit him?"

"Affirmative," Ben said, running through the forest away from the home. "I don't think it was a fatal shot, but I hit the fucker alright. I fired just as he got the engine working, and it affected my aim."

"That's just one of those things," Lee said. "Turn slightly right and keep going. We need to make some distance. Police have already been called, and I couldn't redirect that many calls at one time."

"I'm almost there." Ben hopped over an especially large log, continuing his jog through the dark forest. "It's dark as hell in here." He quickly flipped his goggles back down, assisting his vision during his escape.

"You're almost here," Lee said. "The doors are unlocked. I see you."

"I'm here." Ben rushed over to the car and climbed inside the back. Before he said a single word, the vehicle was in motion and onto the road nearby. "You couldn't wait to leave, could you?"

"Staying around a future police investigation is not high on my priority list. I imagine those Russians thought the same. You don't hear any gunfire anymore. My bet is they're all trying to do what Mikhail managed, get the hell out of Dodge. Where did you hit him?"

"I think I hit him in the side."

"That could be fatal, boss," Lee said. "Depending on how high you hit him. He's out of commission for a while anyway."

"Not if Oleg has surgeons, which we both know he employs regularly. He'll be out a week or two, tops. I failed, Lee. It's alright to say it out loud."

"Not completely," Lee said, turning along the twisted country road toward Toledo. "We have the tracker planted on his bike. We can finish that job tonight if you want. I'd do it quick before he changes vehicles."

"I guess you're right," Ben said.

"Surely you don't think just because we left early that we'd miss out on this plan?" Roger's voice came back onto the call.

"Destroy that phone immediately," Ben said. "Once you're on new hardware, then we can talk." He looked forward to Lee and ripped the device out of his ear, then grabbed a nearby hammer from a toolbox at his feet. He crushed the evidence himself and tossed the rest out of the window toward the tree line. Grabbing a new one sitting nearby, he rejoined the call.

"Yeah, we always do," Bernard said. "We'd already done it. Did you?"

"Of course I did," Ben said. "Who do you think you're talking to? As for you all tagging along, come along. He's a slippery bastard, this Mikhail. He's got the devil's luck, seeing as that bike started up and roared off as soon as I shot."

16

"Ma'am," Warren said. "Ma'am, did you hear me?"

"Huh?" Rachel snapped out of staring at the laptop on top of her desk. She'd been watching the dots representing her husband and son's car out in the middle of the nearby countryside. "What is it?" She looked up at her chief of security.

"I asked how it was going. You seemed quite interested in whoever you're keeping tabs on there."

"It's Ben and his hunting Mikhail. It looks like both cars got away safely," she said.

"Those cars were not nearby, ma'am," Warren said. "It looks like he used the kids to his advantage in that operation, if my eyes aren't deceiving me."

"Apparently so," Rachel said, clearly not happy. "It must have been the only way."

"Those two boys always were stubborn, but your husband knows what he's doing," Warren said. "Are you going to call him and ask what's up?"

"I was about to," Rachel said, grabbing the phone. She dialed the number Ben had given her before he left. She got an automated message, so she hung up and moved to the next one. This one rang.

"Yeah?" Ben asked, answering.

"How did it go?"

"The plan itself went flawlessly," Ben said.

"Good to hear."

"The shot to put Mikhail down, however, was not a clean one. He got away, but we got the bike he was on tagged. We're on our way to finish this."

"We as in you and our kids," Rachel said.

"Is this what the call is for?"

"It's one reason."

"I was lucky to reach them the first time. They nearly marched up to Mikhail's place on foot. I kept them behind cover with vests and helmets. They were nothing more than a mere distraction, firing off shots to lure out the prey. They did their job fine. Without them, I'd have never gotten the opportunity to even take a shot."

"I trust your judgement, but why are they still following you?"

"He's on guard now," Ben said. "It's our only chance of finishing him right now," he said. "We bugged the bike he made his daring escape on. If he switches vehicles, we're screwed and will never find him. He knows he's being hunted now. It's now or never, and I won't take never for an answer."

"As you shouldn't," Rachel said. "Keep them safe at all costs."

"I always do, baby," Ben said. "I'd never put them in harm's way. We both know if I sent them home, they'd simply sneak behind our back and make things worse."

"History would confirm that suspicion," she said. "You know I trust you to get it done. I have a feeling I know who put them up to this stupidity incarnate. I'm going to go have a word with her royal highness. Be careful out there, dear husband."

"You too," Ben said. "She's not to be underestimated, even almost pushing seventy. We know what that woman's capable of when cornered, sweetie."

"Me more than most people," Rachel said. "I got it. I'll be careful." She hung up.

"Problem with the hit?" Warren asked.

"He's taking care of it," Rachel said. "They bugged his getaway vehicle, so they're chasing his wounded ass down to finish him."

"I'd have thought he'd bring him down in one shot," Warren said. "Maybe I'll ask him how it went down when he gets back."

"You do that." Rachel got up from the oversized desk and walked toward the double doors. "I have to speak to Elizabeth. Won't you accompany me, Davis?"

"Sure thing, boss," Warren hurried after her. "Why are we talking to her, anyway?" he asked once he caught up. "Did she do something?"

"I suspect as much," Rachel said. "I told those two teenagers they weren't to kill Mikhail, and then what do they try immediately afterward? They followed him to that hideout and damned near got themselves killed. If it wasn't for Ben, they'd probably be dead. I have it on good authority that Elizabeth encouraged them to disobey my order. You know what that means, right?"

"Undermining your authority is a huge no-no," Warren said.

"That's putting it mildly," she said. "How close are you to her? Are you friends?"

"I like her well enough," he said. "We talk often. I guess you could say we're friends."

"On second thought," Rachel said, stopping at the top of the stairs. "Why don't you reinforce the defenses around the mansion, ensure they're up to snuff. I can handle this myself."

"I can do my job, boss," Warren said.

"Depending on how she answers, things might turn ugly in there, Davis," Rachel said, climbing down the stairs. "If she's your friend, I'd never ask you to do that. I respect you too much to ask. Now do what I ordered and ensure the perimeter is secured. That's an order."

"Alright," Warren said, stopping mid flight of stairs.

Rachel made her way to the front door and circled around the large mansion. She saw the house she'd had built for the older woman with one of the guards she had put on guard duty to make sure she didn't wander off from her solitary confinement. She stopped in front of him. "You," she said. "Come inside with me and follow every order to a T. Is that understood? You are to reveal nothing to anyone, under the pain of death. Is that understood?"

"Yes, ma'am," the young guard said, stepping aside.

"I'll go first." Rachel knocked on the door. "Elizabeth," she called out. "We need to have a little chat."

"One minute, dear," Elizabeth said from inside. She finally opened the door and noticed the two outside. "I'm just preparing some tea. Would you or the junior member enjoy some?"

"No," Rachel said. "We're here on business."

"Let's head into the living area," she said. She entered the kitchen and removed the tea bag from the cup. She tossed it into the nearby trash bin before leading the pair into the living room and sitting down. "Now, what's the problem, dear niece?" She gestured for both to sit.

"You stand watch and repeat nothing you hear in here," Rachel said, sitting across from Elizabeth. She leaned forward and clasped her hands. "I assume you had a hand in ordering this debacle."

"A hand in what, dear?" Elizabeth asked, taking a sip from the steaming cup. "I've been stuck out here for the past few days. You know that better than anyone. I couldn't make a move if I wanted, which I never would disobey you, boss."

"Uh huh," Rachel said. "Just like with Bernard, yeah?"

"Digging up ancient history now, are we?" Elizabeth asked.

"You had your own father killed and used the man you loved to do it. I put nothing past you, not even using your own son and my children."

"Those are some heavy accusations to be making with no proof, dear," Elizabeth said. "First off, how would I manage? I'm stuck here. The only folks I talk to are guards like our guest here." She noticed the sweating young guard desperately trying to find a place to rest his gaze. "They just ask if I need anything."

"Uh huh," Rachel said. "You." She looked at the young man. "Did those teenagers enter in recent days? I'm referring to my son Roger and her son, Bernard? You know who I'm talking about."

"Don't scare the poor young man," Elizabeth said.

"Answer the question," Rachel said.

"To my knowledge, they never entered here, ma'am," the guard said.

"You're sure about that? Think real hard on that answer. Lives hang in the balance."

"Ooh, so mysterious and intriguing how you word that," Elizabeth chuckled into her teacup.

"You're positive the boys didn't bribe you to look the other way? You'd better answer me honestly. The penalty for lying straight to my face is death." She narrowed her eyes at the young man and gave him an intense glare.

"He said no," Elizabeth said. "You're going to give the kid a heart attack, scaring him so much."

"They did not come in here, ma'am."

"See?" Elizabeth said. "You heard it from your guard yourself."

"Phones and emails still exist." Rachel turned her attention back to the aging woman across from her. "I know you like to pretend you're tech illiterate like a grandma, but we both know that's some horse shit. You know as much as I do. It wouldn't be hard for me to get the tech division to investigate your digital traffic."

"Go right ahead, dear," Elizabeth said. "I've been using this vacation to catch up on my soap operas. Oh, did you know Trevelyan is getting back together with Ophelia? I can't wait for the new season of Calendars. I spend little time on my computer. It gives me headaches if I'm on it too long."

"You're just going to sit here and lie to me, huh?"

"You're getting paranoid, dear," Elizabeth said with a polite chuckle. "Trust me, I've been there. Being the head of a major crime syndicate makes one less trusting, but there's one caveat to that, niece. You're supposed to trust your family above all else. You're heading down a dark road of paranoia. I saw Daddy endure the same curse before his unfortunate passing."

"Before you had him killed."

"That's a dirty rumor," Elizabeth said. "Don't scare the young guard so much. I'd never harm my father."

"Oh sure," Rachel said, clearly not believing her. "You." She pointed at the guard. "What's your name?"

"My name is Kyle Evans, Ms. Morris." Kyle barely got the words out without stuttering.

"Well, Kyle Evans, you're going to be on my watch list now. I want you to stand back outside. Don't think I'm done with you yet. You'd better not run. Is that clear?"

"Crystal clear, Ms. Morris," Kyle said, keeping his back straight and giving a salute.

"Now get out of here," she said.

Kyle didn't need to be told twice and ran toward the cottage's door quickly.

"You scared the poor thing half to death," Elizabeth said. "I feel bad for him."

"We both know he's involved," Rachel said after the door closed. "I know they were in here."

"Do you now?"

"Every television has a small camera." Rachel stood and walked over to the muted television. "This one's right here." She placed her finger at the top of the television in the middle, where a tiny black dot could be seen.

"You saw them in here?"

"I saw them in here," Rachel said. "Now either they snuck inside, or Kyle or one of his cohorts let them in here. I know which option I find more likely. I know they were in here and then right afterward they disobeyed me again. We're lucky Ben was there to haul them in and keep them from killing themselves." She paced in front of the older gangster. "It always ends up leading back to you, I find. Now why is that?"

"All I did was give the boys encouragement like any proper mother."

"I don't think so," Rachel said. "In fact, I know so. I didn't come here on a fishing expedition. That's where you're making a critical mistake."

"You don't come in without evidence," Elizabeth said. "I assume if it has a camera, it has a microphone."

"Don't you love smart televisions? You can tell them to switch channels using voice, but it comes with a devastating price - and that's your privacy if experts know how to tune in. I ordered the remaining tech division to do just that. You want to admit you were lying to my face earlier? We both know what happens when you lie to the boss. It's not good for you."

"You're going to do what, exactly?" Elizabeth placed her empty teacup on the table in front of her and stood up. She planted her hands on her hips. "You're going to kill me or something? We both know your teenagers and a lot of the members would revolt."

"Better than having you work against me behind the scenes, I'd imagine," Rachel said. "At least then I wouldn't have to deal with this bullshit anymore."

"You'd be wise to consider all possibilities," Elizabeth said. "If you kill blood family members, this whole Syndicate goes to shit. No one will trust you, and this organization will crumble. Think about what you're doing carefully, dear, for your children if no one else," she said.

"Don't try to threaten me, old woman," Rachel said. "Your time's up, even if you cannot realize it. The era of the gangster from your era is finished. I know you ordered this risky venture. I know you are trying to angle it so your son takes over if anything happens to me. You think you've been sly, but I see right through you and your schemes."

"My boy is the rightful heir, and you know it," Elizabeth said. "What? Is the adopted child from some gangbanger and his baby mama meant to play the face of the Morris Syndicate? Your father would roll over in his grave."

Rachel's hand moved faster than her brain. She slapped Elizabeth hard across the face. "Grandfather never taught you when to shut your big mouth. I knew that already," she said.

Elizabeth spat down on the glass coffee table, tinging it red where it landed. "You little brat. I can't believe you'd hit me."

"You're lucky I don't do worse," Rachel said. "Nobody bad mouths my son."

"He's not your son though, is he?" Elizabeth smirked. "You kidnapped him and stole him away."

"I kept him from growing up in a ghetto and joining some low life street gang where he'd die by age twenty."

"Smashing job on keeping him out of the life of crime," Elizabeth said. "The only difference is, if you hadn't interfered, he'd be with his actual family, and they wouldn't be dead." Elizabeth stepped forward toward her niece. "You like to pretend I'm a monster, but sweetheart, look in the mirror one of these mornings." She poked a finger into Rachel's chest and locked gazes with the younger woman. "You bring more misery to those you claim to love than your father and I ever did. The apple doesn't fall too far from the family tree. My Bernard is the rightful heir to keep it in the Morris family, and you know it as well as I do, unless you want to pass it to Crystal."

"To think you'd keep pushing this even now," Rachel slapped her hand away. "You must want me to harm you more. Why? To go crying to your son and use him as a tool to assassinate me too? It wouldn't be out of your fucking wheelhouse, now would it? You used Roger the same way."

"Just like you used that boy Ben to kill your father," Elizabeth answered in a moment.

Rachel took a step back. "What? I would never," she said.

"Can the denial act, princess," Elizabeth said. "I can put two and two together." She walked over to the window pointing away from the mansion. "Your husband was on ammunition duty that night, wasn't he? No need to answer. We both know I'm correct." Elizabeth turned around, her nose held high. "It was ingenious - really it was. He'd have carte blanche to run around the mansion at will. The gunfire outside would cover the loathsome deed, and he could escape and have a good excuse for no one seeing him. He was also injured, so he could play the tough hero that overcame pain to help the syndicate," she said, quivering her lip for effect. "Isn't that a grand tale to inform the peons? Like I said, it was a genius move - one I'd have devised."

"We are nothing alike," Rachel shook her head, though her voice wavered.

"Give it up, princess." Elizabeth sidled toward her with a cocky grin. "At least admit it to yourself, if no one else. You're no better than I am or your father. You use everyone to further your own ends, noble as they may be sometimes, or contemptible at other times. Obviously you learned how to gain your desires, and that's not terrible. Just don't act all holier than thou. It doesn't play for gangsters like us."

"It's not true," Rachel said. "I only do what I do for my family. I don't do it for power over others like you."

"Merely a means to an end, princess." Elizabeth stopped a few feet away and leaned in closer to her niece. "You already know that, though. You're in denial. It's not a good look. It's better to be honest with yourself."

She reached out and pushed Elizabeth's shoulder, shoving her back a few feet while backing away. "I don't want my child in this. He's just stubborn, that's all. You're putting yours in harm's way for your own gain. I'm trying to stop mine. We're different."

"Whatever you've got to tell yourself to sleep at night," Elizabeth said. "How's his job progressing? Is the bastard dead at least? The sooner Mikhail's dead, the sooner this war ends, and we can return to business as usual."

"Ben stopped them from getting themselves killed. You will know by morning, I suppose." She turned and moved toward the door. "Don't expect to leave anytime soon, and remember, we're always watching and listening. If you say something out of line to Roger or Crystal, I'll know. You will not survive. You want to test me and prove yourself right? Do it. If you believe you're right, you know I'd kill you without batting an eyelash."

"Death threats? So pedestrian," Elizabeth said. "I'm an old woman. That threat doesn't hold near so much weight as it once did."

"Shall I end you right now, then?" Rachel reached down to her belt and pulled a pistol out of its holster. She extended her arm and pointed the barrel toward Elizabeth before pulling the hammer back with a click. "How about it?"

"You either have someone in the tech room watching your ass right now to put that on camera, or it's empty," Elizabeth said. Her smile was gone, now replaced with a straight face. She raised a trembling hand up in front of her. "Lee is gone, isn't he?"

"He's with my dear husband," Rachel said. "No one's inside watching, and little old me knows how to delete video evidence. Isn't that grand, old woman?"

"Do what you desire. I will not beg my niece for my life. I have my dignity still," she said.

"You haven't had dignity since you were eighteen, I imagine," Rachel said. "Fine, I'll do as you say."

"You will? Do it already!" Elizabeth yelled. "Do it!"

The room was silent after the calling of Rachel's bluff. Rachel's arms swayed slightly and trembled, pointing at the older gangster. A click was heard. Elizabeth visibly flinched and turned away.

"No, I'm not stupid enough to kill you face to face," Rachel said. "I'm smarter than that," she said. "It would cast suspicion on me if I did." She holstered her weapon and laughed a genuine chuckle. "You'll live another day, old woman. Count your blessings and know when you're outmatched." She let loose and laughed without abandon.

"Have a pleasant sleep, boss," Elizabeth said in a monotone voice. "I'd hate to see anything happen to the matriarch."

"Oh, I know you would. Sleep well." Rachel approached the door of the cottage and exited without further incident.

17

"You three still with us?" Lee asked. He looked over his shoulder behind their car at the vehicle following them.

"We're with you," Bernard said over the call. "How much farther is it?"

"It looks like this parking garage approaching on our right is where he pulled in and left it."

"I assume he stole another car and left quick," Ben said. "It'd be my plan if I knew how to hot wire a car. He'd have his pick of the cars and could pick out a nice old one to hot-wire. We're going inside. You all find a place to park outside unless you favor spending money for no reason."

"We're heading inside with you," Bernard said. "Pocket change doesn't concern us."

"What if he's lurking inside?" Lee asked. "We can't just drive up on him. He'd start shooting."

"One," Ben said, pulling up to the tollbooth, raising a finger, "he's not in here still, I bet." He lowered the driver's side window, took out the required money, and handed it over to the employee inside. The gate raised, and he brought the car inside the man-made parking haven. "Two," he said, raising another finger, "we need to be close enough for you to access the camera feeds so we can find what car he commandeered. Then we can track him and finally end him."

"Same playbook as before?" Lee asked. "At least this time it should prove easier since we know where he started from. Alright, fine," he said. "It shouldn't take longer than an hour to figure out where he fled from this parking garage, even if it's only me searching."

"Which it wouldn't be," Crystal said.

"Then make it half an hour," Lee said.

"Where does our tracker say the bike's located? I mean, what level in particular?" Ben asked. "I'm not seeing it here on the first level."

"He wouldn't want to steal on the first level," Bernard said. "He'd be in plain eyesight of the employee. I'd want to be at least on the second floor."

"The tracker says the bike is above us," Lee said. "I don't have specifics on altitude, but ascend floor by floor and I'll be able to tell swiftly."

"Works for me," Ben said. He turned the car to climb up the ramp, heading to the next level, and emerged onto a new floor with what looked like brand new cars.

"Still another floor up. It's not on this floor," Lee said.

Ben went up another floor and met an interesting discovery once they were there. "Would you look at that?" he asked.

"What?" Lee asked, looking at the screen. "It's parked on this floor."

"I figured as much," Ben said. "Look." He pointed out the front window. "There's a bloody bandage of sorts over there," he said.

"Looks more like duct tape," Lee said. "Oh hey, look. There's the bike he abandoned, and you're right. It doesn't look like he's here."

"He's a professional and would know not to loiter," Ben said. "He's probably at one of Oleg's properties getting that wound tended to. It makes no difference to us. I'm going to pull into a nearby parking spot and you can start working," he said before pulling into an empty spot nearby and turning off the engine. "Get to work, buddy."

"I'm on it," Lee said. "I'm leeching off a nearby Wi-Fi network, so let's see here," he said. "This should be the camera, judging by the model number, location, and looks. Now, give me a few minutes."

"At least we know you hit him," Roger said. "Is there much blood?"

"Looked like a decent amount of it," Ben said. "I assume he had to change the dressings since he took the time to do it. It means he's careful and worried about it. If only I hadn't waited that extra half second, he'd have gotten that chest shot."

"It might have been a blessing in disguise, Father," Crystal said. "Think about it. A vest covers the front and back of your abdomen, but its protection is sorely lacking in the side department. You probably did some real damage, depending on how high or low you fired."

"He still seemed mobile, and he's alive if he's disappeared this adeptly."

"Possibly," Crystal said. "I was just trying to be positive."

"This fucker is resilient," Bernard said. "Not everybody could shrug off a bullet and drive off using duct tape as wrapping. It would require balls of steel to try."

"Or he had no choice," Ben said. "He's running scared."

"I downloaded the video files from every surveillance

camera, including the last three hours of footage, to be safe. Return us back to the mansion and I'll find where this fucker ran."

"You heard the man. We're heading back home to your mothers."

"I'm sure we're going to get a nice earful, aren't we?" Roger asked.

"Possibly, depending on how she reacts to what I have to say," Ben said. "To your credit, you followed my commands for once. You didn't keep walking when I told you to stop. You followed my commands to a T, and you did your part. I'll tell her you were following my orders tonight. Aren't you lucky your father is such a nice guy?"

"You're damned right they're lucky," Lee said. "Sometimes I wonder if you're too nice, sir," he said.

"That's a phrase I haven't heard nigh on twenty years, Lee," Ben said, backing out of the spot. "Now she'll still be miffed, make no mistake, but I don't think you'll be confined to quarters. I'll make that case for you all if you make me a promise."

"What's that?" Roger asked.

"You know what? What's the point?" Ben asked. "You already promised you wouldn't before and look at you two troublemakers. You did it again. Maybe I should let her. Maybe some quality time to reflect on your actions would change them."

"Seriously?" Roger asked.

"We'll see how I feel when we get back."

18

"It's good to hear from you," Artyom said over the phone. "I was worried when I heard about earlier tonight."

Mikhail was lying on a table with paper on it. Muffled techno music thumped in the background. An older man wearing gloves was at his side, treating the wound. "They got me good, sir, but I'm prepared to do what was ordered."

"Define got you good," Artyom said. "I don't need a half dead man hobbling through the forest and trying one of the most ambitious assassinations of this country's history."

"How bad is it, Doc?" Mikhail asked.

The Doctor had a thick Russian accent. "You're lucky you didn't bleed out on the way here. What is this a remnant of? Duct tape?"

"You use what you have handy," Mikhail said.

"The bullet didn't penetrate too deeply, it looks like," the doctor said. "I got it out already. I'm just checking for any parts that may have broken off. You'll be sore for a few days, but it looks like you'll be fine."

"See?" Mikhail said into the phone. "He says I'm fine. I

can do this, boss. I'll volunteer to be the assassin to perform this monumentally important job. It's personal."

"You always did like your high-profile jobs, and this one doesn't get much higher," Artyom said. "If you're still good to go, then your target is still Elizabeth Morris. Intel says she's in a small cottage outside the main mansion. This is ancient intel, mind you," he said. "They built that thing years ago for her to live in. She may not be there. It could be far more dangerous than you're expecting. I don't want you rushing this job."

"I never do," Mikhail said. "That's a quick method to getting yourself killed."

"Strenuous activity is not advised though," the doctor said.

"That's not going to stop me. Make sure you disinfect it, and I'll return for a follow up," Mikhail said.

"You have weapons for this?" Artyom asked. "That entire house was blown to smithereens according to the survivors I talked to. That was a heavy blow for sure."

"I'm at your nightclub in town right now," Mikhail said. "I'm taking a rifle and scope. That's all. I won't need much if the intel's right. If it's not, I'll return another day and take everything I need. Think of tonight as a scouting trip. Maybe we'll get lucky, maybe we won't; but we won't know until we look personally."

"We know Elizabeth Morris is advising Rachel. She's had far more experience with wars, and Rachel's been fighting back commendably well for a leader during her first war. If we kill her advisor, things become easier. The fate of this whole war rests on you," Artyom said. "Do not take unnecessary risks, and always plan an escape route."

"She's a doddering old gangster in her seventies,"

Mikhail said with a hiss of pain as the doctor set to disinfecting the wound. "How hard could she be to hit?"

"She's also lived through more assassination attempts than almost anybody, so you're trekking on well tread ground. Do not underestimate that woman. Many have, and they're all dead and buried. Just ask the Irish Mafia family of New York, the Enforcers, or any of the many street gangs she's warred with in the past. She's slippery."

"I understand. I'll be heading there this morning after I get out of Doc's grasp." Mikhail looked out the nearby window at the morning light peeking through the blinds. "Painkillers would be nice too, Doc."

"I don't want you intoxicated on the job. Don't take any pills before you leave," Artyom said.

"They're for sleeping after the job, sir," Mikhail said.

"They better be. I don't want your head clouded. Your full effort will be required."

"It's personal now, sir," Mikhail said. "The fuckers shot me. No one's ever landed a shot on me before. I can't let that stand, can I? What's the desired approach vector?"

"I'd recommend the south side. It has a large hill that should give you an acceptable view of the cabin where she's staying. Stay on the ground once you're there." Artyom said. "There are trees everywhere around that would give you a higher altitude, but it'd be tougher to make your escape if you go that route, especially with that wound. You're going to need to exit quickly once you've made your kill shot. They're regimented and disciplined. They'll rush out like a pack of hornets that you just kicked the nest of."

"You're making this job sound more and more appealing." Mikhail leaned forward in the chair at the doctor's behest. He watched as the doctor wrapped the cloth around his body, dressing the wound.

"I can never tell if you're acting sarcastic. I can do this myself if you'd prefer. It's been a while since I've had to, but if you don't want the job, I'll do it myself."

"No," Mikhail said in a firm voice. "I've got this."

"There are probably patrols inside the fence, but they should not prove an issue. Are there questions?" Artyom asked.

"I can't think of any. I'll call once it's done."

"Good," Artyom said. "If you'll excuse me, I have business to attend to. As always, destroy that phone, and good luck, Ghost. You'll need it for this one."

"I don't need such a thing as luck, but I appreciate it, sir." Mikhail hung up after he heard the line click. He looked over at the doctor. "You know what will happen if you repeat a word to anyone, yes?"

"Mr. Artyom was clear when I was put on call," the doctor said. "You'd all send me back to Russia in pieces I believe were the exact words."

"Good, then we have an understanding."

The doctor finished wrapping the wound site and secured it. "You should be fine if you take the antibiotics I gave you earlier. Did you still want the painkillers?" He removed the needle that was stuck in Mikhail's wrist and gingerly wrapped it, too.

"For sleep tonight, yes I would," Mikhail said.

The doctor stood up from the rolling stool and reached into his pocket. He tossed the small bottle to his patient. "There, that should ease the pain to sleep, but you shouldn't be doing whatever job you spoke of. It's not recommended with your injuries. You'll be in agonizing pain just laying down, never mind running."

"Pain is weakness leaving the body, as they say here in America. If we cannot stand it, we're ruled by it." He stood and placed a hand on the nearby table he had just been laying on to steady himself. "Did I lose more blood than I thought?"

"Why do you think I had this blood bag connected to you?" The doctor pointed toward the bag of blood hanging from the IV. Clients rarely bleed that length of time from a bullet wound and insist on gallivanting the same day.

"I'm not your normal man."

A little later that morning...

"I assume since you're all here, you have news." Rachel looked up from her work to watch Ben, Crystal, Roger, and Bernard entering her office. "What happened last night? Why were you all out? I assume my dear husband has a good reason for what he did?"

Warren had an amused face watching the proceedings, but was wise enough to keep his mouth quiet.

"We found him," Ben said. "I needed the boys' help on even flushing him out. It would have been suicide had I tried to infiltrate the building. Someone had to flush out the rats from hiding. I kept them safe and even got a shot off."

"I notice you didn't lead with him being dead," Rachel said. "He's not dead, is he?"

"Negative," Ben said. "He's slippery, but I got him good. We found bloody duct tape in a parking garage inside the city. He ditched the bike he escaped on and stole another in there."

"Do we know where he is now?"

Ben turned around. "Crystal, you want to explain this part? You know the technical details better than I do."

Crystal stepped forward. "We used the traffic camera footage again, but it was easier this time since we knew where he came out of and what car he stole. He's driving a white pickup truck, old by the looks of it. We followed him all the way to a club with some weird ass name."

"Probably one of Oleg's hideouts," Warren said. "If he got winged, he'd be looking for medical attention and more weapons."

"He didn't have weapons other than possibly a pistol when he made his escape," Ben said.

"Anyway, we've been monitoring that specific camera by utilizing a livestream of sorts so we could watch it in real time. About fifteen minutes ago, he left that club. We were following the truck through the city, but he exited the city out of our view. There's just one minor detail," Crystal said, holding up her thumb and index finger for effect.

"Do tell," Rachel said.

"He didn't leave the city in the same direction as before. He exited the city and was headed in this direction." Crystal bit her lip. "We don't know where he's headed, but I have an idea on how we can end this permanently."

"You want to set a trap for him?"

"It'd be nice to hit him before he hits us," Ben said. "I can spearhead the team. Hell, I'll do it myself. I know what car he's driving."

"You're just going to ram him or something?"

"I was going to gauge the situation and do what's needed," Ben said. "It's better than letting him have free rein. He could set up in those woods." He pointed out the window behind Rachel. "I will not take that chance."

"Do what you think is best. Warren, Roger, Bernard, Crystal, you are all dismissed. I have something I need to speak with my husband about privately." She waited for everyone to leave the office before she walked around the desk. "You be careful out there."

"I always am. Now I better hurry, honey. What did you need to speak to me about before I hunted Mikhail?"

"Elizabeth sent the boys out there. I have proof on the camera in her place."

"That bitch," Ben said. "We'll deal with her after this, though." He laid his hands on his wife's shoulders and leaned in for a kiss. "I can't let this guy get close to you or any of us."

"I'll let everyone know to stay away from the windows," Rachel said. "Well, most everyone. Would kind of be nice if he took her old ass out, if I'm being completely honest. It'd save me the headache."

"You do what you feel is best." He gave her a quick hug and backed away toward the door. "I've got work to do, if you'll excuse me."

"Be careful!" she yelled as he exited the door.

Meanwhile...

"Where are you headed?" Roger asked, trying to catch up with Bernard, who was frantically running through corridors toward the stairs. "Hold up a minute, man." He nearly collided with a young man coming out of his quarters, but Roger's quick thinking enabled him to duck to the side and avoid a collision.

"I'm warning Mom," Bernard called over his shoulder.

"I'm coming too," Roger pushed himself into overdrive and caught up with his friend. They slowed down once they came to the bottom of the stairs.

Bernard led him toward the mansion's back exit. "We'll just ignore the asshole Kyle this time and save some money. We'll go in the back. Follow my lead and be quick." He wasted no time and led his friend out into the backyard.

They descended the steps and came to the nearby corner. Bernard peeked around the side. "Come on," he whispered to his side. He ducked low and hurried.

They bypassed Kyle with no problem and reached the back of Elizabeth's cottage. Bernard reached into his pocket to retrieve a key and unlocked it. He opened the door, and the pair entered Elizabeth's cabin...

19

Ben drove down the road near the mansion. He hadn't been looking long; it was his second trip down the familiar road. He knew the winding turns, becoming accustomed over the last almost twenty years. As he turned around a bend, his blood ran cold. A white pickup truck was sitting by the side of the road. He knew the Syndicate's mansion was only a mile away. "He's walking through the woods to get there. Smart," he said.

He stopped near the truck and got out with his pistol at the ready. Though he didn't think he was still inside, safety never hurt. He flung the door open and saw no one inside. "Shit," he said. He leaned down and pulled out his knife, then stabbed every tire before running back to his own car and getting his rifle out. Keeping it at the ready, he started his trek through the woodland toward the mansion.

He's out here somewhere, he thought to himself. *Is his target Rachel? It could be me or Davis. Hell, it might even be Roger. I can't let this maniac reach the mansion. They're all counting on me to take this guy down.*

The underbrush crunched as he quickly made his way.

He was wary of going too fast and giving away his location, but something deep in his gut forced his feet to move faster and faster. *I can't let him get there. I just can't.*

He sped up his pace, making even more noise. He knew these backwoods intimately, but he knew he could walk into a trap with the amount of noise he was making. Seeing no signs of his target, he marched on.

Lucky break, he thought to himself. He kneeled and saw a footprint embedded in the mud. *He went this way. At least I know I'm on the right track.* He followed the footprints in that direction and kept his pistol at the ready. His pace slowed, trying not to make much noise.

Every passed tree brought forth numbers of new potential hiding spots to gauge immediately. His eyes wildly danced around, his neck barely able to keep up with his frantic motions. His mind was full of different ideas swirling, the most prominent scenario being that he might already be in the scopes of his prey. He stopped and leaned his shoulder on a tree. He peeked around, getting a grip on exactly where he was geographically and where Mikhail would choose.

Where would I go to blow off our heads? Ben thought to himself. *I should be getting close.*

He pointed the pistol down toward the ground and used his other hand to pull out his phone. Pulling up his location, he saw he was just south of their property now, maybe half a mile. *He's looking for the highest location near here to make his shot. I'd bet my life. Something that has some brush.* The land below his feet started sloping upward, heading toward the mansion. *He has the advantage*, Ben thought. *I'm in his element now, and I know it. This is foolish to even try.*

He shook his head and shoved the phone back in his pocket. He gripped the pistol in both hands until his knuckles were white. *No choice about it*, he reasoned to himself. He turned the corner and resumed his lone patrol in the wilderness. He was almost at the top of the nearby hill. I *remember this hill*, Ben thought. *It almost became Elizabeth's cottage, but she insisted on being closer to the damn house. Of course he'd pick here. It has a stunning view of the mansion below. Perfect place.*

With every moment, every step, Ben felt dread gnawing at his stomach. His feet did not yield, continuing to bring him to the top of the hill. *There's a plateau here,* he thought. He readied his pistol and got to his knees, crawling toward the top. As he crested the hill with his elbow, he pulled himself forward along with the sound of sliding grass beneath.

He didn't spot Mikhail in any of the few trees, and he didn't see anyone standing. He scanned a few dozen feet away in an open patch. Ben squinted. He saw a patch of grass seem to move. *Don't tell me.* Ben got to his feet and aimed down his gun's sights. He stepped slowly, watching his feet before glancing back at the lump on the ground. His hands trembled as he grew closer. He was within maybe ten feet and had a better view of his target. He raised up his weapon.

The exposed barrel of the rifle roared to life. It kicked back into its wielder.

Ben fired almost like a reflex to the gunshot erupting as he ran to the side and ducked behind a tree. Parts of it came apart beside his head, raining wood down in front of him. He ducked and waited until the bullets stopped coming.

Risking it, he sprang from cover, weapon pointed toward Mikhail's last known location. He could hear a young man's voice nearby, yelling loudly as he moved forward.

"Shot fired on the south side of the mansion! I repeat, shots fired out here! I think they got her!"

Ben heard a click to his side. He dove with reckless abandon forward and heard the gunshot go off. His dive allowed him a chance to fire to his side. He saw his ambusher hiding behind a different tree than he remembered. He chose the course of action that came naturally as he squeezed the trigger as many times as he could manage toward this threat, center mass.

A sharp pain radiated out from his hip as he landed with a thud. "Ah." His left hand fell to the wound. He snapped back toward Mikhail and saw him on the ground. His chest was still moving, but he was flat on his back.

Rapid footsteps drew closer from what he could hear over the accursed ringing inside his ears, along with the same voice from before. He was close. "Over here," he called out.

Ben heard wheezing and what could be described as desperate sucking. Mikhail desperately gathered what little oxygen his lungs could retrieve. The wheezing gave way to coughing, and Mikhail stood, clutching both hands to his chest.

He ejected the empty magazine from his handgun and scrambled for another, rushing to escape death once more. He saw Mikhail reaching for his sidearm as he jammed the spare magazine inside and reached for the slide.

Mikhail's barrel was already facing him.

Ben's eyes widened in realization as another gunshot rang, ending the contest finally.

"Holy fuck," were the words the interloper said. He looked down at the formerly intact skull of the former Moscow Ghost and over toward Ben. "Mr. Adams? What are you doing out here?"

"I was hunting this bastard," Ben said. "Why aren't you inside, Evans?"

Kyle looked back at the dead guy. His head was pieces now. Brain matter was lying on the forest floor, marring the once beautiful landscape into a macabre display of death and blood. "I heard a gunshot, sir," he said. "I wanted to see if I could track the fucker who shot inside our cabin."

"He shot the cabin?" Ben tried to look past Kyle and back toward the mansion. "Oh no," he said. "Call for medical assistance and have it sent out there right this second, Evans. Now means now."

"I understand, sir." He pulled out his phone, nearly dropping it from the sweat coating his bare hands.

"We'll take care of Mikhail's body, or what's left," Ben said. "Get two groups of medical. One for me, and one for Elizabeth in there if she's hit."

"Yes, we need a medical team on the south side and one for Miss Elizabeth's cabin. One's already on route to the cabin? Good. We need one sent to the ridge overlooking the cabin. Mr. Adams has been shot up here. Yes, please hurry." He hung up and filed the device away. He hurried over to his boss, took off his jacket, and pressed the cloth against Ben's injury. "Sorry. I know this hurts, but we need pressure on it."

"You have a wife, Evans?" Ben asked with a hiss of pain.

"Sir?"

"Answer the question."

"No, sir." Kyle kept the pressure on the wound on Ben's hip.

"That's a fortunate thing for you, because she'd kill you if she saw you bloodying up that jacket."

"Some things are worth more than mere objects, sir," Kyle said. He looked over his shoulder and raised a hand

and his voice. "Up here!" He turned back to Ben. "They're almost here, sir. How are you feeling?"

"I have a shooting pain in my hip. How do you think I feel?"

"You're strong enough for comedy, so I guess you're fine."

"Hopefully the bullet either went through or it's shallow. If not, this'll prove dangerous," Ben said.

"A hip shot? You'll probably be fine after a week or two of rest."

"We're in war, Evans. There is no week of rest."

"I guess you're making time for it then, because you're not getting up soon with this…"

20

Rachel and Warren were on the floor, away from her large window. "What the fuck was that?" she asked.

"Sounded like a gunshot set off a bunch more. I'd wager your husband found Mikhail out there. It didn't come from the range."

"I should have never sent him out there alone." Rachel heard the phone on her desk ring. She crawled over and reached up. She stayed seated at the side of the desk as she spoke. "Yes?"

"Ma'am, we found your husband out on the south side of the property with a young man named Kyle Evans. He's been shot, but Mr. Evans' quick thinking has prevented a lot of blood loss. We're moving him to the medical ward as we speak if you want to see him. We've also dispatched a medical team to the cabin in case anyone else was hit."

"What about the shooter? Was there another body?"

"Yes, ma'am," the male voice said. "It's not clear who shot him, but we've confirmed it is, or rather was, Mikhail, the former ghost of Moscow. His head has been blown off. We're gathering the body for disposal as we speak."

"I'm heading there now." Rachel stood and hung up. She looked at Warren below the window. "Mikhail's dead, and Ben's shot. I'm heading to medical to see him. You're welcome to join me." She didn't wait for his answer as she started walking.

"Wait for me," Warren jumped up and struggled to catch up. "Mikhail's dead?"

"That's right," Rachel said. She pushed open the double doors and hurried down the corridor. This time her cell phone rang in her pocket. "Who now, and what's so important?" She dug out her phone and fielded another call. "Yes?"

"Mom?" Roger asked.

"Roger? What is it?"

"We need a medical team out in Elizabeth's cabin. Oh God," he said. "It's bad."

"How do you know that? Are you out there? Don't tell me you were outside when those shots were fired!"

"If it's not one thing, it's another," Warren muttered to himself.

"A team's on the way, Son. Just stay out of their way. Now, where was she hit? Can you put pressure on the wound?"

"Not really," Roger said. "It hit her in the head."

"Oh," Rachel said. "Then don't mess with her head or neck. There might still be a chance. You watch the door. I assume Bernard is with his mother, so you need to be the strong one of you two. He's counting on you. Let him be with her."

"Okay." Quick footsteps from Roger could be heard over the phone. "They're here. I've got to go." The phone call ended suddenly.

By this point, Rachel and Warren were nearly at the medical area they used as a ward. "That was Roger," she said to Warren. "Those two boys snuck out and went to Elizabeth's cabin again."

"It didn't sound like anything pleasant happened."

"No," Rachel said. "It didn't. Elizabeth's been shot in the head. She's dead, I imagine. I couldn't bring myself to tell him the cold, hard truth."

"She was the target?" Warren asked. "Odd choice if I'm honest."

"Not really," Rachel said, turning the last corner. "They know she's experienced leading a syndicate in wartime, and they knew she was an advisor. It makes logical sense. They bet it would put me in chaos and clench the war for them."

"Little did they know you've had her in solitary for the past few days, getting no advice; and we were still breaking their backs." Warren slowed down with his boss as they approached a man outside the ward, standing guard.

"The doctor's not present, ma'am," the guard said. "He should arrive inside a few minutes."

"He'd better fucking hurry," Rachel said. "Let me in to see my husband. Now!"

"Right away, ma'am." The guard side stepped and let her pass.

"I'll stay here and give you two privacy, shall I?" Warren asked.

Rachel closed the door behind and noticed the beds lining the walls. A farther room inside was clearly labeled Operating Room, but it was currently closed.

She saw her husband lying on the nearest bed to her left and rushed to his side, careful to not mess with the IV's set up containing blood connected to him. "Oh my God." She stood towering over Ben and leaned down, placing her hands on the side of the bed.

"It looks worse than it is," Ben said. "I promise. You

should see the fool or what's left of his carcass."

"Where were you hit, baby?" Rachel asked.

"My hip," Ben said with a grunt. "It's a result of my foolish attempt to dodge and shoot at the same time. I'm just lucky I dodged, because that shot would've hit me somewhere worse if I hadn't dove. Was Elizabeth hit in the cabin? No one ever told me. I saw her window was shot through, but little else."

"I'm going to kill that Kyle Evans kid," Rachel said. "He allowed the boys inside Elizabeth's cabin again."

"The boys were in there?" Ben's voice was frantic now. "Are they alright?"

"They're fine." Rachel rested a hand on Ben's forehead and tried to keep him from sitting up. "Now rest up."

"Kyle did nothing wrong, though," Ben said, calming down again.

"Why do you say that? His job was to guard the cabin and allow no one entry."

"Yes," Ben said. "I can guarantee he was guarding the front entrance. I know because I heard him yelling about a shooter when it popped off. He's also the sole reason I'm in this room and not being prepped for burial."

"What?"

"He was the member who secured the kill shot on Mikhail, barely in the nick of time I might add. Mikhail was raising his gun to end me when his head popped like a grape, and I noticed the kid. It was the scariest minute of my whole damned life, but I'd never been as relieved to see any Syndicate member as much as Kyle Evans."

"In the future, if I ever confine anyone there, I'll station more than one guard," Rachel said. "He was the one who shot Mikhail?"

"I saw it clear as day. I was rushing to reload after

emptying my magazine into his chest, which was a rookie mistake because he wore a sturdy vest underneath. Kyle aimed for his head and arrived in time. He also gave me first aid immediately after. I owe him my life, so I'd appreciate if you didn't kill the kid."

"Fine," Rachel said, gingerly sitting down on the side of the bed. "I'll appreciate Mr. Evans a lot more than I did before."

"Good," Ben said. "He's a different breed. Most run away from gunfire. I'm alive because he wanted to chase down the shooter. He's a real go-getter up and comer. I can feel it. Now did he hit anyone in that cabin? You said the boys were fine, but I notice you didn't mention Elizabeth.

"She got shot in her head," Rachel said. "We're pretty sure she's dead."

"Damn," Ben said. "I was too slow to fire my initial shot and now Bernard's lost his mother.

"It's not your fault, sweetness." Rachel used a hand and laid it with great care on the side of Ben's face. "You hunted a sniper in his element, found him, and put him down. No one can blame you for not accomplishing the feat faster."

"I'm not so sure Bernard would agree with that sentiment. He's an orphan now."

"Don't worry about others," Rachel said in a soothing voice. "You focus on getting better after the Doctor arrives. Speaking of which, where is he?"

"He lives like ten minutes away, dear," Ben said. "Unless we house him here, this is the price of a doctor on call."

"Not when it's you, Roger, or Crystal," Rachel said. "I can't be patient then."

The door Rachel entered flew open to reveal a man in casual clothes and a thick pair of glasses. "Sorry about the delay. Is this the one?" He grabbed Rachel's shoulder and got her off the bed. "I need a look at the injury before I do anything else, Ms. Morris. Please move aside."

"You do your job well, Doctor, and everything's fine," Rachel said.

The doctor raised the sheet and saw that Ben's pants had been removed, but he was still wearing underwear underneath the white sheet of the bed. "Oh my," he said. "I'm going to have to ask you to leave, Ms. Morris. This wound needs immediate attention, and I need as few contaminants inside the room as I can manage. Send the nurse in behind you and only him. I'll need his help to move your husband. I don't need a crowd of brutes dirtying everything."

"Right." Rachel backed up toward the door. "You'd better be careful." She exited the room. She spotted an unfamiliar face. "Are you the nurse?" she asked the young man.

"Yes, ma'am."

"Get in there right this minute. The doctor needs you."

The young man hurried past her and went inside the door. She noted the guard who was standing beside the door. "Don't let anyone else inside until the doctor says it's okay. If you switch shifts, relay those orders. No one's allowed inside to contaminate the ward. Is that understood?"

"Crystal clear, ma'am," he said.

"How was he?" Warren asked.

Rachel walked past him. "He seemed fine, but he was shot. It didn't look nice, if that's what you're asking. We need to plan a funeral now."

"The boy won't be happy," Warren said. "Speak of the devil and he shall appear." He nodded down the hall. A large group of members entered the rear door. The pair moved rightward towards the sides of the hallway, making room. Rachel looked back. "Let this group in!"

"Roger that," the guard to the medical ward said, moving aside, gripping the doorknob.

Roger and Bernard trailed behind the procession.

"You two," Rachel said. "You're with me. The doctor's in there, and he wouldn't allow you inside. If there's anyway to save her, he'll find it. Alright?"

Bernard's eyes were red and puffy. He didn't verbally respond.

"Your father is in there too," Rachel said, her voice growing soft. She looked at Roger as she spoke. "He was shot by Mikhail - in the hip."

"Is the guy dead at least?" Roger asked.

"He is indeed," Warren said. "That guard out in front of the cabin was the one who saved your father, from what I'm putting together."

"Guess I'll have to thank him later then," Roger said. "What do we do now?"

"We wait," Rachel said. "It's the hardest thing in the world to hear, but it holds true. We've done all we can. It's in the doctor's hands now. Occupy yourselves however you can for the rest of the day. I'll call either of you if I hear anything. Alright?" Rachel approached Bernard and hugged the stoic, silent young man before turning to her son and embracing him. "We can only pray now. Where is your sister?"

"I don't know," Roger looked around. "She's probably in here somewhere."

Loud footsteps could be heard. Everyone turned and saw her rounding the corner. She slid on the carpet sitting on the hardwood beneath, nearly crashing to the ground as she hurried over to the group. "What happened?"

"I'll explain everything..."

21

A large wreathe had a picture of a younger Elizabeth smiling into the camera. A coffin lay behind the photo. Rows of chairs sat in front of them both. Bernard, Roger, Jackie, Chris, Warren, Crystal and Rachel filled the front row. Syndicate members filled the other rows.

An old preacher walked to the front row and spoke. "We are gathered here today to put another of God's children to rest." The man went on.

Bernard was leaning forward in his seat, staring down at the grass below. He had a hand covering his eyes, trying to not show the tears desperately trying to escape.

Roger placed a hand on his friend's back, not speaking, not daring to interrupt the preacher in front of them. To his left was his sister, Crystal, and his mother was at her side.

"None of us are perfect," the preacher said. "None of us deserves God's forgiveness in the grand scheme of things. However, we're in luck. He is a merciful God. No sin is too grave, except for the sin of rejecting his grace." The sermon continued.

Most in attendance were bowing their heads, showing

respect for the fallen woman. Soft church music was playing alongside the gospel being preached. Wreaths of flowers were adorning the picture and laid on top of the casket.

"We are left wondering why God chose her. Why now? God doesn't intend for us to know the answers to these plaguing questions. We are not privy to God's plans. It may seem unfair, or even cruel, but he has a plan. I know this for a fact. It brings me comfort to know everything happens for a reason. Even if it seems cruel at first. Death is a necessary part of life. I do not pretend to know the Almighty's reasons, and neither should anyone. All we can do is cope with our losses and try to move on. The void we feel in our hearts hurts something fierce. I understand. All we can do is welcome Him into our hearts and trust He'll do right by us. Is there anyone wishing to speak before we continue?"

Bernard stood and walked up to the preacher.

"Ah, Mr. Morris, go ahead."

Bernard turned around, away from the casket. "My mother wasn't exactly the most spiritual person. I don't know what that means regarding this whole service. My mother didn't deserve this fate." Bernard saw many in the crowd nodding along. "She wasn't the nicest woman. She certainly committed more than her fair share of sins. Haven't we all, though? Why did it have to be her?" He composed himself, keeping his voice from breaking. "I've said my piece. I'm done." He moved back to his seat.

"I am sorry, Mr. Morris," the preacher said. "We should find solace in God's holy scripture, not pursuing pleasures of the flesh. I know how tempting getting drunk in a time of unprecedented pain is."

The sermon continued unabated until it reached the end sometime later.

Roger, Warren, Bernard, Kyle, Chris, and Jackie all were

pallbearers. They picked up the casket and held it above their shoulders. They carried it over to the already dug grave and awkwardly lowered it into the hole. The preacher said a few more scriptures and finally dismissed the attendees, leaving just Bernard, Roger, Chris, Jackie, and Rachel.

"I'll get the newer recruits to fill this," Rachel said. "You don't have to worry about it, Bernard."

"I want to fill it in myself, or at least help. It'd give me some closure, I'm hoping."

"Do as you like, but you need rest yourself you know."

"You are not my mother. Sorry," Bernard said after snapping.

"You're going through a rough time. Don't worry about it," Rachel said.

"I'll help as well," Roger said. "I can't leave you by yourself out here."

"Hell, I may as well help then," Chris said. "I'm going to grow too old soon. I may as well use these old bones for something productive."

"Don't tell me you're intending to help?" Rachel turned to Jackie and asked. "I won't need to assign anyone at this rate."

"I will," Jackie said. "She deserves a burial from people she knew."

"I'm going to go check on my husband," Rachel said. "You know where to find me. Bernard, if you ever need to talk, approach me, dear. It's no trouble," she said before turning and heading back to the house.

Chris cracked his knuckles and headed behind the hole. He grabbed a couple of shovels before handing one to each of the volunteers.

Roger and Jackie grabbed one, and everyone got to work.

"You heard anything about your dad?" Chris asked,

looking over at Roger. "You see him after he exited surgery yet?"

"I talked to him this morning before this," Roger said, keeping his eyes on his work. He shoveled another spade full into the hole. "The doctor says he'll make a full recovery. He said he might be slower afterward, but he's fine."

"We all slow in our old age."

"He's almost forty," Jackie said. "He's not pushing sixty like you."

"I never said how old," Chris said. "It's good to hear he's going to be alright. That's something decent resulting from this tragedy."

Bernard took this opportunity to break his silence. "We both saw this happen, you know," he said. "We were inside when Mother got shot. I had barely got the words out when it happened. 'Get away from the window', boom." He piled another heap of dirt on his mother's final resting place. "Next thing I know, she's on the floor and Rog here drags me low."

"Damn," Chris said. "At least you know her killer got what he deserved. That's something. Right?"

"It's what I have," Bernard said. "At least it's better than nothing."

"We'll have this finished before you know it with four members," Chris said. "At least that's something. Then we can return to our apartment."

"I suppose," Bernard said.

Roger gave his friend a long, hard look.

In Rachel's office meanwhile...

"What do you think, Davis?" Rachel asked. "You think Oleg will want this war to end soon? He's lost his ace in the hole, he's lost money laundering businesses, and more than a few personnel. I think he'd be open to negotiate. God knows we could use an end to this war. The heat's rising, and it's getting hard for the rank and file to even walk on the street with all the law enforcement patrolling since this war started."

"It depends on how prideful he is or desperate for money," Warren said. "If he's pressured to create a bunch of return for that Russian investment, he has a plan. I doubt that plan involves an elongated war. He probably wanted to save face on the streets and secure favorable rates."

"Let's hope he isn't stupid enough to think he'd wipe us out." Rachel picked up the phone at her desk.

"Calling and suing for peace?"

"Setting up a meeting. I want a physical meeting, and yes, I'm aware of its inherent dangers. I have contingencies in mind for how we'll plan it safely."

"Let's hope he's in a talking mood," Warren said as she dialed the only number she knew to reach Oleg.

"What do you want?" Oleg asked as soon as he picked up.

"I imagine you're the person to thank for that surprise yesterday," Rachel said.

"Did you enjoy the present? I picked it out special for you. He's a master of his craft, after all."

"So masterful he had his head blown off before he could escape. We thought about feeding his rotting carcass to the dogs, but the canines don't deserve trash for feed. We love our dogs."

Oleg spoke something sharp in Russian. She didn't know what it was, but he didn't sound happy at the news. "Judging by your tone, he wasn't entirely unsuccessful. What's wrong? Did Auntie take a dirt nap today?"

"You want this to continue?" Rachel asked. "I have loads of personnel at the ready. Now you, I doubt you have so much slack looking at this logically."

"Don't assume you know my situation."

"You just received reinforcements, weapons, and, as a corollary, money. Smuggling in that amount of personnel takes lots of capital for briberies, customs, transportation, food, water, etc. The higher ups must believe in your ability," she said. "That's a lot of money to send. Presumably this was to give me a black eye, leave our arrangement, and find more lucrative deals. If you'd like to keep this fighting going, I'm willing to punch blow for blow. I'll burn down every fucking money laundering organization until you have none left. Now, it may cripple us, but it'll outright kill you. No clean money to send back to those old fucks, and suddenly you're replaceable and expendable."

"You presume much," Oleg said. "Who's saying I'm not ready to keep going?"

"You're not as tough and dumb as all that," Rachel said. "You've made your point. No one else is going to stiff you quite as we did. Why keep this pissing match going?"

"What are you proposing?" Oleg asked.

"A meeting tomorrow evening," Rachel said. "Face to face preferably," she said. "I don't want to hash out details over the phone. Just know if you try anything, it won't end well for you."

"I say the same regarding you," Oleg said. "Why would you trust a meetup?"

"I know my men are better fighters than yours," Rachel said. "We both know I possess stronger personnel than you do currently. Other than Artyom, who important do you have remaining? You're running out of personnel and patience. I'm doing you the kindness of backing out of this without further consequences. No other outfits would offer as sweet of a deal, and we both know it. We want to return to making money, same as you."

"That would be the end of it," Oleg said. "We won't deal with you again."

"That's an acceptable term," Rachel said. "We'll nail the rest out tomorrow. I'll have my tech guy send you a location."

The phone call was over as soon as the last sentence left her mouth. "We got us a meeting tomorrow evening, Mr. Davis. I expect the best we have as my guards, including you. I leave the choice in your hands. Scope out the place." Rachel grabbed a nearby notepad before ripping out one page. She grabbed a nearby pen and wrote the address of an old warehouse in the middle of neutral territory. "Scope the place out beforehand. Make sure we position rifles on the roofs. I will have an insurance policy to count on. Is that understood?"

"Nothing will happen to you," Warren said. "I'll make sure of it personally. I'll go gather them now."

"Make it happen," Rachel said, stretching in her chair. "I'm going to go visit my husband. He may be awake now. I wish I could have visited earlier this morning, but Elizabeth's service made it hard." She got up and followed Warren to the doors.

Warren beat her to the door and opened it for her. "I hope he's alright," Warren said. "I bet he'll love to see you."

She watched Warren hurry down the hallway, leaving her to walk at her own pace back to the medical ward. She descended the stairs, and when she reached the bottom, she peeked out a window on her left. Roger, Bernard, Chris, and Jackie were at the grave. "Poor kid," she mumbled to herself.

"I hope Roger has time to see his father. I bet that's where Crystal is."

"You'd be correct, ma'am," Lee said, passing her going up the stairs. "She was last seen headed that way. Have a good day, Ms. Morris."

"Keep working hard, Lee," Rachel called out after the retreating man. "There will be time for rest soon enough, mark my words."

She wasted no more time and rushed over to the medical ward and entered. She could see her husband laying on his back under the white sheet. A steady beep was the only sound other than the rustling of his sheets.

She rushed over. "Don't move," she said in her best soothing voice. "Don't move, honey," she said, reaching his side. She laid a hand on his bare chest and sat beside him on the bed. "You're still in the land of the living, I see. Thank God." Rachel gave a genuine smile.

"Did the doctor say whether I'll walk again?"

"Why wouldn't you be able to walk after a hip injury?"

"I don't know. Hips are connected to my legs physically. I figured it'd affect movement," Ben said, smiling. "Am I alright or not?"

"He said as long as you rest for a month, you'd recover fine. You'll be following that treatment too. I will assign someone to help you out until you do. They'll get you anything you need."

"We're in war," Ben said. "We both know we can't afford to have any personnel sitting here tending to my every beck and whim. Just leave some water by my bed and some snacks. I'll be fine."

"That will not happen," Rachel said, now rubbing her hand over his chest as he lay there under her touch. "I've set up a meeting with Oleg for tomorrow night. This war is going to end."

"What? I can't be lying around while you go out to meet with them."

"You will do just that," Rachel said. "Warren is organizing my team with the best and healthiest we have. You'll have to sit this one out."

"I don't like it," Ben said, narrowing his eyes. "What if it's a trap to get you exposed? They've shown they're willing to assassinate, especially when they're desperate."

"We will have rifles on neighboring roofs," Rachel said. "We're making this as safe as possible, but exposing myself to harm is a show of trust, crucial to negotiations. While we're trying to make it safe, risks are necessary. Our men and women put their lives on the line to fight this war. I should possess the bravery to demonstrate the same, ending this bloodshed. You're not changing my mind, so make your peace with it."

"That doesn't mean I have to like it," Ben said. "You're not bringing Roger and Bernard along, are you?"

"I should hope Davis doesn't rope them along. Bernard needs time to grieve for his mother. I don't want him coming along to a meeting with the same gang who murdered his mother in cold blood. That'd be a recipe for disaster if I ever saw one."

"Send Davis in here when you talk again, would you?" Ben asked. He reached over and grabbed her hand atop his chest, stopping its rubbing. "I want to handpick your protection personnel. It's my job, and I won't let a new person do it. It won't impede my recovery either, so you don't have a good reason to decline."

Rachel pulled her hand away and pinched his cheeks. "If my big man wants to work so badly, I guess I'll have to."

Her voice was patronizing and vaguely maternal. "It's a list of names, yeah." Her voice was back to normal. "I'll send him in. Within a few days, the doctor will allow you to recover inside our room. Put up with the boredom until then. Shall I send someone in to entertain you?" She surveyed the barren room and noticed only beds, a large desk in the corner, and a door leading to the unseen surgical theater. "Because there is nothing entertaining here. I know," she said, snapping her lithe fingers. "I'll arrange for a television to be mounted nearby." She pointed toward the nearby wall. "There works."

"Honey, focus. Send the boys in if you could," Ben said. "Before or after Davis – it doesn't matter. Bernard needs a father figure after his mother died, and Roger is impressionable. We need to address their mindsets about how this is happening. I may as well do something while I'm laid up out of action. Making our young men feel better is at least something. Send Artyom my regards when you see them."

"If you really want that, sure. I guess it'd ease some boredom, so I'll send them in. You're ready for them now? I was going to go find Davis. As soon as they're done burying Elizabeth, I'll send them in."

"Thanks," Ben said. "I can't stand laying here all day and doing nothing with this dull ache."

"Just remember," Rachel said in a doting voice, "you're not Bernard's dad. You can act nice and sympathetic. He's a heart broken young teenager who just lost his mama. He won't act like we all know and are used to."

"Grief does crazy things to some people. He needs to learn how to handle it, and I aim to at least soften that lesson. It's partially my fault his mom's dead anyway." He looked away from Rachel and a frown accompanied the avoidance of her gaze.

"No, it's not," Rachel said. "Mikhail shot her in the skull. You tried to stop it. End of story. Don't even consider telling Bernard it's your fault. He could harbor a grudge, and that won't end pleasantly. Tell him how you chased him through the woods and, if you must apologize, say you're sorry you weren't fast enough. Got it?"

"I suppose that makes sense."

"Good." She stood up from the bed. "Now I have things to do today. I'll be back as soon as I can. Okay, baby?"

"You're the highlight of my day. Hurry back." Ben raised a hand to wave goodbye and watched her leave the room.

Some time later in the medical ward...

The door opened to reveal a sweaty Roger and Bernard entering.

"Boys." Ben raised an arm. "How nice to see you."

"Damn, Dad." Roger made his way over, with Bernard following behind. Standing at the foot of the bed, he studied his father lying in bed. "He did a number on you, didn't he?"

"He might have got a lucky shot," Ben said. "Or maybe your mother's been correct all these years and I am simply lucky when it counts. Don't tell her I'm entertaining that thought. She'd never let me live it down. You two look beat," he said.

"We just finished burying Aunt Elizabeth," Roger said.

"Ah," Ben said, his face losing the smile he had when they walked in. "Yes, I'm sorry. If I was able, I'd have been outside with you."

"What happened out there, sir?" Bernard broke his silence. "Please." He approached Roger and leaned down, gripping the foot of the bed with both hands tight. His eyes locked with Ben's in a fierce gaze. "I have to know."

Ben grunted. "I can tell you from my point of view." He cleared his throat. "I was driving up and down the road leading to the mansion when I saw the truck we were searching for parked beside the road. It wasn't far from the mansion, so I readied my guns and hurried into the forest in hot pursuit."

"Please go on," Bernard said.

"Well, at first I didn't know where he'd be located until I studied my surroundings and put myself in his shoes. Thinking if I was a sniper, where would I choose to secure the best shot kind of concept. I spotted a nearby hill heading in the mansion's direction and it popped into my head. That little hill we can see from our windows? He was probably up there. I wasted no more time and ran."

Ben noticed his story completely captivated Bernard, so he kept going. "I reached the top and searched - first up into the trees, but he wasn't climbing after his injury, so I switched to searching the forest floor. I spotted a weird clump of grass and leaves that didn't look natural across the elevated ground, about forty feet away. It was impossible to tell where his head or his chest was. He had a camouflage suit on that he'd made with local plants. I had to get closer to make sure I ended this in one shot." Ben glanced up at Bernard before back to his son. "I raised my gun immediately, but it was too late. He fired off that shot just before I did."

"Damn," Bernard pushed off the footboard and paced in front of the bed.

"Turns out I'd hit him in the chest, but he was wearing a vest. A firefight ensued. I tried a gutsy play, and that's how I ended up in this bed. There was only one problem. He was still alive since most of my shots hit the vest. You know that guard you both snuck by that was guarding the cabin?"

"Kyle?" Bernard asked. "What about him?"

"He ran toward the gun shots when he first heard them and saved my life out there. He shot him right in the head, just as I saw Mikhail's gun's barrel pointing at me. I nearly saw my life flash before my eyes."

"Damn," Roger said. "I guess I owe Kyle an apology for making his life harder."

"Yes, you do," Ben said. "He saved your old man's life. Bernard." He noticed the younger male stop but not acknowledge him. "I'm sorry I wasn't fast enough in tracking him down, but I tried my best."

"I know you did," Bernard said, his voice even. "Finding a hidden enemy sniper in their territory is difficult, and doing it well on the first try is rare. I don't blame you, sir," he said. "I don't know who to blame, honestly. It feels like it would help to have someone to blame, but I don't have anyone to point to. Initially, I wanted to blame you, but after hearing what happened, I can't."

"Blame Mikhail," Roger said. "The fucker was the one who squeezed the trigger."

"Yeah," Bernard said.

"For what it's worth," Ben said, "if you ever need to talk, I, or I'm sure my blockheaded son here, would be available anytime. I mean that," Ben said. "I'm not your mom, nor could I ever replace her, but I'm always willing to help if I can."

"Right," Bernard said. "Thanks for telling me what happened out there. It means more than you know. What I need is…" Bernard looked over toward the exit. "I need to be alone for today. I'm sorry, but I've got to go." He rushed out of the room, leaving father and son alone.

"That boy is in pain," Ben said after he heard rapid footsteps leaving. "If only I'd been faster out there, his mother would still be alive."

"I don't know what to do. Do I follow him?" Roger asked.

"No, not this time," Ben said. "That boy needs to cry in private. Going in now would only interrupt his grieving process. He won't want to cry in front of his friend. That's the way we men are biologically wired, Son. I imagine Elizabeth raised him that way. Showing no weakness has its disadvantages. You know you don't need to hide emotions from me or your mother, right?"

"Uh huh."

"Just making sure," Ben said. "Now, you should probably see Chris and Jackie. You should know there's something huge in the works. Be ready for anything, alright?"

A knock at the door interrupted Ben. "Come in," he said.

"Hey," Warren opened and entered. "Oh, I didn't mean to interrupt." He had a stack of papers clutched in his right hand. "I had those bodyguard assignments you wanted to review before tomorrow."

"You're still working?" Roger asked. "Does Mom know about this?"

"Of course she does. I was the one who told her to send him in," Ben said. "You underestimate your old man. Now run along. Go find your sister and see what she's doing."

Roger nodded to Warren during his exit and left the two high ranking Syndicate officials.

"Sorry," Warren said, taking a chair lining the nearby wall and pulling it up to the side of the bed. "Here were my first ideas for the operation tomorrow."

Ben took the papers Warren offered him and looked over the names and original positions. "You're not taking Bernard tomorrow," he said. "End of story."

"Why?"

"Because the idiot who ordered his mother killed will attend tomorrow. Hot-headed teenagers should not be posted on a diplomatic mission, especially after that recent trauma."

"Alright, then who do you propose replaces him?"

"Immediate guards should be yourself, Jackie, and Kyle Evans."

"That kid who was guarding the cabin?" Warren asked. "He must have made quite the impression to promote him from shit guard duty to guarding your wife."

"He saved my life," Ben said. "I know he can get it done. He also follows orders to the letter. Trust me."

"Okay. Who should be posted on the rooftops nearby?" Warren asked.

"Chris is a good pick. He's an excellent marksman," Ben said, looking over Warren's choices before checking the next page. "You might take Roger on the marksman squad, but I wouldn't put him up close and personal. Chris could keep him in line on a job like that. He's an excellent shot - not as good as Chris, but he taught the boy well."

"Very good," Warren said. "Then it's settled."

"Let's hope this peace goes through," Ben said. He placed both hands behind his head and shut his eyes. "It always gets scariest before the dawn."

"I think it's supposed to be darkest," Warren said.

"What are you, a fact checker now?" Ben asked. "Don't quit your day job, Davis."

22

"There is a difference between late and fashionably late." Rachel looked at her phone in the cramped interior surrounded by her hand-picked guards.

"He won't show up I bet," Jackie said. "Not after his pet assassin bit the dust."

"He'll be here," Warren said. "We arrived here awfully early is all."

"It's only been five minutes," Kyle said. He saw everyone minus Rachel look at him in the driver's seat. "What? It's true."

"It should go without saying, kid," Warren said. "When we exit, you stay quiet, look scary, and let the boss talk. We're just here as insurance in case they want to try anything. Do not speak, joke, or say a single word."

"I understand," Kyle said.

"Stop trying to scare the kid," Jackie said. "Whatever's going to happen is going to happen. No sense in worrying."

"Looks like the show will start soon," Rachel said. She looked out the front from her middle back seat and watched another car enter the parking lot. "Make sure your safeties are off. Just in case," she said.

"Guards, exit first and then the boss," Warren said. "I don't want any mistakes. Is that clear?"

"Crystal clear," Kyle said.

"We got it," Jackie said.

"Good. Then let's finish this." Warren led by example and climbed outside first. Jackie exited on the opposite side while Kyle left the driver's seat. They were all visibly armed, but none had their weapons in their hands. Rachel did not get out yet. She sat in the back seat, waiting and watching. She saw four guards funnel out of the jeep Oleg's crew had brought before the man himself climbed out. Taking this as her cue, she exited on Warren's side.

"Be careful," Warren whispered loud enough so only she could hear.

"How nice to meet again, Mrs. Morris," Oleg and Artyom took the lead on their side of the parking lot, walking shoulder to shoulder. His muscle trailed behind at his sides, keeping a clear line of sight on Rachel and her crew.

"Sure," Rachel said, with Warren at her side coming up to meet the duo. "Let's go with that for diplomacy's sake."

"Was this little meeting truly necessary?"

"Maybe you don't value good operational security, but we do," Rachel said. "We tend to not like discussing private matters over the phone. If we ever do, we destroy said phone immediately. I like my land line, so that's not an option."

"She likes her landline," Oleg said with a wide smile. "I'm guessing we're out here to divvy up territory and terms? Let's get to the nitty gritty. I don't possess tons of time for mere pleasantries."

"Yes, you're quite the busy man from what I've put together," Rachel said. "Alright then. Here's how this war's ending," she said. "We'll stay out of your way, and you'll stay out of ours."

"That's it?"

"I assume you don't want to get back into business. I know I'd rather skip act two of that play if I had a choice. You ambushed my men and massacred them. It's a little hard to build back trust after that."

"True," Oleg said with a shrug. "Maybe it wasn't the most sporting method of starting this conflict, but it seemed the best option practically. You understand, I'm sure."

"Of course," Rachel said. "The sole reason this meeting is taking place is because of your second-in-command, Oleg." She gestured toward Artyom beside Oleg. "If he'd killed my son and daughter, there would be no peace. There would be many more mysterious tragedies happening at your businesses. You are damned lucky he didn't kill my babies. You owe everything to him."

"Odd point to make," Oleg said. "Alright, I accept that. Artyom here is my second in command after all. I trust him with my business and my life."

"For your sake, that's a good choice. Now all we ask is you don't expand into our part of town, and we stay out of yours. That means no collections, no blackmail, no businesses, and no housing of troops. The same goes for our personnel."

"You're lucky I'm entertaining this at all," Oleg said. He raised a hand and waved toward a nearby rooftop. "Is that your son up there? I understand safety, but at a certain point, you understand this looks like a setup."

"If I wanted you dead, you'd already be on the floor," Rachel said. "They're here as insurance, nothing more," she said. "Don't think I didn't notice your sharpshooter posted on the far side of the street's rooftop." She looked up over Oleg's shoulder.

"Great minds think alike," Oleg said. "I want assurances you won't try to interfere with our business partners."

"I don't even know who your precious business partners are, although I assume we share quite a few. The same could be said for you. We've both lost a great deal of personnel recently. Our organizations are just going separate ways, with no further added bad feelings. We'll never be friendly, but why not at least be cordial?"

"You are quite different as a negotiator than your father was," Oleg said. "You value the carrot; he valued the stick."

"Make no mistake, if you'd rather have the stick, I can oblige. We'd just rather be civilized about this uncivilized business."

"We leave each other alone, we go back to business, and we keep what's ours with no concessions?" Oleg reached out a hand toward Rachel. "Is it a deal, lady Morris?"

Rachel reached forward and shook his hand firmly. "Deal."

He looked over at Artyom. "Call them off."

Artyom turned around, reached above his head, and gave a thumbs up.

"I didn't have time to say before," Oleg said, withdrawing his hand and shoving it in his pocket, "I don't see your husband. Is everything alright with him?"

Rachel grit her teeth but answered in as pleasant a voice as she could manage. "He was injured by your last envoy, before Mikhail's tragic passing."

"I can't believe that guy was the one to put an end to his legacy." Oleg chuckled. "I admit, I didn't see that coming, but he got clipped I assume."

"Something like that," Rachel said. "He sends his regards, especially to Artyom here," she said.

"I knew something was different about him," Artyom said.

"Not having second thoughts on allegiances, old friend?" Oleg asked with a chuckle, rubbing his hands together.

"No such thing," Artyom said. "Never."

"Relax, it was a poor attempt at levity," Oleg said. "So, with that our business is completed. Let's all get on with our degenerate lives and forget this whole ugly mess."

"I'll never forget the lives your men took. I doubt you'll forget our deeds either," Rachel said. "We've dead to bury. You boys have a pleasant night now." Rachel and Warren turned their backs to Oleg and Artyom, who headed back toward their jeep with the other guards beside it.

Rachel entered the jeep along with the other guards.

Warren pulled out a phone as the engine started. He hit the speed dial and waited. "You both should leave and head home. It's done." He opened the door and tossed the phone under the tire. Slamming it shut, he put on his seat belt and they were finally in motion.

"That's one more senseless war behind us," Rachel said. "Now to pick up the pieces."

23

Lee sat at his seat in the large empty room. "They should return soon," he said out loud to himself. "Let's perform a routine check." He tapped the enter button and the prompt on the screen disappeared, replaced by another pop up. "What's this now? Someone was in here and deleting something? What was that?"

He looked at the destination he saw earlier. "I know I have that set to copy itself to an external drive. Maybe they didn't know." Lee got up, leaving the chair rotating in front of the humming computer. He reached around the back of the computer and plucked one cord out. "This is the one," he said. "I think they just erased it off the primary drive, or at least let's hope. We could have a breach, and it'd be my ass." He followed the cord to the hard drive taped underneath the desk and ensured the cord was firmly connected. He moved to sit back at his personal computer and clicked his way through windows until he was at the external drive's screen.

"Let's see here." Lee leaned forward. "Looks like a lot of surveillance footage from Elizabeth's cabin. Wait a minute."

Lee switched back to the original hard drive's storage screen. "This is a smaller file," he said. "It means someone cut a portion out." He opened the footage and skipped forward until he saw something suspicious. "She went to the door and what? Next thing is Elizabeth sitting on her sofa, glaring at her door. What the fuck?"

With shaking hands, he switched back to the other window and opened the file. He successfully found the correct timestamp and watched the rest of the footage play. The argument with Rachel, all the bickering, accusations, everything was on display, including the threat.

He saw Rachel pull out her revolver and point it at the older gangster. "Oh, why me?" he whispered to himself.

"You'll live another day, old woman. Count your blessings and know when you're outmatched," Rachel said. A click made Lee jump alongside the digital depiction of Elizabeth amid Rachel's haughty laugh.

He watched his boss never take her gun off Elizabeth as she backed off. "She deleted this footage," he whispered. "Oh, I've stepped in it now." He closed the window when the nearby door opened.

"Stepped in what, sir?" A young man donning glasses stepped inside the room and closed the door. "I don't mean to interrupt. I just arrived and thought I'd check in."

Lee quickly disconnected the hard drive and picked it up. "Just some more administrative work," he said, holding up the hard drive.

"It didn't sound like it," he said. "Are you going somewhere?"

Lee got up and brushed past him. "I'll be back in a couple of minutes. Don't worry about it. I just forgot my flash drive is all."

"Oh, alright then." The man watched him leave and slam the door.

Lee kept a tight grip on the hard drive as he walked through the hallways. His heartbeat was elevated as assorted different guesses about the contents of the hard drive played out in his head. *The timing lines up with the peace deal right afterward. Was it a concession? Could she have given Elizabeth up to the Russians? Oh hell. The kid should know, shouldn't he? It's his mother, for heaven's sake. If I give it to him, God knows what he'll do. I should keep it a secret when I look at it logically. Hell, I should delete it, but it would be a trump card down the line.*

"You're awfully quiet." Crystal met Lee in the hallway. "Your eyes are shifty, too. You should relax. The war's over. Wait, where are you going anyway?" She stopped going toward her original destination and turned to follow him. "Hold on a minute. What's that hard drive you've got there in your hand?"

"Just a hard drive." Lee stopped and turned around. He held it up and showed off the seemingly mundane device. "Just bringing it to my personal PC to defrag it."

"That'll take forever," Crystal said. "You should just use the one in your lab. Unless you're trying to hide something from me? You're up to something. You never were good at hiding it."

"I don't have the faintest clue what you're blathering about."

"Well, that reaction seals it. I'm going to find out what. Let me see that hard drive if you're not hiding anything."

"No," he said directly. "I can't. It's an order from above. I can't hand it over."

"Hmm," Crystal kept following him, hounding him all the way.

Rachel came out of her office's double doors ahead. She was already facing the pair because of their noise.

"Honey, leave him alone," she said. "He has important work. Speaking of, why are you here, Lee?" Her eyes fell to the hard drive gripped in his hand. "What's that about?"

Lee froze in place, but luckily she didn't pick up on the sudden widening of his eyes or his even further increased heartbeat.

"Are you alright?" Rachel stepped closer. "You're sweating, and we keep it cool at sixty-eight degrees in here. You might be sick."

"I'm fine. I need something inside my room, and I was planning to return straight to work, Mrs. Morris."

"Alright then, but get yourself checked out by medical afterward. I can't have a virus running roughshod over our rank and file because someone doesn't enjoy going to the doctor when they're sick. That'd be just my luck - the entire tech division being bedridden," she said with a chuckle. "Now you." She gave her daughter a stern glare. "I see we need to talk about interrupting personnel on duty again. Get in here."

"Oh, Mom. Seriously?" Despite her words, Crystal was moving into the office as she complained.

"Sorry about her," Rachel said before closing the door.

Lee let loose a long breath and wiped his brow free of the sweat that had gathered there. He ignored the guard that walked past him in the hallway and turned his head. Counting the steps in his mind, he stared at the ground, not wanting to catch anyone else's attention so carelessly. Eventually he made it back to his room and quickly got inside. He ran over toward his personal desk and custom-made computer. He hooked the hard drive up. "Damn it all." He slammed his head on the desk in front of the keyboard and kept it planted there.

"To send it or not to send. That is the question."

That evening back at the boys' apartment...

"Make sure you check your emails," Roger said, taking his shirt off.

"Yeah," Bernard said, and little else. He sat at the desk positioned on his side of the shared room and powered it on. "You'd think they'd come up with an original system so us non-computer users could get used to it. Oh, it looks like I received something. This," he said. "This isn't right. Why is there a video file attached as well as the usual encrypted text? That's not normal, is it?"

"A video file?" Roger approached and leaned forward, trying to look at the screen.

"Put your damned shirt on."

Roger rolled his eyes and did as Bernard ordered. "There. Are you comfortable now? You get touchy about the weirdest crap. Now let me see it. Yes, that is not typical. We should decrypt the text first. If that works, we know it's from someone in the tech division. I'm pretty sure they're the only ones who would have these addresses anyway, but I want to double check before we open a strange email's video file. Now, do that while I keep getting ready. Do not click that video file. I'm going to get Crystal and see what she thinks."

"Yeah, just let me get the paper so I remember the steps." He opened one of the nearby drawers and pulled out a notepad before plopping it onto the table beside the keyboard. He laboriously followed the procedures step by step that he'd written so long ago. "Now I paste it into this, and it should be translated into readable text."

"You think he'll manage?" Crystal's voice was loud enough to be heard, along with the muffled footsteps. "Fat chance," she giggled as the door opened. She rushed inside and came up behind him. "Well, I'll be," she said. "He managed." She looked down at the notepad. "Oh, he cheated. That's why."

"Never mind the how." Roger jockeyed for position around the monitor, trying to read the message his friend had received. "What the hell?"

"You need to see this footage," Crystal read aloud. "It involves your mother the day before she died while you were out in the field, along with some interesting hearsay about your friend. Once you watch this, you will never forget. Do with this what you will. I felt the moral imperative to pass this along. Just don't cause anymore wars, please."

"Cryptic," Roger said. "What do you think, Sis? Should we open it?"

"Let's run a quick virus scan of the file and be sure before clicking it. It could be a test from those egg heads. If we click on it, it could install a virus, and they'd get all uppity. Let's skip that." She slapped Bernard's hand and commandeered the mouse. She right clicked the file and scanned it with that antivirus she herself had installed on his computer.

"Hearsay about me or my sister?" Roger looked between Bernard and Crystal. "I'd be lying if I said I wasn't interested in what it says."

"It's a small file. The scan's almost done. We'll see soon enough," Crystal said. "I don't suppose we could not watch it? Something tells me we don't really want to watch it."

"I'm watching it," Bernard said. "If it has something to do with my mother, I'm watching it. End of story."

"Your mind's made up I see," she said. "Not that I blame you, considering the circumstances. It's done. Let's see what the mystery file shows already. The suspense is killing me."

"Says the girl who just wanted to skip the file," Roger said.

"Sometimes it's easier to remain ignorant, but that's not an option tonight."

"Be quiet." Bernard ensured the speakers were activated and working before clicking the video. A small media window popped up with a play button, along with a forward, back, and a pause button. The interior of Elizabeth's cabin appeared.

"Is this from the television?" Bernard asked. "That angle showing her couch, it has to be."

"Looks like it," Roger said.

Elizabeth came back into the frame, along with Rachel. She went back to the kitchen while Rachel and Kyle entered the frame.

"Kyle?" Bernard asked. "Why's he present?"

"Who knows?" Crystal asked. "Let's keep watching and see."

The group stood transfixed by the video, watching the conversation between the two women play out.

"You had your own father killed and used the man you loved to do it. I put nothing past you, not even using your own son and my children," Rachel said in the video.

Bernard paused the video. "What the hell? Have either of you heard of this?"

"Your mom killed her dad?" Roger asked. "Oof," he said. "Then to boot, she named you after him? I wouldn't put too much stock in nasty rumors. Let's watch how the rest of this video plays."

"My mother would never harm my grandfather,"

Bernard snapped. "She wouldn't do that to family. I know it."

"Like he said," Crystal said, patting Bernard's shoulder. "Let's watch the rest of it before anything. No sense contemplating over a segment when later parts could prove more illuminating."

Bernard hit the play button, and the video continued.

"I know they were in here. Every television has a small camera." Rachel stood and walked toward the muted television. "This one's right here." Her finger covered up much of the screen, blocking their vision.

"You saw them in here?" Elizabeth asked.

"I saw them in here," Rachel said. "Now either they snuck inside, or Kyle or one of his cohorts let them in here. I know which option I find more likely. I know they were in here, and then right afterward they disobeyed me again. We're lucky Ben was there to haul them in and keep them from killing themselves." She paced side to side in front of the older, former gangster. "It always ends up leading back to you, I find. Now why is that?"

"I don't know that I've ever seen her this pissed before." Crystal reached out and paused the video. "It's a little unnerving the way she's talking to her."

"She's not wrong though," Roger said. "We did sneak in there and bribed Kyle."

"This can't be all," Bernard said. "Arguments aren't noteworthy in this line of work. What did they want me to see?" He pressed the play button again, and the video moved forward. It wasn't long before the first bombshell met their ears.

"My boy is the rightful heir, and you know it," Elizabeth said. "What? Is the adopted child from some gangbanger and his baby mama meant to play the face of the Morris Syndicate? Your father would roll in his grave."

Rachel's hand moved quickly, slapping Elizabeth hard across the face. "Grandfather never taught you when to shut your big mouth. I knew that already," she said.

Elizabeth spat down on the glass coffee table, tinging it red where it landed. "You little brat. I can't believe you'd hit me."

"You're lucky I don't do worse," Rachel said. "Nobody bad mouths my son."

"He's not your son though, is he?" Elizabeth smirked. "You kidnapped him and stole him away."

"I kept him from growing up in a ghetto and joining some low life street gang where he'd die by age twenty."

Roger interrupted the video and took a few steps backward. "What?" He brought both hands up, clutching his head. "What the fuck did I just hear? I'm not her son? I'm adopted? What the hell is happening?"

Bernard turned in his chair. "Christ," he said, looking at his stunned friend. "Are you alright?"

"I'm not a Morris?" Roger backed up and sat on his bed. "What the fuck am I then? She said something about a gangbanger and a baby mama, didn't she? That means they killed my actual parents and took me? This can't be real."

Crystal moved to sit near Roger. "Maybe Elizabeth was lying."

"She didn't sound like it," Roger said. He leaned forward, cradling his head in his hands. His voice was eerily calm. "Did you know?"

"Who? Me?" Bernard asked.

"Does everyone but me know about this? Have I been just wandering around while everybody calls me a bastard outsider?"

"I didn't know, dude. Mother never told me," Bernard insisted. "I don't know how many know, probably none of the grunts. I've never heard rumors regarding it."

"She's lying," Roger said. "There's no way that's true. Mom would never do that."

"Come on, we can ask her later." Crystal grabbed one of Roger's arms and tried to pull him back to his feet. "Let's at least see the rest of this before we act in haste. Maybe the rest will shine a light on this video."

Roger's voice was devoid of enthusiasm. "Yeah, fine. Why not?"

She dragged him back to the monitor and hit play again.

"To think you'd keep pushing this even right now." Rachel slapped Elizabeth's hand away. "You must want me to harm you more. Why? To go crying to your son and use him as a tool to assassinate me too? It wouldn't be out of your fucking wheelhouse, now would it? You used Roger the same way."

"Just like you used that boy Ben to kill your father," Elizabeth answered in a moment.

Rachel took a step back. "What? I would never," she said.

"Can the denial act, princess," Elizabeth said. "I can put two and two together."

"Jesus," Bernard said, pausing it again.

"She denied it," Roger said. "She didn't do it before you even insinuate anything. I know she'd never kill a family member."

"My uncle was an outstanding leader," Bernard said. "Why would Mom even consider your mom? There must be a valid reason. She didn't harbor wild ass conspiracy theories."

"Let's just finish this shit show already." Crystal pressed the play button one last time.

"If you say something out of line to Roger or Crystal, I'll know. You will not survive. You want to test me and prove yourself right? Do it. If you believe you're right, you know I'd kill you without batting an eyelash."

"Death threats? So pedestrian," Elizabeth said. "I'm an old woman. That threat doesn't hold near so much weight as it once did."

"Shall I end you right now then?" Rachel reached down to her belt and pulled a pistol out of its holster. She extended her arm and pointed the barrel toward Elizabeth before pulling the hammer back with a click. "How about it?"

"You either have someone in the tech room watching your ass right now to put that on camera, or it's empty," Elizabeth said. Her smile was gone, now replaced with a straight face. She raised a trembling hand up in front of her. "Lee is gone, isn't he?"

"He's with my dear husband," Rachel said. "No one's inside watching, and little old me knows how to delete video evidence. Isn't that grand, old woman?"

"Do what you desire. Hurry! I will not beg my niece for my life. I have my dignity still," she said.

"You haven't had dignity since you were eighteen, I imagine," Rachel said. "Fine, I'll do as you say then?"

"You will? Do it already!" Elizabeth yelled. "Do it!"

The room was silent after the calling of Rachel's bluff. Rachel's arms swayed slightly and trembled, pointing at the older gangster. A click was heard. Elizabeth visibly flinched and turned away.

"No. I'm not stupid enough to kill you face to face," Rachel said. "I'm smarter than that," she said. "It would cast suspicion on me if I did." She holstered her weapon and laughed a genuine chuckle. "You'll live another day, old woman. Count your blessings and know when you're outmatched." She let loose and laughed without abandon.

Bernard stood up and walked away from the computer. "She pulled a fucking gun on my mother." His voice was full of calm rage. "She probably had my uncle killed. She's shown she's willing."

"Watch it," Roger said, stepping up to Bernard.

"Why? She's not even your own mother. You heard it yourself."

"You son of a -" Roger raised his hand but felt Crystal's hands wrap around him, pulling him back.

"Boys, please!" Crystal begged.

"Get off of me." Roger escaped the hold and took a deep breath. "My mother did not kill your uncle or your mother."

"Then what the hell happened?" Bernard's voice was quiet but seething. "You saw as well as I did. She pulled a gun on her and told her specifically that she had one day yet to live. Magically, she died the next day; and the day after, we're negotiating peace with Oleg. It doesn't require a mathematician to add two and two together. She sacrificed my mother as a peace offering and probably seized power in the same way using Ben, like Mom said."

"We don't know," Crystal said. "All we saw was two women arguing. I can tell you from experience, when we're in the thick of bickering, we aim for the proverbial jugular, true or not."

"Fuck this," Bernard said. "I'm going to go visit her."

"Wait a second." Crystal rushed forward and planted herself in front of the door, barring the exit. "Let's calm ourselves and think. Rushing may be what we want, but what will it accomplish? You will not kill my mother, full stop. You'll have to kill me first."

"I'm supposed to simply sit here after learning this?"

Bernard asked. "What kind of worthless son would that make me? I'd be less than a man. My uncle would be ashamed of me."

"He'd be more upset if you harm his daughter, I imagine," Crystal said. "If you insist on retaliation, then think of something less violent."

"Less violent," Bernard muttered under his breath.

"I don't believe any of this anyway," Roger said, sounding emotionally numb.

Bernard's stomping around in the room stopped with a snap of his fingers. His scowl turned to a sly smile. "Why not use this to our advantage? It's what Mom would have wanted."

"I yearn to know the truth," Roger said. "What are you suggesting?"

"You can ask her all the questions you like, and she'll probably lie," Bernard said. "That's not my point. We can use this opportunity and escape from under her thumb. Don't you get it? Even if it's all bullshit, which I doubt," he said, "we can blackmail her with this evidence and grab whatever we wish. I know what I want, and I bet it's the same as you, my friend."

"What are you suggesting? You still haven't spat it out yet."

Bernard went to Roger's bed and sat beside him. "We can start our own branch of the syndicate in a far-off city. We'd get her to send us some personnel, some money for startup costs, and we'd be the bosses. She couldn't say no. If this damning footage was released to the syndicate at large, she and Ben would be finished. Even if it is uncorroborated, it'd be too dangerous to ignore. What's she going to do? Kill all of us? She'll fold."

"Leave?" Crystal left the door. "You two are going to

leave? What about me? You know I can't go with you until I graduate."

"I don't know about you," Bernard said. "My goal is to escape and gain freedom - not be under your mother's thumb the rest of my life, especially considering recent events. I won't hurt her, but if she's doing all this for her family, this is the way to get what we want - our independence. And it'd be payback without physically harming her."

"You think she'd actually go along with it?" Roger asked. "She's stubborn when she wants to be."

"She won't have a choice," Bernard said. "If this video leaked, the rumor mill would go into overdrive. She'd lose all trust, and this syndicate would collapse. She can't risk it. It's why this was sent to us. Someone knew it was morally correct for this tragedy to come to light, whoever it was. They understood we have a right to know."

"This is all rumor and hearsay. The text itself said so," Crystal said. "We might be getting all worked up over nothing."

"Possibly," Bernard said. "I doubt our mole would risk himself sending it if he thought so, though. Regardless, this is an ace we found. We have leverage to get whatever we want."

"What about me, though?" Crystal asked. "You both are going to leave me stranded? I don't want to lose you two as well," she said, her voice growing brittle. "Please, you two are the only two I have left besides Mom and Dad. Sure, the others treat me nice enough, but we always hang out. Without you two, I'd just sit in my room playing games or flying my drones alone. I don't want that."

"If we did this, we'd send for you if you'd like."

"I'm forced to wait a whole year alone until after I graduate, while you two set up a new branch of the Syndicate? You know how hard that'll prove? You'd need to recruit, set up a supply route, find buyers, and oversee a lot of things. It wouldn't simply be you two fools adventuring on your own."

"I'm always up for a challenge," Bernard said. "Look, I don't want to leave you behind either. I just kind of doubt your mom would let that happen."

"Why not?" Roger asked. "We have leverage, right? You'd have to attend a public school for your last year, though. We can't home school you."

"You want to bust into Mom's office and say 'Hey, both your kids are leaving; and by the way, screw you. We have video evidence that would compromise you if you won't allow it?' That'll be a shitshow."

"Then we'd best create copies of this video file. I guarantee you she'll seize whatever we show it to her on," Roger said. "Besides, before we do any blackmailing, I'm going to ask her questions. We'll take it from there."

"When are you two planning to tempt fate? Tomorrow morning I'm guessing?" Crystal asked. "I'm going too."

"Are you sure?" Roger asked. "It will not be a fun conversation."

"I gathered as much," Crystal said, "but I'd make sure this debacle doesn't come to blows."

"I already gave you my word that wouldn't happen," Bernard said.

"Who's talking from you? I'm talking about Mother. We saw her slap the shit out of your mom during a tense exchange, though it looked like no love was lost. I doubt she'd physically strike, but I need to be present. I feel it." A hand went up to her chest, and she bit her lip. "I can't let you two idiots go by yourselves."

"Let's get what sleep we can. We leave at nine. Be sure to

wake early, or I'll drag you out of bed," Bernard said. "That goes for both of you. Now, princess," he said, looking toward Crystal, "you want to sleep in here tonight?"

"What?"

"I assume you still sneak into big brother's bed when something huge happens. That hasn't changed since you were five-years-old. Or are you breaking that habit now since you heard he isn't really your brother? I don't want to hear anything nasty now."

"You jackass," Crystal said.

"You should sleep in your own bed tonight," Roger said. He trudged over to his bed and didn't bother taking his shirt off. He laid down on his bed with the lights still shining above. His voice was monotone. "We could use our time to ponder about tomorrow."

"Fine by me." Bernard stomped over to his own bed and fell into it.

"You two are so childish," Crystal said. "I'm out of here. You'd better not leave me tomorrow morning, or I swear to God I will make your lives hell wherever you end up."

The two boys offered no more words.

"Good night," Crystal's voice was clearly sarcastic. She opened the door, flicked the light switch off, and slammed the door closed.

The two boys laid in their beds in the now dark room. Only the artificial light of the monitor illuminated the large room. Roger rolled on his side, away from Bernard. "What does a guy do when he learns his entire life is a lie?"

Bernard took a moment to answer as he laid on his back and stared up at the ceiling, reaching out toward it and grabbing at the air. "He does what he knows to be correct. He stands by those who stand by him, and he makes his own purpose in life."

"Oh, is that all? Are you sure we could even manage a branch of the syndicate?"

"We'd be fine," Bernard said. "We'd have a few grunts to send off and get everything set up. Personnel would fill once we set up the recruiting protocol and assign someone to initiate people. The hard part would be finding the suppliers in a new location. Unless we smash and grab competitors, starting a war off the bat, I don't see a way we can find the guns necessary to make much cash."

"It's not like we can take a shipment from dear mom's stockpile and sell it. We'd learn the lay of the land quick with that level of merchandise, and we'd make a name for ourselves."

"I doubt she'd let us take it. We'd have to borrow it," Bernard said.

"Borrow it?"

"We'd pay her back. I imagine we'd have to kick a percentage up to her if this works. She'd end up getting hers, don't worry."

"Yeah, we'll just go take a van laden with guns on our pilgrimage - where exactly? I assume you have some idea of where we'd go?"

"Sure, I've got an idea," Bernard said. "Why not another big city somewhere down south? The Morris syndicate has always been in New York, Chicago, and now Ohio, right? Why not diversify and head down south?"

"Hurricanes for one," Roger said.

"Where do you want to go?"

"Why not someplace like LA?" Roger asked.

"Too ambitious," Bernard said. "You know how many gangs and outfits have already set up shop there?"

"It's a gigantic market."

"That they're all fighting over. Let's not get involved in that."

"Look at us," Roger said. "Are we kidding ourselves? It's a pipe dream."

"Our futures are staring us in the face, buddy," Bernard said. "All it takes is the guts to reach out and grab. It won't be easy, but nothing worth having is. We'd be our own bosses, aside from kicking up some money to your mother. Once we get set up, it'd be a sweet gig. We might even find some young, attractive women just for us and create our own dynasty. That'd be nice."

"I'm going to sleep. This daydreaming garbage is for the birds," Roger said.

"Are you with me tomorrow?" Bernard asked, persisting.

"Yeah, I'm with you."

"Alright then..."

24

Rachel and Ben were both in the bed, asleep - a rare treat lately. She'd come to visit him in the morning, but had ended up in bed with her husband. They both were awakened by the door slamming open.

"Damn." Rachel jumped out of bed, unsuccessfully hiding where she had been but moments before. She saw Roger, Crystal, and Bernard file in. Crystal brought up the rear and locked the door behind her. "Is anyone else in here?" she asked.

"No," Rachel said, straightening out her suit. "You all came to visit early this morning. Why'd you lock the door?"

"We figured you'd want privacy," Crystal said. "Sorry for this, Mom."

"Sorry for what?" Rachel asked. She shifted her attention to the two boys standing side by side near the foot of the bed. "You both look like you barely slept last night." She saw the dark bags under her son's eyes and Bernard stifled a yawn. "You came over just to check on your father?"

"Something like that," Roger said.

"You don't look happy," Ben said. "What's wrong, Son?"

"Am I your son, indeed?"

"What's the matter with you?" Rachel asked. "Of course you are. What is this all about?"

"I saw a video yesterday evening," Roger said. "It involved you and Aunt Elizabeth," he said.

"A video?" Rachel asked. "Care to explain that a little more? We have cameras everywhere. What video are you talking about? It wouldn't be hard to find me on some footage."

"Don't play dumb," Bernard said. "You know what we're talking about."

"I don't appreciate that attitude," Rachel said. "What the hell crawled up your collective asses last night? What is this video you're babbling about, and why are you bringing it up here in front of your injured father and causing him more stress?"

"You're not weaseling your way out by hiding behind him," Roger said. He pulled out his phone and moved to the video folder. "Don't bother trying to confiscate this. We've already made off-site copies at an undisclosed location." He extended his arm toward his parents and pressed the play button on the video.

Rachel moved toward her son and grabbed the phone out of his hand. "Where did you get this?" she asked. She heard a line that accursed woman spoke that she'd hoped would never surface.

Elizabeth spoke from beyond the grave. "What? Is the adopted child from some gangbanger and his baby mama meant to play the face of the Morris Syndicate? Your father would roll in his grave."

She quickly stopped the video. She wasn't quick enough, however. "Where did you get this?"

"Is it true?" Roger asked, not budging an inch.

"You are my son," Rachel said.

"From birth?"

"No," Ben said.

"Ben!" Rachel turned around. "What are you doing?"

"The boy deserves to know. He's a grown ass man now, sweetie," Ben said. "Besides, you can tell from his eyes he already knows it's true. We should respect him enough to tell him the truth, don't you think? He is our boy, after all. If not from birth, we are the parents who raised him. I think he knows we love him with everything we have."

"You killed my parents and took me away when I was a baby?" Roger asked.

"They were gangbangers of some nobody street gang, baby," Rachel said. "It would have been a shit life. When I saw you, I just knew I couldn't leave you to that fate. I thought I could do better, but I guess I was wrong. You fell into crime against my wishes, and here you are, already finding out one of my deepest, darkest secrets only very few know."

"Then he's not my blood brother?" Crystal asked.

"Correct," Ben said. "However, you are our baby boy, Son. You know that."

"I don't know anymore," Roger said, shaking his head and taking a step back away from his mother.

"Keep playing the video." Bernard's voice was calm but dangerous, restrained, but barely so. "There's more there," he said.

"I know exactly what's there," Rachel said. "I notice you don't have your gun drawn. That tells me something. I don't even see it on your person. I assume this was my children's doing?"

"What the hell is contained in that damned video?" Ben asked. "Why would he have a gun? What did you do?"

"Go ahead," Bernard said. "Play it for him and enlighten him."

She tossed Ben the phone, and he hit play.

"I used the same method Elizabeth used for your information regarding the gun," Rachel said. "Except I toned it down. She used to play Russian roulette with people under her command who pissed her off. Mine was never loaded."

"What the? When did this all happen?"

"When we were out hunting down Mikhail," Bernard said, his gaze never faltering from Rachel. He never took his eyes off her, even when she looked toward her husband.

"Ah no," Ben watched the screen. "Why are you here? This is a heated argument, sure, but it's in the past."

"It certainly is," Bernard said. "I can't help but notice the timeline laid out in that video you're watching. I believe your wife's words were 'You have another day to live, old woman.' Funny how she died the next day, and then the next day we have peace with Oleg. That is some odd timing there."

"You're suggesting that she was some kind of peace offering?" Rachel asked. She laughed out loud. "Kid, I wish I'd gotten that kind of deal. Your mother was a pain in my ass."

Roger had to restrain Bernard as he tried to rush at his mother, who showed no acknowledgement of the youth's anger.

"She constantly challenged my authority and was a pain in the ass, but no," she said. "Oleg didn't even give a damn about her. He'd never met her. Why would he want her dead, exactly?"

"I'm not here to accuse you of anything," Bernard said. "I'm here with an altogether different goal. Well, we are." He gestured toward Roger.

"Just what is this goal?" Ben asked. "If it's not to accuse her, why show us?"

"Blackmail," Rachel said, answering her husband. "He wants something. In this case, I suppose both do. So what is it, boys? You want a promotion? You want your own little squad? Is that it?"

"Nothing so pedestrian," Bernard said. "We'll found a new branch in a brand-new city."

"That's quite an undertaking for two eighteen-year-olds to manage on their own," Rachel said. "Do you have a clue about the amount of effort that'll be required for your branch to function?"

"You managed at eighteen, as I recall," Roger said.

"I also had my father mentoring me, screwed up as he was," Rachel said. "Aw," she noticed Bernard's eye twitch, "did I annoy you talking about your uncle that way? He was an ass. I had to grow up under him. He was over my shoulder, constantly teaching me things. For you two to succeed, you'd have to have experience watching over your shoulder."

"We will be fine," Bernard said. "All we'd need is startup capital, personnel, and merchandise to sell."

"You expect me to give you two kids crates of guns, manpower, and some money? All so you'll drive who knows where and create a new Syndicate branch? Are you two serious?"

"Hey, if you want this video making the rounds and giving the rumor mill material, refuse. It's no skin off my nose," Bernard said. "It's not the right time for dissent in the ranks while you're recovering from one war. Instability is a dangerous thing in times of rebuilding I heard from Mom."

"I have no reason to think you wouldn't just get yourselves arrested or killed trying to set everything up. You can't simply walk up to random folks and find buyers. You need connections."

"What connections do you have in Tennessee?"

"You're serious?" Rachel asked. "Why there?"

"Never mind why," Roger said. "Do you have contacts there or not?"

"It'd be a sparse list if I did. I know a few contacts who moved away and headed down south," Rachel said. She moved over to Roger and wrapped her arms around him. "You're being loyal to your friend, but you're positive? You don't have to go along with this half-cocked plan. I know you'd never want to blackmail your mother like this."

Roger didn't speak up or even meet his mother's eyes.

"You can't think I have adequate resources to hand over after a war?" Rachel asked.

"I believe you could," Bernard said. "We're not asking for much." Bernard saw Ben holding the phone out toward him. "Keep that phone, sir. We've already made dozens of copies. Use it to entertain yourself in this dreadful room while you recover."

"These idiots have decided, Mom, and they're serious," Crystal said. "I don't guess I could go with them?"

"Hell no, you're not," Rachel said. "You still have a year of high school left."

"A year that I could attend wherever they go and make some friends. I could enjoy a normal life and not be cooped up inside."

"You are my responsibility until you're eighteen, and you are not accompanying these two," Rachel said.

"That means you agree for us to found a new branch?" Roger asked.

"It's not like I have much choice in this matter," Rachel said. "Everybody knows what happens if that video goes public to the rank and file. I never did what it implied, but that wouldn't matter. The rumors alone would be enough."

"Happy for you to see reason," Bernard said. "

"You're not getting any guns to start off with, though," Rachel said. "You'll receive enough money to buy property and with that, you will find some sellers. If you can't, then you'll come back and follow my orders. If you can't even find sellers and buyers, then you're not ready. You two will learn how solitary independence truly is. Without a core group, it's going to be hard to form a branch. I'll tell you what. You can choose who you take, within reason. I need Lee and Davis here. I have enough boots on the ground to spare just about anyone else."

"Deal," Bernard said.

"What? Really?" Roger asked. "That was a first offer. You're supposed to fire back."

"Already a done deal, Son," Rachel said. "I pray you two know what you're doing. You're more likely to end up arrested than anything. I hope you are as resourceful as you think you are. You've never been tested before. I expect a fifteen percent cut off the top. Is that clear? I would offer advice, but I'm not in the mood after being blackmailed by you three children. Leave me alone with my husband, would you?"

"Wait a minute," Ben said. "Don't I get a say?"

"No, baby." Rachel moved back to the bed. "The boys are going to learn this lesson themselves the hard way. They're all grown up and want to be treated like grown ass men. The first lesson is they get no preferential treatment. They get what any ambitious lieutenant would receive, some personnel, startup money, and that's it. Now, boys, go gather your team. Make it quick if you're in such a hurry."

25

"This seems like a bad idea," Roger said, walking beside Bernard toward the Morris property inside the city. He looked over his shoulder at the high rises. "I'm going to miss this place, I have to admit."

"What are we doing here, anyway?" Kyle walked along with the two.

"It's not like we got to see it a lot. I'm sure Memphis has its own charms. Now focus up. What's she going to do? Kill us? We'll be fine. Word hasn't spread throughout the ranks. Act natural. It'll be fine. We're simply securing initial merchandise. What dealers would we be if we didn't have any product to sell? We're showing initiative."

"I don't believe she meant this, but whatever," a female voice said in their ears.

"Molly," Roger said. "Just trust us. You'll follow us down south once we're done here."

"I understand, but don't blame me if something happens."

"Hopefully Lee recommended you for something more than your scathing cynicism," Bernard said.

"I am better than that fat tub," she said. "That's why he was so willing to send me off with you. He's afraid of when I'll show him up and take his job. While I was supporting in the field, he was safe. Once we returned, he couldn't get rid of me fast enough, the fat fuck."

The three young men approached the Morris warehouse and knocked.

"Mr. Morris? One moment please," the voice said. Sliding metal met their ears as the door opened. "Come in," the man said, welcoming them inside. "It's a rare honor that we get to see you two. Do my eyes deceive me? It's the killer of the Ghost of Moscow, too. What an honor," he said.

"You're aware how business is once peace is reestablished," Bernard said, now inside the warehouse. "Business never sleeps."

"You took the words out of my mouth," he said. "How can we assist you three tonight?"

"We're on orders to take two vans full of merchandise to sell."

"I hadn't heard of this." The man stopped with a puzzled look. "Normally we receive some kind of notice."

"It was a spur-of-the-moment decision from Mrs. Morris," Bernard said. "We were stationed at the mansion and drove here in a wicked rush. She said not to interrupt her, and to give you this." He dug into his pockets and handed over a folded up white piece of printer paper.

The man took it, unfolded it, and read. He looked up at the three young Syndicate members. "Alright then. Who am I to doubt the boss and her family? I have the two perfect vans ready over here. Now, regarding merchandise - what type of goods is the buyer searching for?"

"They want a sampling of sorts," Bernard said. "We need handguns, vests, helmets, rifles, some modifications - basically a little of everything, including explosives if we can spare any."

"That will take time to pack fully, but it shouldn't prove a problem. You can accompany me if you like. I'll get someone to help fast track this shipment. You can help if you're especially in a hurry."

"I think we will," Roger said. "We're the ones troubling you. It's proper we help pack on a rush assignment."

"I don't mind work, sir," Kyle said, keeping up with the group.

"It's good to see the boss taught her son manners." The man led them over to their work area full of tables and crates. He cupped a hand around his mouth to amplify his voice. "Hey!"

A worker clear across the warehouse turned.

"Yeah, you," their host said. "Fetch the two vans in the rear and prep them for loading. We've got another order - on the double."

"Yes, sir!" the other yelled before running to fulfill the request.

"Sorry about the skeleton crew," the guy said. "Most of my workers headed home for the night."

"No trouble at all," Bernard said. "The men need rest after the war. There's nothing wrong with us putting in some elbow grease."

The three, along with the two workers, filled the vans to their brim with crates containing every sort of merchandise that the syndicate sold. Every type of protective article, every modification, every type of ammunition - all were stuffed inside those two vans. It was a meticulous process, but time passed quickly as the men bantered.

"This must be one rich customer wanting to try everything out on the first buy," their host said, putting the finishing touches on the last crate.

"We always aim to please," Roger said.

"We appreciate you two helping us out," Bernard said.

"It's no trouble at all, gentlemen," he said. "Let us get that. I insist," he said. "There we are. You're all set," he said with a wipe of his brow. He reached into his pocket and tossed a key to Bernard and one to Roger. "Here are the keys. Best of luck on the sale, gentlemen."

"Roger, you and Kyle take that one. I'll take this one and Molly will take our vehicle outside and follow."

"What about our cars?" Roger asked, leading the group outside into the night air.

"It's like an eight-hour drive, dude. We can return and get them. Focus on the job at hand and not your little four-door," Bernard said, walking toward his designated van. "Is everyone clear on the plan?"

"It's not complicated," Molly's monotone voice said. "Yeah, boss."

"A little less sarcasm, please." Bernard climbed into his and slammed the door shut.

Roger did similar and started the engine before looking at Kyle in the front passenger seat. "Guess it's you and me for this car trip, kid."

"I believe I'm older than you, sir," Kyle said.

"Sorry," Roger said, following Bernard out of the warehouse and giving a wave to their hosts they'd just swindled. Roger saw him pull out a phone. "There we go," he said. "We need to leave quickly. I think he's calling this in."

The caravan met up in the parking lot and got onto the road.

"I never got the chance to thank you, Evans," Roger said.

"For what, sir?"

"You saved..." Roger paused mid-sentence. "You saved my father. He'd have been dead without you rushing out there. I owe you for that. I'd be lying if I said I didn't want you to join our little outfit because of it. You deserve a chance at paving your way and not being a cog in that already built machine."

"I was just doing my job," Kyle said.

"Your job was guarding the cabin, not running out into the woods toward a sniper. That was above and beyond," Roger said. "Anyway, I'm sure you don't want to relive that day. None of us do."

His phone interrupted him, vibrating on the dashboard. "I knew it would come, but I was at least hoping we'd be halfway through Ohio before it rang." He answered and put the irate caller on speakerphone so he could drive with both hands placed on the steering wheel. "Hello, dear Mother. Are you having a good night?"

"What are you two doing?" Rachel asked. "I just received a phone call from one of our warehouses."

Roger gave a quick glance over at Kyle before returning his focus to the road. "Is that right?"

"They also told me about this deal I sent you over there for," she said.

"Right, and?"

"And I didn't fucking send you two there to get any damned guns, and you know it," Rachel said.

"It's already done," Roger said. "Besides, you'll get your cut."

"Well, thanks to this little stunt, your first shipment's tax is being upped from fifteen percent to twenty-five percent to cover the costs."

"Love you too, Mom," Roger said in as pleasant a voice as he could.

"Never pull something like this again. I raised you better than this." The line went dead with that warning and scolding. Roger disconnected the call and sighed.

"That was milder than I was expecting," Kyle said. "I was expecting full on yelling and threats if I'm honest."

"Know how and when to pick your battles, Mr. Evans," Roger said. "We had a favorable outcome. It was a calculated gamble, and it paid off."

Molly's voice interrupted the duo. "Sounded like it's going to pay off ten percent less."

"Molly?" Roger asked. "How did you hear this?"

"I have my ways," she said. "I enjoy hearing everything and being ready for anything. It's impressive you two pulled this off with only a onetime extra tax to show for a black eye. That's all I have to say. I'll leave you two alone now. I was aiming to annoy Bernard for a while, anyway."

"She's a unique person," Kyle said. "Not that it's a bad thing," he said. "Just a little creepy sometimes."

"Most people proficient with tech are odd," Roger said. "I can't believe she insisted we take Chris and Jackie with us. They should already be driving south."

"I'm sure your sister will miss you," Kyle said.

"That tearful goodbye hurt," Roger said. "She said she'd follow us when she turned eighteen."

"You think she will, sir?" Kyle asked.

"As surely as the sun rises and sets."

THANKS FOR READING!

The Morris family adventure continues next year. If you wish to support this work, please consider leaving an honest review on Amazon. Thank you and have a great day!

ABOUT THE AUTHOR

Alex J Fischer has released 14 action/adventure novels thus far with plans for more.

Alex grew up in a small town in Ohio and still resides there. Hobbies include writing, video games, and watching crime shows.

ALSO BY ALEX J FISCHER